Patricia Elliott writes:

'The French Revolution was a time of exhilarating ideals and violent upheaval, which paved the way for the freedoms we take for granted today. Old rules were broken for ever, and the aristocrats who had indulged themselves in lives of luxury and extravagance faced ruin or death. Yet there were those among them who were eager to rid France of her corrupt *ancien régime* and to recognize the rights of ordinary people.

'Eugénie de Boncoeur is far more concerned with clothes, romance and her social life, than with the Revolution. Born to a life of privilege, can she survive in a changed world?'

PIMPERNELLES

The Pale Assassin

Patricia Elliott

Hodder Children's Books

A division of Hachette Children's Books

First published in Great Britain in 2009
by Hodder Children's Books

1

A Catalogue record for this book is available from the British Library

ISBN 978 0 340 95676 2

Typeset in Garamond by Avon DataSet Ltd,
Bidford on Avon, Warwickshire

Printed in the UK by CPI Bookmarque, Croydon, CR0 4TD

The paper and board used in this paperback by Hodder Children's Books
are natural recyclable products made from wood grown in
sustainable forests. The manufacturing processes conform to the
environmental regulations of the country of origin.

Hodder Children's Books
A division of Hachette Children's Books
338 Euston Road, London NW1 3BH
An Hachette UK Company

For my agent, Elizabeth Roy, with love and gratitude

My thanks to Rachel Wade of Hodder Children's Books, for a conversation during a train journey that stuck in my mind; to Gillian Wayne of the City of London School for Girls, for an enlightening initial reading list; to Edwina Ehrman of the Victoria and Albert Museum; and with thanks and apologies to the late Baroness Orczy, for appropriating the title of her famous novel, *The Scarlet Pimpernel*.

'From my earliest days I had a feeling that adventures lay in store for me.'

From the memoirs of Lucy de la Tour du Pin (1770–1853)

THE BEGINNING

July 1779

One summer evening outside Paris, a coach drawn by four black horses was creaking and swaying through the soft country twilight. Cool grassy scents drifted in through the windows, refreshing after the stench of the capital, but the cold-eyed man seated inside was oblivious to them. His mind was on murder.

His name was Raoul Goullet, and he had killed before. Tonight he would kill Sébastien de Boncoeur, the Marquis of Chauvais.

The Marquis had beaten him at cards. His hard-won fortune, accumulated over years, had been lost in an evening to a mere novice. He pictured for the umpteenth time those mocking young aristocratic faces round the green-topped gaming table as he, Raoul Goullet, experienced gambler, discovered he was left with –

nothing. In desperation he had tried to cheat, and then – the humiliation of it! – they had stripped him of his breeches and booted him naked into the street.

But tonight he intended both to keep his money and to be avenged.

The coach turned into a long avenue shadowed by trees, and the chateau of Chauvais, built of white stone, rose ghostly in the distance. The rising moon shone on pointed towers, lines of shuttered windows, steps leading to a terrace bordered by a balustrade.

The assassin sat back and gave a tight-lipped smile. As the coach rolled to a halt and from somewhere dogs began to bark, his gloved fingers felt the outline of the dagger in the pocket of his white brocade coat.

It was the young Marquis himself who opened the great wooden doors. He appeared much taken aback to see who it was, though he bowed stiffly. There was a tiny, ravishingly pretty child clinging to his silk breeches; she gave the visitor a baleful glare from sky-blue eyes.

'I did not expect you, monsieur,' the Marquis said, holding a candlestick aloft in the echoing stone hall and quietening the pair of tall wolfhounds with a single raised finger of his other hand. He bent to whisper to the child. 'Eugénie, *chérie*, run along to Nurse.' She pouted but obeyed, skipping off into the shadows.

'You wish for satisfaction, I take it?' said the Marquis reluctantly, once the soft sound of her slippers on the stone floor had died away. He did not wish to be challenged to a duel, but he knew that he and his friends had gone too far the other night, and he had been the ringleader. This man was a cheat, but he was dangerous, and the Marquis had a wife and two young children to consider.

Goullet shook his head. 'I have brought the money I owe you,' he said, his pale face glistening in the candlelight; it was an unattractive face, almost reptilian.

He beckoned, and his coachman appeared, eyeing the dogs nervously, a money-bag hanging heavily from each hand.

'In the library, please,' said the Marquis. He did not want his wife to know of an evening spent at the notorious gaming-house run by the Baron de Batz. Indeed, he would much rather have forgone his winnings altogether, for now he would have to think of somewhere to hide them away. *Cheat's gold*, he thought with revulsion. He could never touch it.

But already the coachman had hauled the money-bags into the library and returned for more; and now they sat beneath the bookshelves like a row of malignant and bloated slugs while the coachman himself, a powerfully built and disconcertingly savage-looking fellow, lurked over them as if on guard.

Raoul Goullet eyed the dogs askance. 'I do not like dogs. Shut them away if you please, while we check the money.'

'Of course,' said the Marquis, and he shut the dogs the other side of the library door.

But his sense of danger was alerted. He had recently returned on leave from fighting the British in America, but he had never seen such malevolence in a man's eyes.

Goullet waved towards the bags. 'All that I owe you is there. Go ahead and count. Gaston will open the bags for you.'

'There is no need. I am sure the amount is correct.'

'No, I insist.'

The Marquis went across to the money-bags and appeared to bend over them. Out of the corner of his eye he saw the candles flicker on the card table. There was a minute movement of air behind him.

He whirled.

The flash of a blade.

An experienced army officer, the Marquis's reactions were swift. The dagger dropped to the waxed floorboards and slid with a whisper to the wall.

'I do not understand your game this time, monsieur,' said the Marquis evenly, though he was breathing fast and had hold of the visitor's arm in a vice-like grip.

'But I believe you have just tried to cheat again.'

'I do not lose twice!' hissed the assassin. He jerked his head at the coachman. 'Gaston!'

Snarling something, the coachman moved forward to tackle the Marquis, but before he could reach him, the Marquis gave a long, low whistle. The library door shook, as heavy weights were thrust against it from the other side, then with a shower of wood splinters it burst open and the dogs hurled themselves through. At the Marquis's command they halted, paws juddering, ready to spring; jaws open and dripping; their eyes moving from their master to their two quarries, and back again.

'Go, before I set them on you,' said the Marquis curtly.

The coachman gave one horrified glance at the dogs, turned and ran.

Burning with fury and humiliation, the assassin followed him, stumbling through the darkness of the hall to the great doors. As they were slammed behind him, he lost his footing and fell heavily on to the flagged stones of the terrace.

In the hall the Marquis fondled his two hounds. They were the gentlest bitches he had ever trained, brought over from England by his wife. 'Bravo, *mes belles*,' he murmured as they fawned around him. 'What a show you put on!'

Outside, the assassin brushed dirt from his coat, his eyes glittering in the moonlight. At that moment he looked what he truly was: an extremely dangerous man who had been thwarted of revenge.

A wail came from an unshuttered window high above his head. The child Eugénie, protesting at being put to bed. The assassin cocked his head to listen.

'I shall win yet, Marquis,' he said softly, venomously, his words creeping like a curse along the moonlit terrace. 'I shall destroy you and your family.'

And the thought of what he would do made him grind his teeth with pleasure.

PART ONE

Watched

ONE

12 July 1789

Ten years later, on a sultry Sunday afternoon in Paris, Eugénie de Boncoeur was walking with her governess beneath the horse-chestnut trees in the gardens of the Palais-Royal, gorging herself on marshmallow. In half an hour, though she did not know it yet, a revolution would ignite around her as if lighted kindling had been pushed into a vast, waiting bonfire.

'I think we should sit down, Mademoiselle Eugénie,' said her governess, Hortense, whose pale olive face had flushed unusually pink with the heat. 'There are empty chairs in the shade over there.'

Eugénie spoke thickly through another delicious mouthful of her marshmallow, *pâté de guimauve*. 'We could go into a café and have some lemonade.'

Hortense shook her head, but Eugénie pretended

not to notice. She was wearing her new dress *à la reine*, in the simple shepherdess style made fashionable by the Queen, and as she walked its white muslin skirts floated out so that she felt she was walking in the middle of a cloud. She was far too excited to care about being hot.

All around her the crowds were flooding through the arcades and tented pavilions. She had never seen so many people, nor heard such a din. As they went on groups began to gather, and they had to skirt round them; she could not even hear the water playing in the little fountains any more above the angry voices.

'See, what did I tell you?' whispered Hortense. 'I said this was not a good time to come!'

It was true that earlier, back at her guardian's old mansion-house near the Tuileries Gardens, Eugénie had had a great deal of trouble persuading her governess that today was the day for their long-planned secret expedition. Eugénie was not used to being thwarted, and she had longed for this visit to the Palais-Royal ever since Hortense had told her about its shops and stalls, cafés, restaurants and entertainments, all packed together beneath covered walkways. It was where you went to hear the latest news and to listen to revolutionary speeches. Hortense had been there and so had everyone in Paris, it seemed, except for Eugénie.

But Hortense had looked grave at first.

'I'm certain that Monsieur le Comte would not approve, mademoiselle! It's not a suitable place for young girls.'

'But the Duc d'Orléans opened it for everyone,' protested Eugénie. 'Didn't you tell me it's called the People's Palace now? Besides, it's our only chance, with my guardian away at his estate! Oh, please, Hortense!'

And so eventually Hortense had agreed.

But it had been impossible to walk to the Palais-Royal through the Tuileries Gardens because it was blocked with crowds, milling about in a threatening way. They had had to catch a hansom cab. As it bowled away, Eugénie had caught a glimpse of the great dusty square of the Place Louis XV, lined with the figures of soldiers on horseback, shimmering darkly in the heat. The sun glinted on their swords.

'Why are they there?' she said, already a little unnerved by the crowds in the Tuileries.

'German cavalry!' said Hortense with contempt. 'The King has filled Paris with foreign troops to make him feel safer. He thinks they will stop the people rioting about the price of bread, but it's only made them angrier. They've formed their own militia to defend Paris from the troops. They've even begun to hack down the customs wall!'

The hated customs wall that snaked round Paris had

been built to levy high duties on farmers' produce entering the city, and made food very expensive. But there was always plenty to eat in her guardian's house; Eugénie knew she would never starve like the beggars in the street. Forgetting the angry crowds and the soldiers, she craned forward in the cab, impatient to see her first glimpse of the Palais-Royal.

But she had not expected to see quite so many people there as well.

She began to be frightened by the wild look in their eyes and the raised voices above her head. In the oppressive heat they stank of sweat and fear.

Looking down she saw with dismay that her white shoes and the hem of her new dress were covered in dust.

'Why is everyone shouting, Hortense?'

'The King has dismissed his Finance Minister.'

'Everyone is always cross with King Louis, aren't they?' said Eugénie tiredly.

'He has got rid of the only man who could have saved the country from bankruptcy,' said Hortense, sounding cross herself. 'Monsieur Necker. The people call him the Miracle Maker.'

'Then why did the King dismiss him?'

'They say the King is trying to prevent the reform of

taxes. The poor people pay too much and starve while the nobility pays nothing. It's not right.'

Hortense always knew everything. She pored over all the newspapers and political pamphlets as they came out and tried to pass the information on to Eugénie, whose education was her responsibility. But the news did not interest Eugénie in the slightest; she could not see that it had anything to do with her.

'I think we should go home before things get worse, mademoiselle.'

But Eugénie had noticed a gilded salon where people sat at marble-topped tables around a counter laden with bottles. Its doors were open on to its own gardens. 'Can we have a glass of lemonade first? Please, Hortense.'

'The Café Foy. The most expensive,' sighed Hortense, but she set off up the path because, as Eugénie knew, she too was thirsty. 'Don't move, mademoiselle!' she shouted back over her shoulder.

Eugénie had wanted to drink her lemonade inside the Café Foy, for she had never been in a café before; but she could see that all the tables were taken. Indeed, there were people pressed up against them, listening or talking to those sitting down. So, instead, she stayed motionless on the sun-parched grass, clinging to the rough bark of a tree in case she was crushed underfoot by all the hot bodies pushing past her.

Then the church clocks all over Paris began to strike three and she had the strangest feeling: she thought she could feel the vibration through the tree, and stretching out all around her, as if the whole city was shaking itself to destruction.

There was a man in a white coat standing at one of the upper windows of the Café Foy. His gaze travelled around and lighted on Eugénie, clutching her tree in the middle of a swelling sea of people. She felt a curious sense of chill in spite of the fact that sweat was trickling down her back. But by the time Hortense returned, flustered, but triumphantly bearing two lemonades that had half spilt from their glasses, he was not looking in her direction any more. He was staring at a young man who had come out on to the terrace.

Hortense, too, looked at the young man, who had long dark curls and a thin, pale face. A green ribbon was tied around his hat and its ends fluttered in the hot breeze.

'I have seen him here before,' Hortense said. 'Camille Desmoulins, a journalist. He writes the most stirring articles.' Her eyes shone, and she paused in handing Eugénie her lemonade.

'Robert will be jealous,' teased Eugénie.

Robert was one of her guardian's footmen. Eugénie had surprised Hortense and Robert together, kissing, and had somehow been rather shocked that her governess, with her gravely beautiful face and passionate, intellectual ideas, should succumb to such an ordinary emotion as love.

'Shall you marry Robert, Hortense?'

Hortense made a little face. 'Pouf! Robert! He is nothing to me. I want to be free!' A faraway look came into her dark eyes. 'One day I'll visit England. Even a governess may find freedom there.' She added, with sudden disconcerting fierceness, 'In England the king has to listen to his people. He doesn't hold all the power to govern and impose taxes like our king, but is bound by a constitution.'

'What's a constitution?' said Eugénie, but she only half listened to Hortense's answer. A stab of jealousy went through her as she pictured Hortense showing an English girl newspaper articles and pamphlets, or even that book by Monsieur Rousseau, that she, Eugénie, had found so dull. Perhaps an English girl would be cleverer than she was, and Hortense would love her more.

'A constitution prevents the king having complete power and allows the people their say,' said Hortense.

'But England is so far away! I may never see you again.'

Hortense looked at Eugénie with pity. 'Soon there

will be no governesses in Paris, *ma petite mademoiselle*. Nor in the countryside. And perhaps no footmen like Robert, who can tell? Unless things change.'

'What do you mean?'

'Why do you think your guardian has left Paris for his estate at the moment? He's worried that the peasants may seize and destroy it. In the country they're taking power into their own hands, rebelling against the tyranny of the aristocrats they work for and refusing to pay them rent.'

'But surely not at Haut-bois?' said Eugénie, distressed. 'They are loyal on my guardian's estate – and at Chauvais too.'

Hortense looked at her intently, then put her mouth close to Eugénie's ear.

'But there are also many aristocrats who want change,' Hortense whispered, making Eugénie's ear hot and wet. 'They want a fair constitution like everyone else. Your guardian is one of them, and your brother, Armand. I keep my ears open, listen to servants' talk so I know.' She paused. 'If nobles, like your guardian, could talk to the King, perhaps they could persuade him . . .'

There was sudden commotion over by the doorway of the Café Foy, where some men were bringing out a table. The dark young man, who had been talking and gesticulating excitedly and had drawn a small crowd around him, was lifted up on to it, and then someone brought a chair and he climbed precariously on to that. He was now so high that even Eugénie could see him.

'What's he going to do, Hortense?' she asked, wondering if he was an acrobat and would suddenly stand on his hands, like the circus performers she had heard came to the Palais-Royal.

'He's going to make a speech!' There was a glazed, exalted look in Hortense's eyes and she clasped her hands together, taking a step forward as if to be nearer the speaker. Eugénie, frightened that she had forgotten her and that she would be abandoned to the crowd, clutched at her skirts. Waves of people were bearing down on them to join the throng around the young man's table. He had a pistol in each hand and was making wild movements so that they flashed silver in the sun.

Hortense grabbed at Eugénie's arm. 'Come!' she said urgently.

The crowd was yelling, hoarse with passion, and the upper-storey windows of the cafés all around were filled with people hanging out and shouting, too; only the man who still watched from his window did not open his mouth.

'To arms! We need weapons!'

'Let's protect ourselves against the foreigners!'

'To the arsenal, then! To Les Invalides!'

A ragged boy leapt up into the chestnut tree above Eugénie's head and began tearing off the bright-green papery leaves. He threw them out to the crowd; broken twigs almost hit her. People began to stuff them into their hats like cockades: green, the colour of hope and liberty.

'Come!' cried Hortense again, and pulled Eugénie away.

Clinging together, they battled through an oncoming surge of people, eager to hear the rest of the speech. An old man was knocked to the ground. No one stopped to help him and he was trampled over as if he were a piece of rubbish. A red wound opened in his bald, sunburnt head.

Eugénie gasped and bit her tongue. The inside of her mouth, coated with sweetness from marshmallow and lemonade, filled with blood.

The crowd had become a mob: a bellowing, mindless beast.

It took them a long time to escape and they were forced to go in the wrong direction. In the theatre district Hortense looked for a cab. They were both dishevelled and exhausted, their clothes and hair sticking to them with sweat and dust. Hortense had stuck leaves in their hats to avoid the crowds molesting them, and these had turned into wilting green rags. It was no cooler, though dark clouds hid the sun.

They passed empty theatres, their façades barricaded. At the top of the street they paused, frozen by the sound of commotion behind them: shouts and yells and unearthly cries.

Hortense gasped and put her hand to her mouth. She had gone white with shock.

'Don't look, mademoiselle!' Then her colour came back patchily and her hand dropped. 'They must have broken into Monsieur Curteius's waxworks.' She dragged Eugénie on. 'Hurry! Hurry before they are on us!'

Eugénie looked back and, in a single instant that she never forgot, saw the waxen heads on poles carried by the triumphant mob: disembodied heads, jerking and bobbing against the darkening sky.

And that was when Raoul Goullet, the pale assassin, encountered Eugénie de Boncoeur again: on his way from the Palais-Royal, his coach taking the back streets behind the theatre district to avoid the mob.

He did not, of course, recognize her at first. He looked out and saw a dark-haired young woman pulling a girl in a white dress over the dusty cobbles, and as he saw them, the young woman raised her hand in a pleading way.

He ordered the driver to stop and opened the door reluctantly: he did not like children.

'Thank you, monsieur!' exclaimed the young woman. She sank down trembling on the seat opposite and clutched the girl to her. 'They are going to Les Invalides to search for muskets! There'll be a riot!'

'The Revolution has begun,' said Goullet.

There was satisfaction in his tone, and Hortense looked at him with interest.

He was richly dressed in a white brocade coat and lace ruffles, but the coach bore no aristocratic crest. Under his powdered hair his face was unhealthy-looking in its extreme pallor and with something chilling about it, the cruel mouth, perhaps, or the cold, narrowed eyes.

All the same she ventured, 'You would support a revolution then, monsieur?'

'I believe that it will present ... opportunities,' Goullet said.

His gaze was caught by the child, who was staring at his black-gloved fingers. She looked away as if she knew she had been rude. She was exquisite, even though her dress was dirty and her mouth crusted with sugar. Her skin was like porcelain, smooth, unblemished, translucent; she reminded him of one of his own precious figurines. He had the largest and most valuable collection of china in Paris, kept in locked glass cabinets.

'You like *pâté de guimauve*?' he said to the child, who had pulled an empty *papier* from the pocket hanging on her blue sash.

The governess nudged her, and she nodded her head unsmiling.

'Where shall I take you?' he said to the governess.

Flustered, Hortense told him, and belatedly introduced them both. She saw something enter the man's icy eyes, but he said nothing more and when they reached the lane off the rue Saint-Honoré and the coach had stopped, he pulled out the steps and helped Hortense down, taking her hand in his gloved one. She tried to suppress a shudder; inside the black silk, there was something very wrong with his fingers.

The pale assassin leant back as the coach swayed away, and a small smile played on his thin lips. He had been watching the brother for some time, but now fate had brought him the sister too.

Eugénie de Boncoeur might be a child now, but one day she would grow up.

He had only to wait a little.

Two

14 July 1789–September 1790

On the 14th July, two days after Eugénie and Hortense had fled the uproar in the Palais-Royal, the people destroyed the old fortress-prison of the Bastille, the hated symbol of oppression. Initially they were searching for gunpowder and cartridges for the muskets they had stolen from Les Invalides, but in the turmoil the men defending the prison were savagely killed.

On the 17th, there was a special ceremony at the Hôtel de Ville - the town hall. Hortense took Eugénie to see the King acknowledge both the new National Guard, formed from the citizens' militia, and a revolutionary council, called the Commune, that would now govern Paris. The King's carriage arrived first; General Lafayette, the people's war hero, who had been appointed Commander of the National Guard, rode behind it on a white horse, his beaky nose pointing the way. Sixty thousand citizens followed him noisily, armed with muskets, pikes and cudgels.

Eugénie watched as the King stumbled out on to the balcony. He mumbled a few words and a tricolour cockade was stuffed into his hat. He had lost most of his personal army, most of his power to the National Assembly, and his aura of royal invulnerability. He looked bemused – belittled – as he blinked short-sightedly at the shouting crowds.

Eugénie thought he did not look like a king at all.

The King had been forced to agree that the National Assembly should prepare a constitution. In the streets strangers fell on each other's necks in joy: the Revolution was over – or so it was generally thought.

But the country was still bankrupt, and still the people starved. In the sweltering heat of summer they ransacked the empty bakers' shops; they accused the aristocrats of hoarding grain. While the Comte and Eugénie's older brother Armand were away at Haut-bois, Eugénie and Hortense hid indoors with the shutters tightly closed, while the mob roared through the streets, overturning any carriage that bore the crest of a nobleman.

Eugénie stood in the dim, stifling withdrawing room on the first floor of her guardian's mansion-house. Her silk dress, limp with the heat, clung to her as she peered down through a crack in the shutters. A group of men with pitchforks were running along the lane below in the hot sunlight, their filthy faces streaming with sweat: workmen or *sans culottes*, in long, dirty trousers. The sinister words of the 'Ça Ira', the revolutionary song, came hoarsely up to her.

'*Ah, ça ira! Les aristocrats à la lanterne!*'

The street lanterns hung from iron supports that jutted out at right angles from the houses; they were used by the mob as convenient gibbets. Eugénie trembled as she listened. *Why do they hate us so much?* she thought. *What have we done?*

She asked Hortense, who was standing silently in the shadows behind her.

'The people hear about the extravagances of the King's court, while they wear rags and can't afford to eat.' Hortense shrugged. 'The nobility have too many privileges. And they do not pay the *taille*.'

The *taille* was the main tax, and Eugénie could see it was unfair that only poor people had to pay it. 'But will a new constitution change things?' she said, staring through the shutters again. 'Will they stop threatening us then?'

'People have long memories,' said Hortense. 'There's a chasm between the aristocrats and the poor. It's so deep it can only be resolved by something great and terrible.'

Hortense was not given to affection, but Eugénie felt her hand touch her back lightly. 'Many aristocrats are emigrating, fleeing the country before it is too late. You and your brother should do the same, mademoiselle.'

The men, still singing raucously, had disappeared into the rue Saint-Honoré.

'Armand will never leave,' Eugénie said firmly. 'He is not a coward.' She turned from the shutters, but her voice wavered as she looked into Hortense's intelligent, pitying eyes.

'What would those men have done if I had gone out into the lane?' She put her hands to her face. 'Would they have hanged me? Yet I have done nothing. Have I, Hortense?'

For the next few months there was a deceptive calm in Paris. The National Assembly drew up the principles of a constitution: the Declaration of the Rights of Man and the Citizen. 'All men were born free and equal, in their rights.' The Paris season was the most glittering that it had ever been – either a feast before famine or a celebration, depending on one's viewpoint.

Then on the 5th October, a crowd of market women stormed the Hôtel de Ville, which had become the headquarters of the Commune. They demanded bread for their starving families. In the wild wet night they gathered in the Place Louis XV, waving pitchforks, broomsticks and flaming torches, determined to march to Versailles and put their complaints to the King. They made such a fearful noise when they set off the following morning that it woke Eugénie as she lay between her lace-edged sheets, sleeping late after a visit to the Comédie-Française.

The King, the Queen and their two children were forced from their gilded palace in Versailles to the draughty and decaying Tuileries Palace, not far from the house belonging to Eugénie's guardian. King Louis XVI had become a prisoner of the people in all but name. The great and terrible thing of which Hortense had spoken was starting to happen.

One September morning the following year, Eugénie's brother Armand and their guardian, Comte Lefaurie of Haut-bois, were talking in the withdrawing room of the mansion-house.

The elderly Comte had lowered his great girth on to an armless chair that he knew from experience would take his weight, despite its delicate-looking carved legs.

His young ward Armand was standing facing him, before the mantelpiece. Earlier that morning he had been fencing with his friend, Julien de Fortin, and his skin was still flushed with heat; but he had come down from his rooms with alacrity when a servant brought him the Comte's summons. It was best to stay on the right side of the Comte, who was still paying him an allowance and permitting him to stay in his house. He wondered a little apprehensively why his guardian wanted to see him.

The Comte yawned. 'I declare, long evenings, such as we endured last night, are too much at my age. Give me my dinner at five. Ten o'clock and I am asleep!'

'It was a glittering gathering, though, was it not, monsieur?' Armand had been dazzled and thrilled by it, but thought it would appear naive to say so. His blue eyes, set wide apart, had a perpetual expression of wonder and delight in the world.

The Comte snorted in derision. He rubbed his right leg in its white silk stocking, and rested it on a footstool; he suffered from gout.

'Madame de Staël's salons are always like that. Boudoir politics! Be careful. You'll be sucked in. She likes young men, particularly young lawyers.'

'It's true that I have now become a bourgeois!' said Armand, nervously trying a joke. Unlike the middle classes – the bourgeousie – it was most unusual for a member of the *noblesse de court* to take up the profession of law, but Armand wanted to rebuild his family fortune. At the moment that was far off: he was still studying for his bar exams.

'A bourgeois is not a bad thing to be nowadays,' said the Comte thoughtfully. 'They are stronger than us economically, now that the nobility has been stripped of its tax privileges and feudal dues.' He regarded Armand with his sharp eyes. 'Your poor father would be proud of you. You must qualify, and not become distracted by the Revolution. I know you go to the Jacobin Club, that hotbed of Freemasons and revolutionaries!'

'I go to find out what mayhem they plan next,' protested Armand, flushing. Was this why the Comte wanted to see him? 'But I am no radical, I do assure you, monsieur! I desire a liberal constitution – as you do – but I'm also a royalist.'

'Soon it may not be possible to be both, Armand.'

'Soon? Then you do not think the Revolution over?'

The Comte shook his head. 'The people have learnt a dangerous thing – that violence and bloodshed bring power.' He leant forward.

'Louis is well guarded in the Tuileries Palace. But are they preventing an attack on him, or his escape? He will be forced to sign the constitution when it is finally drawn up. When I visited him last week there was a hunted look in his eyes. What will happen next, I wonder?'

The Comte sighed, took off his wig and put it over his foot. His scalp was baby pink, with a fringe of sparse white hair. 'At least I'll not be here to see it. I am retiring to Haut-bois. The peasants are still loyal to me at the moment. Let us hope that they will remain so in a year's time!'

'We'll miss you in Paris,' said Armand politely. He did not love his guardian, but he respected him.

'Tosh! I am too old for all this. The world I know has been destroyed almost overnight. I'm a relic of the past. Even my servants have become sullen and lazy.' The Comte wiped his hand over the surface of the rosewood bureau beside him and blew the dust from his fingers in disgust.

'But the new house on the Champs-Elysées? I thought you were planning to move there?'

'Paris is covered with holes where grand new buildings were to rise before the Revolution. My house on the Champs-Elysées is one of them. All work has stopped on it. I trust you to visit it from time to time in my stead and supervise the builders when they begin again – if they ever do. I shall go on paying your allowance so that you can continue your studies, of course.'

'Thank you, monsieur,' Armand said gratefully, relieved that the Comte had said nothing more about his revolutionary activities and that the conversation seemed at an end. 'While you're away I shall live a studious life and look after my sister.'

He was startled when the Comte said abruptly, 'That won't be necessary.'

Armand, about to make his farewell bow, stared at him.

'It is high time Eugénie went to a convent to finish her education, like other young girls of her class,' said the Comte. 'She must learn some self-discipline. I have selected the Convent of the Sacred Spirit, which my own sister attended years ago. Eugénie will be safe within its walls whatever happens in Paris.'

Armand hesitated. 'But Hortense, her governess? They are very close. Eugénie will be devastated to bid her farewell!'

The Comte's frown made deep folds in his fleshy forehead.

'The governess is one of the reasons I have made my decision. She has no regard for her position or place. She reads revolutionary newspapers, articles inciting violence – one of the servants told me so. I have seen her attending the National Assembly with a tricolour rosette pinned to her hat.'

'There is no law against women attending its sessions, monsieur,' said Armand mildly. 'I believe many do – aristocratic ladies among them, who wear the tricolour.'

'She fills Eugénie's head with nonsense!' retorted the Comte.

'I doubt my little sister pays attention. I suspect she is more interested in the pretty clothes and trinkets you lavish on her so generously, monsieur!'

But the Comte was not to be stopped. He held up a pudgy hand that sparkled with diamonds. 'Women should not be involved in politics. They do not have the vote. Women have already had far too much to do with this revolution. Meanwhile, I do not believe Hortense spends any time with Eugénie on embroidery or mending. The child has no accomplishments at all!'

'I taught her to fence at Chauvais,' Armand offered, feeling he should defend his sister. 'And she learnt to ride and shoot there as well as any youth.'

The Comte glared. 'Was it you who involved her in those inappropriate pastimes?'

'No, monsieur.' Armand cleared his throat. 'Her groom.'

'That is exactly what I mean. After the death of her mother, she was allowed to run wild at Chauvais, and your father indulged her. Now she must learn the proper duties of a woman of her class.'

Armand was silent, his face doubtful.

The Comte shifted his gouty leg irritably. 'Do you not understand? Eugénie has no title – not that that means much, now that we've been stripped of them – but worse, with the estate bankrupt, she has no money coming to her when she is of age. Her only chance is to make a good marriage with a wealthy husband.'

'But I'll protect her, monsieur,' said Armand eagerly. 'Soon I'll be earning.'

'The road is long and hard for a young barrister before he can make a name for himself, and who knows what the future holds for the profession now. No, Eugénie must marry and marry well.' The Comte paused.

'Raoul Goullet has observed her out walking with her governess in the Tuileries Gardens. He has asked for her hand.'

Armand's face fell in shock. 'Raoul Goullet? But he is so much older, monsieur! You cannot allow such a thing!'

The Comte's frown deepened. 'I am Eugénie's guardian. I am concerned for her future welfare. Goullet is the richest man in Paris. And he is in excellent health. I have stipulated that no marriage can take place until Eugénie is sixteen.'

'But Raoul Goullet must be fifty!' cried Armand.

'I have never spoken to the man, but he has no rank or breeding.'

The Comte's sharp eyes grew very cold. 'Titles mean nothing any more, since we are forbidden to use them. Eugénie does not need to love Goullet. If she carries out her wifely duties, she will be more than well provided for. She can take lovers.'

'Monsieur, there is something about Goullet I do not like. You know what they call him?'

'Le Fantôme?' said the Comte impatiently. 'The name signifies nothing. He is a well-known figure in Parisian society, attends every occasion.'

'That is exactly it,' said Armand desperately. 'He is like a ghost, always listening in the shadows. I believe he confers with the Watching Eye, the brotherhood of Freemasons he has formed. Whose side is he on?'

The Comte sighed wearily. 'He is like you and me, Armand, trying to support both the King and the people's constitution.'

Armand bit his lip. 'Monsieur, I beg you, reconsider.'

The diamonds flashed with a hard glitter as the Comte waved his plump fingers again dismissively. 'It is too late. That is why I wished to see you. I signed the marriage contract last night.'

'You should not have done such a thing!' Armand burst out. 'Have you told Eugénie?'

'Of course not. She is still a child, she would not understand my reasons. And I forbid you to mention it to her either.'

Armand stood rigid, the blood draining from his face. He was mute, not daring to defy the Comte, yet shamefully aware of his own cowardice.

The Comte's lips tightened. 'I have taken you and your sister in, regardless of the inconvenience, for your father saved my life in that benighted war against the British in America that helped to bankrupt our country. But I mean to carry out my duties as guardian until you come of age, Armand. If you qualify as a barrister, which you cannot do without my money, and Eugénie marries, then I will know I have done my best for you both and repaid the debt I owe your father in full.'

He took the wig off his foot and thrust it back on his head, where it hung down lopsidedly above his fiercely glinting eyes.

'Now ring the bell. First we need to dismiss the governess.'

Eugénie had been standing at the window of her little salon on the third floor of the Comte's old mansion-house.

If she craned her head sideways she could see the

trees of the Tuileries Gardens, already looking dry and yellow after the hot summer, and the roof of the *manège*, the former riding school, where Hortense went so often to watch the National Assembly meet. If she opened her window and leant out, she could even see the gloomy façade of the Tuileries Palace at the end of the Gardens, where the royal family lived now. By all accounts it was a very draughty and uncomfortable place: she would hate it herself.

She looked around her comfortable sitting room with complacency; the Comte gave her everything she wanted. Except love . . .

There was a familiar step on the stairs outside her door.

'Armand!' She skipped joyfully across the room and flung her arms around her brother. 'I am so glad you are come to see me! It has been so dull all morning! Can we take the *berline* and drive out to the Bois de Boulogne this afternoon? Will you ask Monsieur le Comte? He will allow it, I'm sure! I shall wear the new hat Madame Rose Bertin designed for me!'

Armand disengaged himself gently; his face was grave.

Her arms dropped to her sides, and her heart filled with a terrible foreboding. He looked as he had at Chauvais when he came to tell her that Papa had died.

'Why, Armand,' she faltered. 'Whatever is the matter?'

Armand had watched as the Comte dismissed Hortense. The young woman did not flinch, or shed a tear or beg him to reconsider. She merely nodded, as if she had been expecting such a thing. A small ironic smile played over her lips.

I know you are a revolutionary like me, Hortense, Armand thought. *But there is such a difference between us!* He was in awe of her strength and self-control, yet almost frightened by it.

When he went upstairs to tell Eugénie that Hortense was to leave and she would have to continue her education at the convent, he had never seen his sister turn so white, not even when Papa died.

Minutes later, Hortense herself came into the little salon. Eugénie ran to her without speaking and flung her arms around her. Tears streamed down her face.

Hortense stood as straight and stiff as a pillar, unmoving. Finally, one of her hands came up to touch Eugénie's shining hair. 'Be careful, *ma petite*,' Armand heard her whisper. 'Be very careful. Things are going to change.'

After she had left and Eugénie had huddled, weeping, into an armchair, Armand found he could not bring himself to tell his sister about the secret marriage contract. He stared at her, the words sticking in his throat. *There is time*, he thought. *I will do it later, when she is not so distressed.*

Eugénie looked up at him through tear-drenched eyes. She had lost Hortense, and soon she would have to say goodbye to Armand as well. She had passed the Convent of the Sacred Spirit in the *berline* once, with Hortense.

It looked like a prison.

THREE

March 1791

Eugénie was sitting on a bench in the dank, weedy little courtyard that lay behind the high front gates of the Convent of the Sacred Spirit. There was a chill wind, but she could not bear to be cloistered inside any longer. She ignored the book of devotion open on her lap; she was waiting for someone – anyone – to walk by the gates so that she could watch them. Any reminder of the outside world, even the clatter of a carriage, was thrilling to her now.

I might as well be a nun myself, she thought dolefully, in the hanging silence.

No noise was allowed in the convent, nothing that would disturb the nuns' daily routine of prayer and meditation, except the gloomy clanging of chapel bells to mark the services. Even during needlework and the making of altar lace, conversation between the six boarders was forbidden, so from the first it had been difficult for Eugénie to make friends, though the other girls were all aristocrats of her own age.

There was growing menace in the streets, an upsurge of resentment against the clergy. The girls whispered about it to each other, but no one really understood its reason. Their music and singing lessons stopped; the tutor was too afraid to walk through the streets to the convent. Then a carriage belonging to the Abbot was overturned. In the convent, the nuns murmured and turned away when they thought the boarders were listening, though Eugénie did her best to overhear.

One by one the girls went home, and Eugénie wondered if she would ever see them again.

Now she was the only one left.

She had surreptitiously tucked a letter from her English uncle into her book of devotion, and now she pulled it out to read again. It was the first letter she had received at the convent in the months she had been there, and though she wished it might have been from Hortense instead, it was better than no letter at all.

> My dearest niece,
> It concerns me greatly to read reports of the Revolution in the newspapers here. I am certain

that Paris is a dangerous city for a young girl at this time. It is possible that your guardian, being elderly and living so far away from the capital, has not heard of all the momentous events affecting your poor country. I beg you to consider taking refuge in England with us until the whole affair is over. I know your late mother, my own dear sister, would have wanted it, had she lived to see such turbulent times. Your cousin Henrietta and I would gladly welcome you here on the coast in Deal . . .

Escape! thought Eugénie. If she never had to make another border of altar lace she would thank God for ever! But how could she leave Armand?

As she tucked the letter back between the pages, the wind played with a weedy sapling by the gates and lifted the hem of her dress. She thought suddenly that she caught a hint of greening in the air, the promise of spring. Putting down her book, she jumped up.

This won't always be my life, she thought, as she lifted her skirts and pointed her foot. *I mustn't forget my dance steps!* And she began to whirl around in the wind, humming under her breath.

One of the elderly nuns, Sister Marie, paused in passing an upstairs window that overlooked the courtyard, saw Eugénie dancing and brought a thin, papery hand to her mouth in horror. She had a soft spot for the wilful child, but all the same – such improper behaviour in a convent! Men might look through the gates and see her. She should hurry down at once and reprimand her.

And yet she found herself reluctant to move. For a moment she was caught by an emotion she scarcely remembered, as the small, youthful figure below her, fair hair flying in the wind, danced on, alone and oblivious in the grey courtyard.

Armand came to visit later that day.

'Why can't I come home with you?' whispered Eugénie. She put out her hand and gripped his arm with her sore, pricked fingers. 'All the other girls have gone and the nuns are such dull company!'

He hesitated a moment. 'You can't stay in the Comte's house alone. I have moved out and taken rooms with Julien de Fortin in the rue Saint-Antoine.'

'Oh,' said Eugénie in surprise, her hand falling. For a moment she was at a loss, then she said brightly, 'But the servants will look after me, as always.'

She noticed he did not look at her. 'There are few left there, Eugénie.'

'Then can't I come and stay with you and Julien?'

'It wouldn't be suitable without a chaperone,' Armand said gently. He looked at her downcast face. 'I promise I will arrange a visit soon, Eugénie.'

They had brought their chairs close together in the visiting chamber, a small, chill room without windows, off the cloisters. Facing each other, their heads close together, they spoke English, not French. Their mother had been English and they had grown up speaking both languages. They had no fear of being understood at the moment, but still they whispered; outside the open door the dark figures of nuns glided past over the stone with bent heads and expressionless faces, their hands tucked into their flowing sleeves.

'They don't even allow me out with them to take alms to the poor. They say it is too dangerous now.' Eugénie made a face. 'Life is boring beyond belief, Armand!'

'Think of what you are learning.'

'Nothing of any importance. How I wish I'd listened to Hortense! She knew so much.' She paused and said carefully, 'What has befallen poor Hortense? Do you know? I've had no letter.' She could not stop the hurt creeping into her voice.

'For a while I saw her sitting in the public gallery at the National Assembly. I think she is well able to look after herself. You shouldn't fear for her.'

Eugénie sighed. 'The books she wanted me to read – I rejected them all. There are no books here, except Bibles and prayer books and devotional texts.'

Armand smiled. 'Then think how you'll be able to improve your husband in due course! You'll make an excellent god-fearing wife.'

'A wife?' said Eugénie in disgust. 'Is that all there is in life for a woman? I must have adventures first!' She tossed her head. 'I shall marry late, if at all.'

His smile faded and a curious expression crossed his face. He shook his head. 'But how would you support yourself? Be sensible, Eugénie. What else can there be for you but marriage, in your situation?'

She changed the subject quickly because he looked so sad. 'Is there news of Monsieur le Comte?'

'He writes that he is well, but suffering sorely from the pain in his leg. He will not return to Paris, I think. He has been sent a parcel of white feathers.'

'White feathers? But don't they symbolize cowardice?'

'It is because he hasn't shown his disapproval of the Revolution by emigrating to England.'

'To my mind it is much more cowardly to leave France than to stay!'

'Many nobles think by emigrating they show their loyalty to the crown.' Armand shook his head and his wide, dreaming eyes shone. 'I could never desert my country. Besides, things are happening that may strengthen the King's position.' He stopped abruptly.

'What things?' demanded Eugénie.

'Secret plans.' He looked at her intently. 'I can't say more.'

She was agog. 'Are you involved?'

He shook his head and put a finger to his lips, frowning.

Eugénie tried not to look as if she minded that something that sounded so much more exciting than her own dull days was being kept from her. But then she thought of something interesting to tell him.

'I've received a present from an anonymous sender, Armand – isn't that mysterious? At first I thought it was from you, and indeed, so did the nuns, else they wouldn't have given me it, I'm sure.' She began to laugh and then clapped her hand over her mouth to suppress it. 'Of course, they didn't know what was in it!'

Armand looked taken aback and almost apprehensive, she thought. 'What was it?'

'My favourite *pâté de guimauve*!'

'With no message?'

'Nothing. Perhaps he forgot.'

'He? You think the sender is a man?' said Armand sharply.

'At first I wondered if someone had glimpsed me through the gates. A secret admirer, perhaps!' Her eyes sparkled. 'But the package was addressed to me by name. It must have been Monsieur le Comte. It was kind, and I greatly enjoyed it. I did not tell the nuns what it was, of course.'

He seemed oddly alarmed. 'Eugénie, that was wrong. You should not have eaten it.'

'It's much too late now, Armand!' she said mischievously.

But even then he did not smile.

Early that evening Eugénie was sitting on her narrow wooden bed, trying to memorize the prayer she had been given to learn. Over her head a dark crucifix lowered down from the wall. Each boarder had her own cell for prayer, study and sleep, unheated and sparsely furnished. The stern Mistress of Novices, whose responsibility they were, believed in treating the rich, aristocratic boarders exactly as she treated the novice nuns.

Her door was shut, but she judged that any minute she would hear the tolling of the next bell and after that the strange swishing sound, like a retreating tide over sand, that the nuns' habits always made as they passed on their way to prayers in the church. She, Eugénie, would have to join them.

She waited, but the bell did not sound. That was most singular.

It was still light outside, though dusk would soon fall. Her cell was shadowed and she had lit a candle. The bare plastered walls and the few pieces of furniture were suffused in its warm golden glow, so that she could almost persuade herself that the air was less chill, though she had put on a heavy shawl over her dress.

She was warm at last and almost falling asleep over the prayer book, when she heard a knocking at her door, not loud, but urgent and repeated, and then her name whispered by an old, tremulous voice.

'Mademoiselle de Boncoeur! Mademoiselle Eugénie!'

Startled, Eugénie padded barefoot to the door. She must be late for prayers.

Sister Marie was clutching her rosary in one hand and a candlestick in the other. Her lined face was yellow as parchment in the candle's flame. 'My child . . .'

Eugénie liked Sister Marie, who had comforted her during her first desperate days of homesickness. 'What is it, Sister?' she said puzzled, putting her hand on the nun's thin arm to soothe her, though she knew such touch was forbidden.

The elderly nun controlled herself with an effort. 'You must flee, child. They are coming for us!'

'Who?'

'The mob.' She swallowed. 'Our abbot – he didn't agree to the Civil Constitution, which puts the state before the Church and King. We are all in danger now. I am so sorry, mademoiselle, that you should be with us . . .'

Eugénie stared at her in disbelief. Surely the mob would never break into a sacred place? She could hear nothing, but the convent walls were thick. Then old hands grasped her, something cold and heavy was pushed into her hand.

'Take this key, child. Run to the church. Go out through the east door. It leads to a lane. Whatever you do, lock the door behind you.'

She could not move.

'Take nothing. Go!' Sister Marie's voice rose. 'Go!'

Eugénie caught her fear. Her heartbeat quickened. She began to tremble, as if her body knew it was in danger before her mind could take it in. 'But what of you and the other nuns? How will you escape?'

Sister Marie seemed to gather herself together and her voice was calm.

'The handmaidens of Christ do not fear death. This is the time of His great sacrifice and example. We shall remain in our cells and pray. But you, child, have lived but a short while in Christ.' With firm fingers she made the sign of the cross over Eugénie's head. 'Now hurry!'

Outside the moon had risen over the ancient city. Tonight it wore a devil's face. The narrow street in front of the convent was empty, but soon it would be full of moving light and shadow. There was the sound of harsh voices, the ring of boots, the flare of torches. A crowd was surging over the cobbles towards it, beneath the tightly closed shutters of the houses.

But in one of the tall houses the shutters had not been fastened. A ghostly figure, more like a spectre than a man, looked down on the mob unseen. For a moment he was outlined by the moon's light as his gloved fingers crawled over the window sill.

The convent's iron gates were closed and locked, but someone had an axe. The mob would tear its holy atmosphere apart before the night was over. The moon gleamed in each man's eye and made him mad.

Four

Eugénie slipped through the heavy wooden door that led out of the boarders' quarters. Across the courtyard lay the dark, empty arches of the cloisters; beyond them, the church was outlined by moonlight. As she stepped out on to the cobbles and away from the thick stone walls, she heard terrifying sounds. Crazed laughter, the mad roaring of many voices, a rhythmic thudding and clanging that echoed across the cobbles.

The mob was destroying the convent gates.

On the sharp night air unfamiliar, frightening smells came to her – the tang of burning lanterns, the thick dark stench of men's unwashed bodies.

Run! I must run! But her heart was beating so fast it was difficult to breathe. She gripped the key with a clammy hand. Her legs felt too weak to move. It was the hardest thing she had ever done, to leave the solid stone building for the open courtyard. But the door behind her would soon be hacked to pieces, the quiet passages would reverberate with violence.

Clutching the key to her, she grabbed up her skirts with her other hand and fled for her life.

The church always stood open in case any nun wanted to pray alone. Eugénie hesitated on the threshold and felt her scalp prickle with a different kind of fear. She had never been in here alone, but even by daylight it had always seemed sinister, with its black-beamed roof and rich wall-hangings depicting some of the most violent events of the Bible.

The nuns must have been interrupted in their preparation for Complin, the last office of the day. At the far end of the nave she could see candles burning at each end of the altar table, on which stood the heavy gold cross, the golden chalice and the great burnished communion dish; behind the table, twisted, crucified limbs glowed milkily from an ornate frame. But the gold candelabra that hung all the way down the nave to the rood screen were unlit and the church lay in heavy, incense-laden darkness, except for the eerie glimmer of the gilded statues in their niches along the side aisles and the gleaming whites of their painted eyes. All the riches of the convent had been poured into its church down the ages, and soon the mob would discover them. Even now she could hear that inhuman noise drawing closer.

At the head of the nave she bobbed in the direction of the altar from long habit and crossed herself hastily. From the open door behind her a high scream came on the night air, followed by another and another. Her heart pounding, she began to fumble her way in the darkness past the benches and prayer mats to the aisle that would take her to the east door.

Shouts, yells, the heavy tread of boots over the stone flags. Swinging light around the doorway, dark figures in the light. She shrank behind a pillar.

The voices became distinguishable, one from another. One louder than the others, the leader perhaps, shouted back, his voice booming and echoing through the church. 'Gold, look at that gold!'

Shapes clustered around him. The weapons they carried − sticks, pitchforks − made them look like strange, antlered beasts in the shadows.

'This is where they've hoarded it, those women.'

'Feed the families of Paris for a lifetime!'

'What are we waiting for then?' That was a voice, growling deep, but coming from the figure of a woman, wrapped around with ragged skirts, her head covered by a shawl. She was the first to move towards the altar, swishing over the stones with dreadful intent. Halfway down she turned in triumph, one beckoning arm raised. The shawl fell back. Beneath it was a man's bearded face.

They had dragged a novice nun with them, a young girl. Eugénie had seen her play the organ during services. She was forced to it now, weeping. The dreadful notes of the 'Ça Ira', the anthem of the Revolution, sounded through the church. Figures capered about the little nun, howling out the words of the song drunkenly. A man bent over her and fondled her breasts.

Eugénie began to creep away behind the pillars, keeping to the dark. There was so much noise in the church that there was no danger she would be heard, but with her pale-grey dress, the white shawl around her shoulders and arms, and her long fair hair she was frightened of being seen.

She was in the darkness by the little east door when she heard them seize the gilded statues in the side aisles. There was a crash as one toppled to the flagstones, a blood-curdling oath. The wall-hangings were ripped down to see if anything of value was hidden behind them; she heard shouts of triumph as the tapestries tore, fury as bare stone walls were exposed, the chinking of gold and brass thrown carelessly together as they wrapped their loot, quarrelled over it. A fight started somewhere in the nave.

The east door was small, only as high as her head, and even in the dark she could see there were no bolts, only a vast keyhole. She was trembling from head to foot, her hand shaking so much she could not fit the key in the lock. It was a heavy iron key, greasy from her sweating fingers.

It was in at last. There was a sharp click as the latch slid back. She held her breath, but the sound had not been heard in the uproar behind her. Someone was trying to lift the gold communion cup.

Then there was the tread of feet very close, and light swung towards her: a man, carrying a lantern.

There was nowhere to hide. She felt powerless to move. She whimpered with fear. She stood with her back to the door, her palms against the wood, and felt it give behind her; at the same time as she saw the man's underlit face, a skull on thin shoulders that were clothed in darkly stained rags. He carried a block of wood that glistened black with blood.

His jaw dropped in shock as he took in the pale apparition before him, its streaming golden hair and white, feathered wings outstretched against the door. Lantern and cudgel fell from his fingers as instinctively he tried to make the sign of the cross.

There was a crash on the stone and the candle went out. Eugénie pushed against the door violently, and it opened behind her. She tumbled backwards into nothing.

She found herself lying in the cold, soft mud of a deep ditch. Above her the moon shone down; a few stars glittered from a black sky. She was dazed, all the air knocked from her lungs by her fall, and weak with shock. Scarcely able to raise her head, the fear of even now being discovered by the mob made her struggle to a crouching position. She was covered in foul-smelling mud, up to her ankles in it, her stockings and shoes soaked through and her wet, stinking skirts clinging to her.

The door to the church still hung open on the darkness inside and that terrible raucous noise boomed and echoed from within, but distanced, as if it came from under water. Eugénie began to scuttle along the ditch like a frightened animal, keeping her head low. She wanted to leave the east door as far behind her as possible before she ventured on to the lane itself. Finding she was moaning softly under her breath, she clamped her jaws shut; tears streamed down her face, but she was unaware of them.

Beyond the convent walls a row of mean little houses

were pressed together, and tightly shuttered in the darkness. She could make out another line of buildings opposite. There was not a soul to be seen, no one to help her. An apprehensive silence trembled over the lane, as if the occupants of the hovels that bordered it were holding their breath, in case breathing should make too much noise and alert the mob.

Had Sister Marie been one of the mob's victims? A thin wail escaped Eugénie before she could stop it. And then, at her lowest ebb, as she clambered out of the ditch, she heard the miraculous sound of wheels churning and splashing towards her along the narrow lane. Only the rich could afford a carriage, and the rich were not part of the mob.

She raised an arm desperately. In her sorry state, she must look like a beggar-girl. She tried to mouth, *Please help me*, but no sound came out. If the carriage did not stop, she would be knocked down, for it took up the entire width of the lane, narrowly avoiding the ditches.

She saw the occupant pull down the window and shout something at the driver. There was sudden yellow light on her face and a frantic jingling of harnesses as the horses were reined in. The gleaming black door was opened by an arm in a satin sleeve.

The voice of a gentleman said, 'Mademoiselle? Are you in trouble? May I assist you?'

She could not see his face in the darkness, but before she could hesitate he had let down the step and she felt her hands grasped. The next moment she was lifted up and pulled inside.

'Do not be frightened,' said her saviour softly. 'You are safe now.' It was a young man's voice. 'I thought I knew you, and indeed I do. Are you not the little sister of my friend, Armand de Boncoeur? Whatever are you doing in such a place, on such a night?'

Eugénie could not answer. She shook her head, and leant back on the leather as the young man rapped smartly on the front panel of the carriage and they jerked away over the ruts. She was shivering violently from the chill of her wet clothes.

'Tuck this around you, mademoiselle.' He was offering her a fur rug. Eugénie made a feeble protest, all too dreadfully aware of her reeking state, but he pressed it upon her. She tried to whisper her thanks.

Behind them the convent glowed red, and acrid smoke drifted after them on the night air.

'My name is Guy Deschamps,' said the young man, as they left the lane behind and drove into a wider thoroughfare where the hanging street lanterns had been lit. 'I have met you with your brother on several occasions, walking in the Tuileries Gardens and at the Festival of the Federation last summer. He has talked of you so often, and I believe he told me you were to be a boarder at the Convent of the Sacred Spirit. You were lucky to escape with your life tonight.'

In the half-light Eugénie remembered him now, a tall young man, with auburn hair that he wore unpowdered. He was older than Armand and had already qualified as a lawyer. Last summer at the festival when she had been a whole nine months younger he had charmed her by treating her as an adult. When Armand had introduced her, he had bowed low and kissed her hand.

'It was my good fortune you saw me,' she whispered. 'I am most grateful, monsieur.'

'I had an appointment nearby, but all the gates in that quarter are shut against the mob now. We took our lives in our hands, the driver and I, set off at the speed of lightning through a back way and kept the carriage darkened.'

'I thought the Revolution was over,' wailed Eugénie.

He shook his head. 'Oh no, mademoiselle, it's not ended yet.'

Suddenly, unexpectedly, she began to cry.

'You poor little thing, I shall take you straight to Armand,' said Monsieur Deschamps. 'He'll be at

Madame de Staël's salon tonight, I do not doubt. I am invited myself.'

The prospect of seeing Armand and so soon was almost painful. Eugénie longed to be safe in his arms and fussed over by him. He would be aghast to hear what had happened to her. She began to cry in earnest, trembling with horror inside the fur rug.

Guy Deschamps calmly passed her a lace handkerchief and made no comment. At last she managed to sob, 'Thank you, monsieur. You are most kind.'

'Our arrival will cause some consternation among those complacent guests, I think.' He gave a wry smile. 'They'll meet someone who has experienced the Revolution at first hand instead of merely talking about it!'

He leant forward to knock again. 'The rue du Bac!'

Eugénie's weeping subsided. She felt an overwhelming fatigue as they rattled over the Pont Royal. Beneath half-closed lids she saw the dark watery shine of the Seine. She was not sure then if she slept, or fainted.

The next time she became conscious it was to feel strong arms beneath her, scooping her up in the fur rug, like a parcel. She was lifted through the carriage door and chill night air touched her cheeks. With a little moan she buried her face in Guy Deschamps's shoulder, shielding her eyes from the dazzle of candles as he carried her into golden warmth and what seemed to be a thousand voices all talking at once.

Then there was silence.

FIVE

Later, a shadow fell across Eugénie's sleeping body. She had been laid down gently in the huge bed in Madame de Staël's own chamber, generously offered by the hostess herself, who felt it was the least she could do for dear Armand's little sister after such an appalling experience. Now marble, gilt and firelight surrounded Eugénie, and was reflected in the great ornate mirrors so that there seemed no need for candles.

The young maid, sent to watch over her while the guests partook of supper, lowered her eyes as a gentleman guest entered unexpectedly, lost among Madame's many rooms, perhaps. He stayed merely a moment, staring over at the sleeping girl, then left without a word. Out of the corner of her eye, the maid noticed that he was wearing black gloves.

* * *

Eugénie did not know how long she had been asleep, but when she awoke it was to find she was lying in an enormous bed, with sumptuously gilded corner posts. The heavy silk hangings were drawn back and Armand sat with her, gripping her hand.

'Armand?'

'You are safe, Eugénie. There's nothing to fear here.'

She lay comfortably for a moment, content to be with him, as she sleepily traced the patterning of the canopy over her head with her eyes. Beneath the bedclothes, the embroidered sheets and the padded silk coverlet, she was wearing clean underlinen and a shift. Her filthy clothes had been taken away. Someone had washed her as she lay there, for her hair was still damp. That someone must have also seen her naked, but at the moment she scarcely cared.

Madame de Staël must still be entertaining, though Eugénie had no notion what hour of the night it was; there were voices somewhere, and music, and she could distinctly smell food on the air. She was exceedingly hungry, she realized, and her mouth watered as she thought of the supper tables laid out with great dishes of delicacies – chicken, young lamb, sweetbreads, tenderly cooked vegetables, each with its own rich sauce or shining glaze.

Armand had covered his eyes with his free hand. 'How could I have let such terrible things happen to you?'

Eugénie took his hand away gently. 'But it wasn't your fault, Armand. I was so fortunate – your friend – that he should come along in his carriage and see me . . .'

'I owe Guy so much for rescuing you.' Armand shook his head bitterly. 'Those monsters betray the spirit of the Revolution!'

Eugénie thought of the skeletal face she had seen, the desperate eyes. *A man, not a monster.* If she was hungry now, how much hungrier must he be?

Then all at once she was surrounded by people. The room with its gold embroidered wallpaper seemed full of silk French coats, foaming lace, white stockings; the rustle and gleam of dresses. Out of the midst of the chattering throng came two footmen, bowing low, who placed a laden tray on her knees.

A large young woman with poppy-red cheeks and dishevelled dark hair, wearing a chemise with a shockingly low neckline, stood with her back to the fireplace, talking non-stop to a group of guests while she surveyed Eugénie in a proprietorial way. This was Madame de Staël herself. Several more gentlemen and ladies had wandered in, and were now examining

Eugénie as she lay in bed, just as if she were an exhibit at one of the new botanical lectures, one elderly gentleman even quizzing her through his lorgnette, his goggling eye huge and glassy. What was worse was that they were talking over her head about her in pitying whispers, as if she could not hear what they were saying perfectly well.

'Armand,' whispered Eugénie uncomfortably. 'I do not think it is proper for all these strangers to see me like this!'

'There's no need to concern yourself.' Armand nodded towards the young woman by the fire and leant closer. 'Our hostess allows visitors in when she takes her milk-bath. It is the done thing, Eugénie, you may be sure of it!'

He rose hastily and bowed, as Madame de Staël advanced to the bed. She had beautiful, intelligent dark eyes, which brimmed with kindness as she looked at Eugénie. 'My poor little creature! How do you do?'

Eugénie sat up straighter, feeling an impossible urge to curtsy and trying not to unbalance the tray of food. The smell of roast quail made her mouth water. 'I am much recovered, madame,' she said with as much dignity as she could muster, 'and obliged to you for your hospitality.'

A woman held a glass of watered wine to Eugénie's

lips, as if she could not do it for herself. 'Oh, my dear, how I sympathize!' she cried. 'A gaggle of *poissardes*, those dreadful market women, stopped my carriage in the Bois de Boulogne recently in broad daylight and demanded money for bread in the most terrifying way.'

'What did you do, madame?' said Eugénie politely, eyeing her food.

'Why, I gave it to them! It would have been my life otherwise, I'm sure of it. All I had was a handful of francs. They wanted it doubled. That women should behave in such a way, even common women like those!'

'Perhaps we should envy them their courage, Victoire,' said Madame de Staël lightly. 'They did it so that their husbands and children shouldn't starve. The Revolution is giving women the chance to think independently at last.'

'Oh, we all know your views, Germaine!' said the woman sulkily. 'You would desire women to have the vote even if they have no fortune or education.'

A tall gentleman with hair-powder in his ears leant over and said mildly, 'Either no individual has genuine rights, Victoire, or they all have the same ones, be they man or woman, rich or poor, educated or not.'

'But do you not agree that such a society would be lawless and violent, Condorcet? Yet I do believe that is the kind of society Germaine wishes to see!'

'If you understood my views, Victoire,' said Madame de Staël, her fine eyes flashing, 'you would know that I desire a balance between liberty and order. I wish for moderation, not more bloodshed.'

Eugénie tried not to yawn at all this dull conversation going on over her head, and continued eating.

'There will be change, Germaine,' said the gentleman called Condorcet. 'There's violence in the streets again. What the changes will be I cannot tell, but once begun, a revolution has its own momentum.'

'Then I am confused, Marquis,' said the woman called Victoire crossly. 'I had thought the Revolution over.'

'Me too, madame!' Eugénie piped up through a mouthful of quail. For some reason that made them all laugh, and she was patted on the head by the Marquis de Condorcet's bony hand.

'Why, once this is over, no doubt your brother will find you a husband, you pretty little thing,' said Victoire with a smile.

'But I don't wish to be married, madame!' said Eugénie in alarm.

She saw that Armand looked uncomfortable, but Victoire was continuing, 'What else is there for you, but a husband, my dear? That is the lot of us women, whatever greater freedoms Germaine desires for us.'

Eugénie's tray was removed by bowing footmen. She

began to feel sleepy; the guests passing before her were dreamlike, insubstantial figures that clustered about her bed and disappeared. Old men with powdered wigs; young women in loose dresses, hair curling artlessly on their shoulders; older women dressed in the old, elaborate style of corseted bodices and wide, panniered skirts, their faces patched and hectically rouged and their piled hair decorated with extraordinary ornaments – one a miniature of the Bastille: they all viewed her most particularly, and were gone.

Then there was no one in the great golden chamber except for herself, drowsing in the bed, and Armand and another young man sitting by the fire. Their voices were a lulling murmur. Looking beneath her lids, she could see that the young man was Armand's great friend, Julien de Fortin, who often used to visit Armand at their guardian's mansion-house.

Julien de Fortin was a little older than Armand, slight, with a shock of dark hair falling over a thin, intense face. He had come to Paris all the way from Gascony, and had studied at the prestigious Collège Louis-le-Grand as a scholarship boy. People said he would make a brilliant lawyer, but on the occasions Eugénie had met him she had thought him dull in the extreme. He had no humour or charm, and frowned out at the world beneath curved black brows. She had never been able to make out what it was that her gregarious brother with all his enthusiasm and energy saw in Julien, who was so quiet that he appeared morose.

They would be talking about nothing that interested her, she thought, merely politics as usual: that was all Julien could talk about. She wriggled into a more comfortable position and closed her eyes. Sleep came at once.

Julien leant towards Armand. He spoke urgently, but kept his voice low.

'If we let him in, it could be dangerous. We know little about him – his politics, his aims, his convictions. Does he believe in the ideals of the Revolution, as we do?'

'He's offered us an introduction to the Baron de Batz! Don't you realize how valuable that could be to us? The Baron's contacts . . .' Armand shifted irritably in his chair. 'Dammit, Julien, Guy has just saved my sister! Of course he can be trusted!'

'At the moment we know our members,' Julien protested. 'We've known each other since the start of the Revolution and before – since our schooldays. Guy is older, he left college before we began.'

'Are you saying that because he is not an old friend he cannot be admitted?'

'I believe the reason Guy wants to introduce the

Baron to us is that he sees it as a way in for himself.'

Armand spread his hands. 'Then we should be flattered that he wishes to join us!'

'You are dazzled by Guy Deschamps, Armand,' said Julien sourly. 'You are too quick to like and admire.' Their voices were growing louder.

'And why not?' demanded Armand. 'Guy is doing well as a barrister, he has plenty of satisfied clients and wealthy patrons. Germaine de Staël is one of them!'

'And of course Madame de Staël can do no wrong in your eyes,' said Julien sarcastically.

'Hush, Julien! She is our hostess!'

'But at least *I* have no illusions about why she has invited me!' Julien retorted, but he lowered his voice fractionally. 'She likes to keep all us royalists together. She would dearly like to be in control, but as a woman she can only influence us with her words. But she is honest, at least, while the Baron is the most unsavoury character! Do we really want to become involved with him?'

'It is too late, Julien. I have told Guy that we would be delighted to meet him.'

'Then you are a fool, Armand! I thought we took decisions together.'

Armand began to bluster. 'He's a royalist, Julien! What is there to fear? His contacts could be very useful.'

There was suspicion still in Julien's voice. 'Do you know what dealings Guy has had with him in the past?'

Armand pushed his chair back in exasperation. 'Anyone who is successful in Paris has come across the Baron at some time.' He sighed elaborately. 'Julien, you distrust everyone! It is in your nature. You have an unfriendly soul.'

'Mock me if you like, but you know well enough how the Baron made his money,' said Julien fiercely. 'Through introducing trusting innocents like your father to his gambling houses, and turning them into bankrupt addicts!'

There was a dreadful silence.

'You go too far,' said Armand at last, in a choked voice. 'If you were not my friend I would call you out for that!'

Julien laughed coldly. 'What, and have me run you through? You know I am the better swordsman, Armand!'

At that fortunate moment Guy Deschamps himself entered the room and their conversation was forced to end. As Armand rose to pull up a chair for Guy, neither he nor Julien looked at each other.

Two men, intent on their own business, almost collided as they passed between the marble pillars of Madame de

Staël's thronged withdrawing room.

They knew each other of old. They were rivals, two of the richest men in Paris.

Around them the room quietened.

They bowed cordially one to another, Monsieur Goullet's bow altogether more cursory than the Baron de Batz's extravagant sweep. Their eyes met, wintry pale-blue and gleaming raisin-brown, and flicked away at once.

'Baron,' Goullet said pleasantly, through gritted teeth. Was de Batz mocking him with that bow?

'Monsieur,' replied de Batz with deepest courtesy.

Then they walked away from each other.

The room sighed, and conversation continued.

Goullet's steps took him to the chamber he had entered earlier. He looked in as he passed by. There were three young men he knew sitting by the fireside, talking in low voices; Armand de Boncoeur was waving his hands as he spoke. He was not noticed by any of them. Nor was he seen by the girl, who was awake now, her beautiful hair spread over the pillow.

Eugénie felt somewhat put out. Guy had not even glanced over at her to see if she was awake. Why wasn't he attending her bedside? Wasn't he concerned to see how she fared after her experiences?

Julien rose and went out while the other two waited, and eventually he came back with a much older man, short, thickset and swarthy. A pungent smell of cigars and snuff came drifting over to Eugénie as they went over to the fire. Armand and Guy rose to their feet at once and bowed, and the man bowed back. Then the low conversation resumed once more, until abruptly it stopped.

At last Guy had noticed that she was watching them. He was holding a warning finger to his lips.

'You need not hush yourselves on my account, for I am quite awake!' Eugénie called out.

Guy glanced at the others. 'Our business is finished, is it not?' He rose to his feet. 'Then I shall come and see how well you are recovered, mademoiselle!'

And indeed he did, bowing to her gracefully as he arrived at her bedside, and looking most handsome in the candlelight. Eugénie had not been able to examine him properly in the carriage but, now she could do so, she found she liked the twinkle in his hazel eyes and the way his long mouth curved into a smile as he saw her, propped up hopefully against the pillows.

'So, Armand's little sister, I am glad to say your recovery appears to be progressing well.'

Eugénie nodded fervently, unsure whether he was

teasing her or not. She was suddenly shy and did not know what to say. Out of the corner of her eye she saw that the older man had left the room.

'I believe you saved my life tonight, monsieur,' she managed at last.

Guy bowed his head. 'It was nothing, mademoiselle.'

Hearing that, Armand came over. 'Nothing?' He clapped Guy on the back, his eyes shining. 'We cannot thank you enough!'

'No doubt you'll want Eugénie safe at your side after what happened,' said Guy.

'We will be together now, Armand, won't we?' cried Eugénie eagerly. 'I cannot bear to be sent away again. Will you tell monsieur our guardian so?'

Armand smiled at her awkwardly, then turned away, murmuring to Guy, 'As you know, there are difficulties . . . I must talk to Eugénie.'

At that moment, Julien de Fortin left the fireside and joined them, making Eugénie a stiff bow. 'You are recovered, I trust, mademoiselle?'

'Yes, yes,' said Eugénie, scowling impatiently. How different Guy, with his delightful manners and easy conversation, was from Julien! 'You've come to see me at the wrong time, monsieur, for Armand wants to talk to me – alone,' she added, then realized that this would mean Guy would disappear as well.

Guy took Julien's arm, smiling. 'I hear the musicians striking up again. Let us go and make intelligent conversation with Lafayette over supper. I believe I saw his nose sticking out of a group of admirers earlier.' He bowed to Eugénie, his eyes lingering on hers. '*Au revoir*, mademoiselle.'

'We will meet again, monsieur?' whispered Eugénie.

'Oh, yes, mademoiselle,' he said. 'You may be sure of that.'

Then he had gone, steering a reluctant Julien from the room.

'What were you and Guy saying?' said Eugénie.

'It is not important now,' said Armand.

'You said you had to talk to me about it so it must be.' She moved her legs plaintively. 'Can't you take me home? This bed is too big. I shall be so much better in my own!'

Armand stared at her a moment and shook his head. He sat down on the edge of the bed as if he were considering what to say next. Then he blurted out, 'Eugénie, Eugénie - my dearest sister, I hate to tell you this when you have already been through so much tonight, but since you asked . . .'

'Yes?' said Eugénie, gazing up at him, startled.

He stopped, biting his lip. It seemed very quiet suddenly, the crackling of the fire, the music and voices,

73

too far away to fill the vast spaces of Madame de Stael's boudoir.

Then he spoke again, more quietly. 'The truth is, you cannot go home. We have no home any more.'

Six

Six weeks before, Armand had returned to the mansion-house belonging to his guardian after working late at law school.

It was a bitter February night, and thin flakes of snow flew through the lamplight. He was looking forward to warming himself before a fire and eating a late supper.

He saw immediately that something was wrong. The front doors were hanging open and the house was in darkness. He called out in alarm, but no servants came.

He stepped into the hall, raising his lantern. Then he saw.

There was nothing there any more. Everything gold or silver had been stolen, only a few pictures remained, slashed through with knives; the mirrors and great hanging chandeliers were in shards, littering the floor. The gold clocks, the silver candlesticks, the Sèvres dinner service, the gilded furniture had all been looted. The vandals had hacked the staircase apart. In the kitchen they had even seized the pots and pans for their copper and iron.

Armand spent the night huddled on the kitchen floor, clutching a banister for protection, but they did not come back.

There was nothing left to come back for.

At first Eugénie could not take it in. She stared at Armand, her heart beating uncomfortably hard. She had already seen the mob too close.

Finally she whispered, 'Oh, Armand! If you'd been there when they arrived ... We've both had such fortunate escapes.'

'It must have been one of the servants who betrayed our guardian's trust and let them in,' said Armand bitterly.

Eugénie put her hands to her face. Tears trickled down her fingers. 'My beautiful dresses, my hats and shoes – all gone?'

Armand nodded sombrely. 'The house was completely ransacked. It is an empty shell now.' He put his arm around her and held her close. 'I didn't want to to tell you until you left the convent. But that was why I couldn't bring you home. Oh, Eugénie, I am so sorry. I had thought you safe inside the convent walls.'

'We have no home!' she cried in a muffled, desperate voice into his shoulder. 'What are we to do, Armand?'

'I shall think of something.'

She took her hands from her face and looked at him wildly. 'But I have nothing now – no clothes, nothing to wear!'

'I shall buy you new dresses,' he said soothingly. 'You'll have whatever you want. I have my allowance from Monsieur le Comte.'

She blinked back her tears. She had not even thought of her guardian. How selfish she was! 'Monsieur le Comte? He must be so much dismayed. Is he returning to Paris?'

'What can he do? It's too late now. He tells me he intends to remain at Haut-bois. He has raised my allowance so that I can afford rooms in Paris.' He smiled tightly.

Eugénie brightened. 'So we can live together again, Armand! We can be together and none of this will signify.' She paused and thought. 'I did not much care for that old house anyway. It was full of dark corners and smelt of damp, and there were spiders in Hortense's room.' She added quickly, in case Armand should think her heartless, 'But I am sorry for our guardian's loss. It is only that –' she hesitated '– our own loss seems so much worse. To be without a home altogether . . .'

She stared at him suddenly, her face alight. 'But we have one! We have the château at Chauvais! Let us leave Paris and go back to the country together.'

To her dismay, he shook his head. 'I cannot do that yet, Eugénie. I must qualify first. The Comte would stop my allowance if he thought I wasn't pursuing my studies. And Chauvais is bankrupt, as you know. I want to be able to put money back into it, to see it flourish again. I have to earn to be able to do that.'

Eugénie's mouth turned down. Her head was in a whirl. She knew only that she wanted to stay with Armand and that she felt tired, so tired.

'We'll talk further in the morning and decide what's best,' said Armand gently. 'You must sleep now.'

'I shall never sleep again!' declared Eugénie, but she fell back against the pillows. 'Won't Madame de Staël need her bed?' she asked weakly.

'No doubt she'll be with her lover, the Comte de Narbonne, in another chamber. Hush, now. I will stay by your side while you sleep.'

'I think you should accept our uncle's invitation,' said

Armand seriously, the following morning. 'You'll be safe in England, Eugénie.'

After they had been brought breakfast, they had returned to discussing the future. There was no sign of Madame de Staël, who was still abed and would not rise until noon, but Eugénie had been brought a set of her clothes to wear. The maid was waiting discreetly in a corner to dress her when she was ready.

'But I don't know our uncle!' said Eugénie, frowning.

'Thomas Coveney. He is a surgeon, I believe, and lives in a little place called Deal, on the Kent coast. You visited him once with Maman, when you were very small.'

Eugénie remembered only a heaving grey sea, a scudding sky to match and a town of tiny houses. An ugly little girl had pinched her in secret and made her visit a misery.

'I want to stay with you, Armand,' she said firmly.

He sighed. 'Why not go to the Comte, if you do not wish to go to England? Once he knows what befell you at the convent, he'll want you safe at Hautbois, I'm certain. The Revolution may grow more dangerous still.'

'I don't care! I don't want to leave you. Don't send me away again, I beg you!'

Something in her voice must have touched him. He

nodded wearily. 'Very well. I must think where you can go.'

'Am I not to live with you then?' cried Eugénie passionately. 'But Armand, why ever not?'

He shifted uncomfortably. 'I've told you, I've taken rooms with Julien.'

'Does Julien de Fortin mean more to you than your sister?'

Now he looked annoyed, cornered. 'Of course not, but who would look after you while I'm at law school? Who would see you did not come to harm in the streets of Paris? Be sensible, Eugénie. Julien and I – we have much to do together –' he waved a vague hand '– politicking, and such things. I cannot be a nursemaid, and I do not have the funds to employ a chaperone for you.'

She felt stricken. 'I understand, Armand,' she said sadly. But she did not.

His face softened.

'My poor little sister, what a brute I am! Of course you needn't leave Paris if you don't wish to do so. Let me give it further thought while you dress.'

Then he left her and the maid to cope with the clothes so kindly lent by Madame de Staël, but singularly voluminous on Eugénie's slight body.

* * *

Their carriage swerved to avoid yet another careering one-horse cabriolet and almost hit a laden cart blocking a street entrance. Beggars and richly dressed pedestrians alike fled from horses' hooves. The Paris traffic was as chaotic as usual.

Eugénie stared out at the bookstalls lining the Pont Royal, the pages of books and pamphlets fluttering in the cold breeze. A ragged boy ran after a ballad sheet that had blown away. It all looked so normal. The news about last night's sacking of the convent would not have spread far; the various districts of the city were cut off from each other by the difficulties of transport and traffic.

'Where are we going?' she asked dully.

'You remember Jean-Paul Vivier?' said Armand.

She nodded, puzzled. She had met young Monsieur Vivier once. He was a member of Armand's circle, another law student.

'Jean-Paul knows a milliner called Isobelle Fleurie,' said Armand. His face was shining with satisfaction; he had solved the problem of Eugénie. 'I met Belle through Jean-Paul because he rents a house in the same street, the rue des Signes. I know Belle will be delighted to take you in as a lodger. So many of her customers have emigrated she needs the money.'

'A milliner?' said Eugénie doubtfully. Such people

had always come to her guardian's house to fit her for hats; she had no idea how they lived.

'Belle is a respectable woman,' said Armand, growing more eager by the minute. 'I am sure she will be happy to have you. She has an elderly woman who cooks and keeps the house clean, and a couple of young girls in the workshop. Of course, it is not exactly what you are used to, but my allowance must do for us both now.' He looked at her hopefully and added, to tempt her, 'Belle used to work for Rose Bertin.'

Eugénie cheered up a little at the mention of Madame Bertin's celebrated name. But then she thought of the hats Madame Bertin had made for her, now all lost to her for ever, and her eyes filled with tears. She looked out of the carriage window at the thin sunlight outlining the angles of the deep roofs as they went by on either side of the street. She was going to have to live with a strange woman, instead of Armand. His exasperated tone earlier had implied that she was a nuisance, a burden, with which he could well do without.

She knew the truth now: that his friends – Julien, Guy, the Baron de Batz, Madame de Staël and all her wealthy, well-connected guests – were far more important to him than his younger sister.

When had this happened? When Armand started at

law school two years ago? There was some influence in his life that was so much stronger than she had ever been, even when their relationship had been at its closest, after their father's death.

And then suddenly she knew what it was: the Revolution. It was filling him with its ideas, its glamour, its danger, and it was taking him away from her.

She hated it.

Once they had left the Seine with its grand buildings on both banks and crossed the Place Louis XV and the rue de Saint-Honoré, she lost her sense of direction at once.

The carriage slowed in a long cobbled street, scarcely wide enough for two carts to pass each other, where the houses were hung with signs, darkened by time and weather, like a line of wooden washing. Piglets feeding from their sow mother – that was a wine shop; a wheel, a wheelwright's; a bear drinking from a bottle, another wine shop; a boot, a shoemaker's; a knife for a grinder's.

The children playing barefoot in the mud leapt away to the safety of doorsteps as soon as they saw their carriage approach; too many had been injured by the heavy wheels of heedless drivers. Above them the deep-roofed timbered houses leant out over the street, their gables cutting out the light.

They stopped outside a tall house wedged between

its neighbours; its sign was a feather, in a heavy wooden frame.

Eugénie looked out in dismay. Where were the elegant ladies she had expected, arriving to order their hats? Where were the gentlemen accompanying them, and the grand carriages parked in a row? The only inhabitant of the street, apart from the children, appeared to be an old woman, with a shawl wrapped round her head and a wicker basket on her arm.

The woman who opened the door to them looked middle-aged, although she was dressed in a youthful fashion and had not put her chestnut-brown hair up, but wore it tumbling unpowdered around her bare shoulders. Her large grey eyes widened with pleasure when she saw Armand, and she dipped a curtsy.

'Ah, *le petit marquis*, the friend of Jean-Paul, is it not?' She put a thin freckled hand, laden with rings, on Armand's arm. 'What brings you here? Not a new hat, sadly!'

Her gaze took in Eugénie, who was clutching Armand's hand. 'This must be your sister. You are so alike!'

'Eugénie has been studying at a convent, the Convent of the Sacred Spirit.'

'No!' Belle exclaimed in horror, her beautiful eyes larger than ever. 'But that was broken into last night, was it not? Oh, *ma pauvre!*'

And suddenly Eugénie, stiff with embarrassment, found herself swept into Belle's perfumed embrace, with Belle's curls tickling her cheeks and Belle's breasts in the loose chemise soft against her. She stood awkwardly, tilting her face so she should not touch Belle's rouged one, and looked away.

There was a strong fishy smell in the room competing with Belle's perfume and the woodsmoke from the small stove in the corner; later Eugénie would recognize this as glue, but now she wrinkled her nose while she examined the workshop critically. Her first impression was one of extreme untidiness, the sort of mess of which Hortense would never have approved, but struck Eugénie as delightfully exotic.

A large table took up most of the room, and there was a young seamstress working at it, her nimble fingers flying as she twisted a tricolour rosette from equal lengths of red, white and blue dimity. The clear spring light from the window picked out the hat bases surrounding her, elaborate and extraordinary concoctions of gauze and wire, perched on papier mâché busts.

Scattered over the table haphazardly were containers of glue and dye and brilliantly coloured spangles, bundles of feathered plumes, rolls of ribbon, scraps of lace and fringed trims, boxes of pins, canvas tapes coiled within wooden measures, even two exquisite fashion dolls lying sprawled on their stomachs, their white-stockinged legs sticking out.

Eugénie's gaze moved on and up. Behind the faceless heads on the table, bolts of brilliantly coloured silks, satins, taffetas and velvet spilt out from shelves on the walls. The light lingered on a stream of scarlet satin that seemed to ripple and flow like a river of blood.

She stared at it, clasped unresisting but frozen, in Belle's arms.

Belle let her go. '*Ma pauvre*, you look quite white with shock still!' she exclaimed. 'But that is scarce surprising. So what is it that you have come to me for, monsieur?' She smiled at Armand flirtatiously. 'You want a hat for your pretty sister? Perhaps in the new simple style – a cotton bonnet with a single ribbon, for spring? I have a length of Indian cotton, so fresh and light and youthful.'

Armand shifted his feet sheepishly. 'Not today, Belle. Today I have a favour to ask you.'

Belle's eyes sparkled with genuine delight as Armand explained their predicament.

'But of course, *chéri*!' she exclaimed. 'Mademoiselle Eugénie must lodge here with me. There are plenty of rooms upstairs, and Fabrice will be delighted I'm not on my own when he's away. One of the girls can chaperone her about town. Manon, I think. She was lady's maid to a noblewoman who has recently emigrated to Coblenz. Her stitches are so exquisite that I employed her at once.'

'Won't your husband mind me being here?' said Eugénie timidly, somewhat overwhelmed by Belle's enthuasiasm.

Belle looked startled. 'My husband? He is long dead, *ma petite*, but he always had an eye for pretty girls. His ghost will be smiling at you!'

'Your son then?' stammered Eugénie. 'The Fabrice you mentioned, Madame?'

Belle put back her head and laughed, showing small stained teeth. 'Fabrice is not my husband and will never be, for I am quite cured of marriage. But he makes me happy from time to time, when he has it to spare.' She winked at Armand.

'Oh,' said Eugénie, a little shocked but deeply curious.

'And as for you, *ma petite* −' Belle looked Eugénie's borrowed clothes up and down with some disdain '− you have certainly come to the right place. First we shall attend to your costume, for you cannot go about Paris in clothes that are so ill-fitting − you, the sister of a marquis!'

'They belong to Madame de Staël,' said Eugénie defensively.

'Ah, that explains it,' Belle declared. 'So much money, so little taste! You must return them at once. I shall get Loulette to take them back tomorrow,' and the young girl sewing the rosette at the table looked up and grinned beneath her cap at the prospect of an excursion away from the workshop.

'Wait, Belle,' protested Armand, half laughing. 'There is the question of payment for Eugénie's room and board . . .'

'I will take nothing,' delared Belle grandly, but then she hesitated and her big eyes looked askance at Armand. 'Well, perhaps a few sous. Life has become harder for me since the Revolution, not easier. As it has for so many of us,' she added with a sigh.

'Then you need not worry any more,' said Armand, but Belle was not to be stopped. Tears began to gather in her eyes.

'To think that I, who once made hats for Louis XV's mistress, have come to this,' she gestured dramatically at the cramped workroom. 'Why, Madame du Barry would send her very own carriage to my workshop in the rue de Saint-Honoré to take me to her at Versailles. I had a dozen seamstresses working for me then, not just my Manon and Loulette. And now they say that

Versailles is no more – that the great palace stands looted and ruined, just like your guardian's mansion, *mes enfants*. Fate – we never know what she has in store for us, do we? Me, a widow, with little custom, and you, homeless orphans, *mes pauvres chéris*.' She took a lace handkerchief from her bosom and blew her nose delicately.

'That is not quite true, Belle,' murmured Armand. 'We have the estate, my sister and I – we have Chauvais.'

'Oh, *that*,' said Belle, pouting. 'But that is in the country. It does not count!'

Shortly after her arrival at Belle's house in the rue des Signes, Eugénie wrote a polite letter to her uncle, Mr Thomas Coveney.

> It was indeed kind of you to invite me to Deal, but please do not worry on my account. I have left the convent and am now safely lodged with a respectable widow, Madame Isobelle Fleurie, at the above address.
>
> Nor is my education wholly neglected. Armand has arranged lessons in the pianoforte, I learn composition from Monsieur Pradère, the composer, and take drawing and painting

classes with the great artist, Monsieur David. Indeed, what with my Italian lessons in addition, my days are completely full!

Armand and I converse in English when together, so that we do not forget it and may speak it easily with you when we visit England on some future occasion.

Meanwhile, I hope you and my dear cousin, Henrietta, are well.

Your affectionate niece . . .

SEVEN

April 1791

Belle's tall, narrow house was a warren of dark, empty rooms squashed together on each floor. They were all somewhat small after the Comte's mansion-house. Eugénie slept in one of them, on a wide wooden bedstead, with a feather mattress that kept her warm. Every morning Manon came to wake her, since the green serge hanging around the bed blocked out all the light and even at noon it seemed deepest night inside her curtained box.

She was afraid the first few nights; she dreamt of the burning convent, the nuns' screams. After that, Manon moved in and slept in the next room. Each time Eugénie struggled awake from a nightmare, fighting the bedclothes, she would hear Manon snoring.

Manon was large and plain, and an excellent maid. She said little to Eugénie, but in the night she would comfort her, hushing her sobbing. During the day she seemed happy to do Eugénie's bidding. She knew Paris well. That, thought Eugénie, might prove extremely useful.

Belle allowed Eugénie to pick out whatever she wanted to wear from the old display costumes hanging in the workshop wardrobes, and Loulette altered them and brought them up to date for her. Eugénie fancied she appeared quite the young lady of fashion, as she paraded before the downstairs looking glass.

As she swished her skirts out to see their colours shimmer in the candlelight, she caught sight of Loulette watching silently from the shadows.

After that she became more aware of Loulette's hostility. It bristled from her whenever Eugénie was near. Though the workroom was cramped, she would deliberately move her chair away from Eugénie, or turn her back on her, her sharp little face pinched and sour.

Is it because I am an aristocrat? thought Eugénie uncomfortably.

One afternoon when the dinner was cleared away, she came upon Loulette fastening her hat in front of the looking glass before going home. Unusually, they were alone in the workshop.

'I believe I never thanked you properly for altering

my clothes, Loulette,' Eugénie said.

Loulette grunted, and turned to the door. Eugénie tried again. 'Do you have far to go?'

Loulette stopped and stared at her. Something sparked in her eyes. 'Croix-Rouge, south of the river, mademoiselle. It would mean nothing to the likes of you.'

Eugénie tried to ignore the contempt in her voice. 'You have brothers and sisters there?'

A harsh rush of words burst from Loulette.

'Eight of us, sleeping in one room at the top of a tenement building, and nothing to eat. The building next door toppled over the other day. Too tall, see? It killed the people. Ours could be next.'

Eugénie gazed at her in horror. 'How dreadful!'

'Dreadful!' Loulette mimicked her fiercely. 'You know nothing!'

Eugénie hesitated; she desperately wanted to find the right words. 'I know,' she said humbly, 'but I'd like to understand.'

'Understand this then,' said Loulette savagely. 'It is your sort who have spent all the money and taken all the food so that we have none! It is your sort who live grand lives in grand houses and never look at us!'

'But we are fighting a revolution to change that . . .' Eugénie began helplessly. 'Many aristocrats want—'

'No, it is we who fight the Revolution and who will win!' said Loulette. She came across to Eugénie, grabbed her arm and dragged her to the looking glass.

'What are you doing?' Eugénie gasped.

Loulette pulled back her own sleeve to reveal a scrawny arm, a thin knobbly wrist. She put it beside Eugénie's rounded forearm. For a moment they both stared into the looking glass, at their reflections side by side.

'We workers fight for *bread*,' Loulette spat out at last. 'Something to fill our bellies and make us fat as the aristos. That's more important than high ideals!'

Then she left.

Eugénie sank down at the worktable. She had never felt so desolate, nor so guilty.

Armand came to see her.

'Are you happy here, Eugénie? I do so want you to be!'

She did not wish to disappoint him. She nodded, and a smile spread across his face.

She fiddled with the tricolour rosette on the lapel of her pierrot jacket. 'It is a little lonely.'

'But your lessons must take up most of your day?'

She nodded reluctantly. Yes, her days were busy. After bread and coffee each morning, she left the house with the silent Manon to go first to Monsieur Pradère's house for pianoforte, then to art classes with Monsieur David. They took a tin container of bouillon and bread soup and did not return until three, when her art class was finished. Then it was time for dinner.

But she missed Armand. She looked at him sideways, wistfully. 'I would be truly happy if I could see you more.'

He sighed. 'That is not possible, Eugénie.'

'It is because of the Revolution, isn't it? I know it is!'

'It is true that much of my time is taken up with writing pamphlets,' he said carefully. 'I hope to have something published soon.' He began to stride around the workroom, his face alight.

'This is such a time to be alive, Eugénie! To be young! It is the young who will change France. We are the ones with the ideas. There is so much to do! Liberty, equality, fraternity! Those words have such a brave ring, do they not? They are the watchwords of our Revolution, Eugénie, and we must make them come true for our beloved country!'

'But can words feed the people?' she asked.

For a moment he looked startled. 'Of course, eventually.'

She watched him doubtfully, as he continued talking,

gesticulating, knocking a hat from the table. Then he noticed that she was silent and appeared sad.

'I have ordered you a piano,' he said to divert her, 'a fine new Érard, for you to practise on.'

She clapped her hands together. 'Oh, Armand!' she breathed, then said anxiously, 'Can we afford it? Was it not very dear?'

'One hundred and fifty livres,' he said in an offhand way. 'Only the best for my sister!'

She wondered briefly whether he should have spent so much, but then he suggested an excursion to the boulevard de la Comédie-Italienne to breathe the fresh air from the country, and in her delight she said nothing. That particular boulevard, built like the others on the old ramparts of the city, was the most fashionable promenade, and its music and theatres the most popular: the shaded walks with their stalls and entertainments were so crowded that Eugénie ended up quite ruining a pair of heels.

It did not disconcert her in the least, for just before they began walking, Guy Deschamps had passed their carriage in a cabriolet and reined in the horse to raise his high-crowned hat to her.

'Why, Mademoiselle Eugénie, I am overjoyed to see you are now in the best of health.'

Eugénie was tongue-tied. He was scrutinizing her

new riding costume – with a look of admiration, she thought. She blushed in confusion.

Armand rescued her unwittingly by interrupting with, 'Guy, my dear fellow! How splendid to see you! Will you take some refreshment with us? We are intending to visit a coffee-house.'

Eugénie's heart beat faster, in hope.

'Alas, I am otherwise engaged.' His eyes met Eugénie's. It was true: he looked most disappointed. 'Another time, mademoiselle.' He had spoken to her directly!

It was an altogether thrilling day.

But Armand had looked at the crowds as if he did not see them, and seemed to simmer with secret excitement. She knew he was still thinking about the Revolution.

Over the following weeks more convents were sacked. It happened south of the river and the news did not reach the rue des Signes until some days later. Once or twice the church bells of Paris clamoured forth in alarm, warning of unrest somewhere, and they stayed inside, waiting anxiously for someone to bring news that it was safe to venture out again.

There were some things about the Revolution that Eugénie found even more of a nuisance – the lack of hackney carriages to hire, the boring food, the expense of wax candles. The currency was being steadily devalued and paper assignats were now in circulation; the wealthy hoarded any coins they could, as they prepared to emigrate.

She wondered if Armand paid Belle enough rent money. She had never had to use tallow candles before, and they gave a poor light and smelt disgusting. Belle's house stank of tallow and glue, and the smell had entered all her precious new clothes, even her hair, which could not be washed so often now water was considered a luxury.

On the Monday after Palm Sunday, Eugénie, accompanied by Manon as usual, left the house in the rue des Signes for her Italian lesson. They always walked through the Tuileries Gardens because it reminded Eugénie of her old life, but today people were streaming in through the gates on every side. The broad, sunny walks she had always known, where respectable, well-dressed couples strolled through the formal gardens on fine days, were filled with people who looked poor and half starved, and more were pushing in behind them.

The crowds caught the two girls up and swept them along in a vast wave. Eugénie, pinioned in the darkness, could see nothing but people's bodies blocking the sunlight. She clung to Manon, terrified they would both be trampled.

'What's happening, Manon?' she screamed.

'I've heard nothing, mademoiselle. Keep hold of me!'

They became trapped close to the palace, wedged in on either side, unable to move. Around them the crowd was immobile now, row upon row of staring faces. Several large carriages sat marooned in the forecourt of the Grand Caroussel. A heavy-chinned, pale face peered through one of the carriage windows. Eugénie recognized the King. He was so close she could see that he looked ill, defeated. Sitting behind the King, a proud-eyed woman held a weeping little boy.

A cry went up. 'The King was trying to escape!'

Howls of abuse came from the crowds.

'Thought you'd go to Saint-Cloud, did you? With that Austrian bitch beside you?'

Eugénie covered her ears, trembling. She knew the people hated Queen Marie-Antoinette, who was from Austria, France's age-old enemy. They accused her of bankrupting the country through her extravagant spending on clothes. Insults flew over Eugénie's head, growing more ribald; she was appalled, though she did not understand them. Neither could she understand why the members of the National Guard were standing about, doing nothing.

A jeering mob began to flood through the gates, which had been opened to let the carriages pass. A man in court dress climbed down from one carriage and tried to run to the King's. Someone raised a stick to beat him back.

'Save him!' shrieked the little boy inside the King's carriage, but the stick came down and down remorselessly.

Dark blood stained the pale stones. Eugénie looked through her fingers; she felt sick.

The King pushed down his window. In a voice he struggled to keep calm, he called out, 'It is strange that we who have granted the nation liberty are not allowed it ourselves . . .' but his words were lost in the ferocious roaring around him.

Eugénie and Manon were forced to remain where they were for two hours, until the crowd began to thin at last and they were able to make their way back to the rue des Signes. Both of them were trembling.

'You must hate us, the aristocrats, for what we have been in the past,' whispered Eugénie. 'And the King, too, for his indulgence then.'

Manon looked at her, and to Eugénie's surprise her normally stolid face was full of compassion. 'I know that not all aristocrats are bad. The lady I used to work for was the kindest, most generous person I have ever known, mademoiselle. And now she has gone, escaped this revolution, and I think soon the King must go too, poor man. If he stays, he will die.'

That night Eugénie had another nightmare. She had never spoken to Armand about the sacking of the Convent of the Sacred Spirit. But she had thought about the young nun playing the terrible 'Ça Ira' on the organ, and most of all she had wondered about Sister Marie. Sometimes in the night an unspoken cry would rise from her heart. *Were you murdered, Sister Marie?*

That night she stared, wild-eyed, into the rectangle of thick, heavy darkness around her, listening, listening, for an answer. She did not know that she was sobbing, until the curtain was drawn back and Manon was there.

EIGHT

May 1791

Soon after coming to live at the rue des Signes,
Eugénie met Fabrice.

He was a plump, jovial man, considerably shorter
than Belle, with smiling, long-lashed, liquid-brown
eyes and an air of extraordinary energy about him.
He blew in unexpectedly one evening, throwing Belle
into hysteria and causing her to flee at once into the
kitchen (for the red-armed cook, without regular
pay, had departed), where she began to prepare an
omelette while shouting loving insults back through to
the workshop.

Fabrice seated himself among the hats, and looked
quite at home.

Eugénie had been practising at the new pianoforte,
which was crammed into a corner. She knew that

Armand was only a few doors away, visiting his friend Jean-Paul, and she had been hoping that when the door opened it was Armand, come to see her before he returned to the rue Saint-Antoine. Manon was sitting close by, sewing, screwing up her eyes to see by candlelight. Loulette had gone home.

'You send me no message, you great good-for-nothing bear of a man!' came Belle's furious voice. 'Where is your *politesse*, your manners? Do you not love me, that you treat me so?'

'I do, and soon I shall show you how much, my pigeon,' Fabrice shouted back, grinning widely across the hats at Eugénie, who dropped her head, and blushed. She could not help looking at him sideways though, because of his colourful clothes.

'Are you an actor, monsieur?' She left the pianoforte with relief and ventured closer to the table.

Fabrice laughed. 'I am a balloonist, a king of the air!'

Belle snorted as she put an omelette before him with a flourish. 'Let us have no talk of kings in this household, Fabrice! I've heard that ours is one no longer, but allows the people to rule him. They stopped him from going to Easter communion at Saint-Cloud, did you know that?'

'A balloonist!' said Eugénie. 'Why, I've heard people say it's a miracle – to see the balloon rise up supported by nothing at all, and then not fall back on the earth and kill those men in the basket below it!'

Fabrice nodded solemnly. 'It is indeed a miracle. That is what I like people to believe, then they flock to my displays. But there is a scientific explanation for it that is just as wondrous.'

Belle was standing with her arms akimbo, watching with gratification while Fabrice shovelled in his food. 'Luck!' she declared. 'It is only luck that holds it up. One day that luck may run out for you, Fabrice le Brun, and, crash, that will be the end of you. And then what will I do, your Belle? I shall have no one.' Her voice trembled.

Fabrice winked at Eugénie. 'A beautiful woman is never alone for long. That is why I do not intend to die, my cabbage, and have some other gentleman take my place!'

Belle pouted and touched her hair. 'You think you own me, Fabrice, is that it?' But her eyes were shining with delight, and Eugénie saw that she did indeed look beautiful.

'Women are there to be possessed by men,' declared Fabrice, 'to be wives and mistresses. What else is their use? Their beauty would be wasted.' He slid an arm around Belle's waist and she slapped it away.

'But not all women are beautiful, monsieur,' said

Eugénie. She lowered her voice in case Manon heard, and thought Eugénie referred to her.

'All women are beautiful to me,' said Fabrice gaily.

'But even the beautiful ones might not want to be a wife or mistress.'

'Pah, what else is there for them? It is men who do things in this world.'

'Was it not women who wrote to the King, pleading for a better education so they might do just that?' demanded Belle, her hands on her hips and her eyes sparking. 'Was it not women who marched to Versailles, demanding bread for their families? Is it not some of the most eloquent women in Paris who are even now using their influence with the great political figures, and writing pamphlets to change the world? When we have the vote, the things we women will do!'

She began to cuff him about the head while Eugénie watched, open-mouthed, unsure whether Belle was truly angry or not.

'Peace!' cried Armand, holding his hands up to protect himself. 'I agree. Women are remarkable, and so we must prevent them from ever voting, else they will rule us, weak creatures that we are! Meanwhile – ' he stood up and unrolled a poster triumphantly, 'you see what your poor man is about to do?'

The poster advertised a balloon demonstration in the

Tuileries Gardens the following month.

'Oh, Fabrice, your name is writ so large!' breathed Belle.

'That is because I designed the poster myself,' said Fabrice with satisfaction. 'Letters tall as a house, I told the printer.'

He scattered a handful of tickets over the table in front of Eugénie in a careless way. 'Ask your friends, as many as you like, mademoiselle.'

A thrill of excitement and purpose ran through Eugénie. 'I shall ask my brother. He'll come with me, I know, and Manon, my maid, of course.'

A little gleam entered Manon's eye.

'Come then, Manon!' cried Eugénie. 'We'll go and tell Armand now! What a happy coincidence that he is with Jean-Paul tonight!'

She grabbed up some tickets, seized her cloak and hat from the chair where a few hours ago she had cast them down, and tugged on Manon's arm.

'It's dark outside, Eugénie,' protested Belle. But it was in a half-hearted fashion, for Eugénie could see that she was eager to be alone with Fabrice.

'Jean-Paul is only a few doors from us,' said Eugénie, and she pulled Manon after her, while the maid struggled to tie her her shawl around her shoulders.

'Be quick, then, *mes petites*,' called Belle, but Eugénie

already had the outside door open on to the street, and she and Manon were gone.

The hanging lanterns that jutted from the walls of the houses were lit. It was not a cold night; there was a smell of spring in the air, sweetening the stench of the central gutter.

It was still a relief to reach Jean-Paul's doorstep, which was in darkness. The whole house was tightly shuttered, and from the outside appeared empty. Puzzled, Eugénie knocked, but no one came. When she pressed on the door, it gave, and she stumbled over the step, Manon following her in.

Eugénie had been to the house several times before and knew the pattern of the rooms. The parlour was deserted, though one or more people had been eating a meal and candles were still burning in the centre of the table surrounded by empty plates.

'Armand!' she cried, running through, taking a candle as she went. 'Armand!' but there was no answer. She went up the narrow wooden stairs and to her surprise heard voices arguing behind Jean-Paul's closed door. She caught a few words as she put her hand on the door latch.

'. . . desperate and foolhardy plan . . .'

'We do not know for certain . . .'

Then a name: 'Count von Fersen, the Queen's supposed lover . . .'

'. . . obvious that he is planning the escape,' said another voice.

'But why does he not trust us . . .?'

That was Armand's voice, impatient, frustrated. Eugénie pushed the door open a crack, meaning to peep through and see who was there with her brother. She knew most of his friends by sight. She looked at once for Guy Deschamps, but he was not there. She could see Julien de Fortin, and the darkly fleshy face of the Baron de Batz, whom she remembered from Madame de Staël's salon. Jean-Paul Vivier was sitting next to Armand, and a youth she remembered was called François. But to her confusion there were several older men she did not recognize.

They were seated at a round table, one Armand had brought from Chauvais, in a scatter of wine glasses, paper and pens. Only a few candles were lit, so the room was shadowy and cheerless. It did not seem like a casual gathering of friends, but something else entirely. She sensed tension, argument, and she hesitated. She shook her head at Manon and turned to leave but, as she did so, the hem of her gown caught under the door and she had to pull the material away.

Armand looked up, startled at the ripping sound, a

strangely frightened look on his face. Then he saw it was Eugénie. Her heart sank to see his look of dismay.

He rose from his chair, papers flying, and came swiftly across to her. The others, seeing her, stood up, pushing their chairs back with sudden noise to bow to her. Armand waved his hand impatiently for them to sit again.

'Eugénie, what are you doing here after dark?'

'It's not late, Armand,' she whispered, overcome with shyness that so many male eyes should be on her. 'I have something . . .'

She waved the tickets but he scarcely seemed to notice, interrupting her with, 'Can you not see I am engaged? You must go home.'

'It's not my home, you know that,' Eugénie hissed. She wanted him to share in her excitement, as he would have done in the old days, but here he was, as usual too busy with his friends for her.

'Leave now, Eugénie,' he said urgently. 'You shouldn't be here tonight. What is it you want?'

'I've tickets for a hot-air balloon demonstration! Belle's friend is an aeronaut. Oh, Armand, will you come with me?'

He took a ticket under the candlelight and stared at it. His whole body seemed to stiffen, and he called for Julien to come over. 'Look at this,' he said in a low voice, showing Julien the ticket. 'See the date? If we are right, this will prove an excellent distraction for the public.'

'Then will you come with me, Armand?' Eugénie repeated, still hopeful.

'I believe I may be needed elsewhere at that time,' he said. He shot a look at Julien.

'Where?' Eugénie said, bewildered. 'Chauvais?'

He shook his head.

'It cannot be more interesting than seeing a balloon demonstration!'

'Hush, Eugénie,' he said, compressing his lips and flashing a glance back at the gathering. 'I cannot come.'

'Then I won't be able to go,' she wailed, 'for Belle is to be Fabrice's dresser that morning, and Manon and I cannot venture through such mixed crowds on our own!'

'Let me escort your sister,' Julien said unexpectedly to Armand. 'It will be a good thing for one of us to be seen at such a public event that day, especially if things turn out as we think they may.' He bowed awkwardly to Eugénie, unsmiling, bending his brilliant dark eyes on her – so dark she could not read their expression. 'Will you permit me to take you, mademoiselle?'

Her heart sank. Why wasn't Guy there tonight? This grave, intense young man was not at all the companion she wanted. But at least she would have Manon with her. Manners forced her to curtsy and feign some words of gratitude, through a mouth like a prune.

And still Armand did not tell her where he would be going.

Eugénie met Guy Deschamps unexpectedly at an art exhibition a few days later. Her art teacher, Monsieur David, was showing a number of his paintings privately at his studio in the Louvre, and it seemed all Paris society had been invited to admire them. The room was crowded, its high windows tightly shut. Eugénie was feeling decidedly hot and much like leaving, and was about to say so to Manon, when she saw Guy approach. He looked so nonchalant, so in command and so very handsome that her heart began to race.

'Mademoiselle! What a pleasure indeed!' He bowed low, took her hand and brought it to his lips while he gazed at her with the slanting eyes that looked sometimes green, sometimes hazel, depending on the light.

'Monsieur Deschamps!' She could not think of anything to say. She stared at him helplessly, longing to keep him with her but fearing to bore him. She felt painfully aware of how young she was, and he so much older, so sophisticated. But he began to talk easily about the paintings, leading her from one to another, pointing out details, ignoring her confusion.

Finally he glanced at her flushed face. 'I rather think that is enough culture for the moment, mademoiselle. Shall we go outside for a breath of air?'

'Oh, yes, monsieur! If you please . . .'

He tucked her hand into the crook of his arm and led her through the double doors. Manon followed them a few paces behind, her face inscrutable.

It was a perfect spring day, made all the more so by the courteous attention of her companion. The sky was a cloudless blue, the spring sunshine gentle on the great stone face of the Louvre. She was wearing a dress of sprigged muslin in green and white, with a fichu of palest yellow around her shoulders.

He looked at her standing beside him in the sunlight, and smiled. 'You look a veritable goddess of spring!'

'Do I?' she said, blushing. She wanted to tell him that he, too, looked godlike to her. He was so tall, his English frockcoat in grey silk so beautifully cut.

'Let us walk a little,' he said.

They walked in the dappled shade beneath the trees, Manon dogging their footsteps.

'May I take you home?' he said after a while. 'I do not think we wish to return inside, do we?'

He had asked her opinion and in the most delightful way, as if it were a joint decision. She shook her head and was about to accept his offer, when she hesitated in confusion. She did not want Guy Deschamps, so smartly dressed, so debonair, to see the rue des Signes and the shabby workshop. She found herself gabbling.

'I am much obliged to you, monsieur, but please do not trouble yourself! My maid and I prefer to walk on such a lovely day.'

He looked a little taken aback, but bowed low over her hand. 'As you wish, mademoiselle.'

'But perhaps,' she said quickly, 'perhaps I may see you at the balloon demonstration?'

'Balloon demonstration?'

'In the Tuileries, on the 21st of next month?'

'Ah.' He straightened and looked at her. She noticed there were golden flecks in his eyes. 'It sounds delightful. May I accompany you to it, mademoiselle?'

A sickening regret filled her. 'Alas, monsieur, Julien de Fortin has already offered to do so.'

His long mouth smiled. 'Then we will meet there instead, mademoiselle.'

For the duration of the long, winding walk back to the rue des Signes, Eugénie and Manon were followed. They did not see their pursuer, nor would they have known him. He was a small beggar-boy, bribed with a handful of sous, to give details of Eugénie's whereabouts to a man who had been at the exhibition.

'There will be more for you when you return to me with the information,' the man had said to the boy, and he jingled the coins in his pocket with his black-gloved fingers.

NINE

Early June 1791

As spring turned into summer, the days grew
warmer and drier. The mud of Paris turned to
dust that blew about the city. Heavy carriage wheels
sent clouds of it billowing along the cavernous streets
and lanes, choking pedestrians and covering their
clothes and hats with a fine grey powder. It entered the
old houses through holes in the plasterwork and cracks
in the wooden beams; indoors, it lay on furniture and
food unless they were covered by cloths. It flew into the
glue in Belle's workshop. Each day Loulette blew on the
feather plumes and shook out the ribbons, but still the
dust came, seeping through the shutters, as it always
did, each summer.

Belle herself was hard at work on Fabrice's new
costume, tight-fitting black satin, with a red cloak

covered in sequins. Occasionally Fabrice would burst in and try everything on, preening himself before the looking glass in the workshop, while Belle clucked around his knees with pins in her mouth, taking in, letting out.

'*Mon Dieu*, you have eaten too much since last week, Fabrice! How is that possible with bread at fourteen sous now? You have some other woman feeding you, a rich woman!'

'No, never, I swear it! Only you, *mon petit chou*. Here I have the best omelette in all Paris.'

'So that is all you come for – your stomach, not your heart!' And she would slap his belly and pinch his bottom, so that Eugénie had to look away to hide her confusion.

Meanwhile, in the sunlight, daisies opened their petals on the grassy triangles of the Place Louis XV and in the spring dusk, plots to rescue the King from his present predicament bloomed in unlit, secret rooms; while each group, royalist or revolutionary, watched warily for any sign that might give the others away.

In an imposing house in the Faubourg Saint-Germain, two men sat opposite each other one June evening, talking in low voices. The candelabra had not yet been lit, for the footman had been sent away until the meeting was over.

Le Fantôme's pale coat and the white rectangle of the map lying on the table between them glimmered out of the semi-darkness. Around them, precious objects caught the remaining light: glass-fronted cabinets of porcelain from Sèvres and Dresden, the ornate gilt frames of oil paintings, the gold-leaf tooling on leather-bound books, the heavy mirrors on the walls. Le Fantôme had spent years wrenching himself up from humiliation in the gutters of Paris, both in the most disreputable gaming-houses of Europe and in the shadiest dealings of the stock market. He had remade his fortune out of dirty money, but beauty was what he had spent it on.

He had no fear of his house being ransacked by the mob, as so many other fine houses had been: he knew the mob leaders and had spies among them. Fear was a powerful deterrent; they knew he could report them to the government.

This evening the others who formed the Brotherhood of the Watching Eye had all left. Only Le Scalpel remained, the youngest member of his ring of spies.

Le Fantôme spoke to him as an equal; he had come to respect Le Scalpel's intellect and cunning.

'Ever since the crowds prevented the King from travelling to Saint-Cloud, the rumours have grown. He's planning to flee with the Queen and children. You know what this means for us? If the King escapes the country, the Revolution is over. We shall be thwarted and neither of us will come out of it rich men. It's turbulence that creates financial opportunities, and the longer that continues, the better.'

'One of us is somewhat wealthy already,' observed Le Scalpel drily. 'You are unlikely to lose your money whatever happens.'

'Ah, but greater wealth brings greater power.'

Le Scalpel observed the shadowed face with cool curiosity. 'Is that really what you want – power?' Greatly daring, he added, 'Power to manipulate? The thrill of bending others to your will?'

Le Fantôme did not answer directly. 'You think I've motives other than money? Perhaps you're right. But what are yours, I wonder?'

Money and women, thought Le Scalpel. And the feeling of triumph that came when he possessed both. But he smiled and said nothing.

'Now what have you to tell me, Le Scalpel?'

'Very little, I fear. I believe de Boncoeur may have secret plans of his own regarding the King to which only a few of his closest companions are privy.'

'We know de Batz is game for any attempt to rescue the King from the Tuileries Palace. Can you find nothing out from him?'

Le Scalpel shook his head. 'He has proved extraordinarily elusive since I introduced him to Boncoeur. But I believe he's waiting to see if it's worth collaborating with Boncoeur's circle of royalists. Batz is an opportunist. He'll only act if there's money in it.'

Le Fantôme shifted impatiently. 'You have no need to tell me that. I want real news, Le Scalpel. Boncoeur's an idealistic young fool, but he has the support of powerful nobles, like Condorcet. There's no doubt he's a leader despite his youth.'

'Would it be simplest to get rid of him altogether?'

That would take away the pleasure of hunting him down, thought Le Fantôme. He wanted that to last as long as possible. He wanted de Boncoeur to suffer as he had. 'Not yet, I think. We shall keep de Boncoeur alive. He could be useful to us.'

'How?'

'His attempt to rescue the King will cause great disturbance. The people will be outraged that their king should be fleeing his country. Disturbance is what we need. We must make sure de Boncoeur's plans fail, now and in the future.' He paused thoughtfully. 'De Boncoeur is not the brains behind his group. The ideas are provided by Julien de Fortin. Together the two of them are a formidable pair. Charisma *and* brains, eh?'

The black-gloved fingers crawled across the map and

came to rest on the Tuileries Palace. 'It won't be long before this stands empty. Meanwhile, without an intelligent guiding hand, de Boncoeur's idealistic ventures are more likely to fail.'

'Go after de Fortin, then?'

Le Fantôme nodded. 'In suitable circumstances, of course.' He smiled grimly. 'Crowds can so easily turn into mobs in the present climate, mobs turn violent, and no one can see who is being attacked.'

'You mean . . . ?' Le Scalpel touched his throat.

Le Fantôme nodded. 'Exactly.'

He took off his right glove and held out his naked hand in the darkness.

Le Scalpel reached over and took it. He had never touched Le Fantôme's flesh before, and could not prevent a shudder. The fingers were icy, and did not release their grip. He could feel hard knobs where the broken bones had healed. Fleetingly, he wondered when it had happened and why.

'But don't harm the girl,' said Le Fantôme. 'I want her kept safe. For me.'

TEN

21 June 1791

Eugénie, Belle and Manon had breakfast together in the workshop early on the morning of Fabrice's balloon demonstration. Fabrice himself had left before dawn for the Tuileries Gardens, where *la Liberté*, the green taffeta of her balloon brighter, even, than the midsummer trees, was tethered ready for inflation inside the circular wooden fence that had been especially erected to protect her from the spectators.

Early sunshine edged in through the slats in the shutters of the old house in the rue des Signes, drawing lines from hat to hat on the workshop table and coming to rest on the two new Liberty caps decorated with vivid red ribbons, in the fashionable shade known as 'Foullon's Blood', that Belle had made for herself and Eugénie to wear that day. Eugénie, drinking her dish of coffee too quickly in excitement and burning her tongue, thought of the balloon rising up and up through the windless air, drawn in a straight line to the sun, while she and Belle watched in their beautiful new hats.

Belle took Fabrice's costume down from its hanger, and packed it into the red silk bag she had made to carry it to the Gardens, admiring her own handiwork as she did so.

'See my stitches on these breeches?' she said to Eugénie. 'Smaller even than Loulette's, although her eyes are younger!'

Loulette, who had just arrived to guard the workshop while they were all out, made a disrespectful face at Manon.

And then it happened.

A wild clamour of church bells pealed suddenly somewhere outside, not far away. Eugénie clutched the table in alarm and felt it vibrate. As they stared at each other in shock, other bells joined the insistent ringing. It was the tocsin, the familiar discordant, jarring sound of alarm to alert the people of Paris. It had not rung for some time, lulling them all into a sense of false security. For Eugénie it seemed to carry with it the threat of indefinable but terrifying violence. She thought of Sister Marie and felt her stomach churn with dread; the aftertaste of milky coffee turned sour in her mouth.

Belle was pale. '*Mon Dieu*, what can have happened?'

She rushed to the door and flung it open, peering out, as if to find her answer in the street. Eugénie jumped up and ran after Belle as she stepped into the dust. Manon and Loulette followed, open-mouthed and blinking in the sunlight. The air trembled with sound.

'We shall have to wait for the newspapers to tell us!' cried Belle in frustration.

There was, indeed, nothing and no one outside to tell them what had happened. The street was unusually empty. The old woman with her basin of coffee and tin jug had vanished. None of the shops was open. Opposite, shutters parted to show frightened faces looking out, then were slammed shut again and remained closed. No one was willing to take any chances once the tocsin had sounded.

But there was someone – someone hastening along the dusty cobbles, his boots raising little white eddies like smoke. As the figure came closer, Eugénie recognized Julien de Fortin, his face haggard in the sunlight, deepset eyes dark beneath the curved black brows that seemed always drawn together in a frown. He gave a perfunctory bow as he reached them.

'Mademoiselle Eugénie?' he said loudly, above the bells. 'Thank God you've not left for the Tuileries!'

'What has happened, monsieur?' said Belle, forgetting to curtsy in her agitation.

'The royal family have fled the palace,' he said abruptly. 'A *valet de chambre* discovered the King's bed empty first thing this morning. The Queen, the Princess and the Dauphin are missing too.'

They stared at him in amazement. 'But won't they be recognized?' Eugénie said, feeling a sense of guilty relief that the tocsin signified nothing worse. 'Then they'll be brought back, poor things.'

'Poor things!' snorted Belle. 'That is no behaviour for a king – to run away like a coward! He'll soon be discovered, him with his crown and robes.' She glared down the end of the street, as if the King might be crossing there that very moment.

'Somehow I don't think he'll be wearing his regalia, madame,' said Julien gravely. 'That would be most unwise.'

'He'll be in disguise, won't he?' said Eugénie eagerly. 'So will the Queen, too.' She wanted the King's bid for freedom to succeed: how terrible it must be to be cooped up in the grim Tuileries Palace, prevented from ruling properly because a constitution had been forced upon you and you didn't agree with parts of it.

'King Louis XVI in disguise – unbelievable!' exclaimed Belle. 'Now he'll know what it's like to be a commoner in common clothes. Let's hope common fleas and lice bite him! So he'll be mingling with the likes of us now, will he? We'll watch out for him, won't we, Loulette, in case he runs away past our shop?'

Loulette nodded and giggled.

'He may well be out of the city by now, madame,' said Julien, his voice level. 'They must have left hours ago. Meanwhile, the Marquis de Lafayette has put it out that the King has been kidnapped by enemies of the Revolution.'

'Rubbish!' sneered Belle. 'The Queen is behind this, you mark my words, monsieur. The King's been persuaded by her, and willingly, and we won't see him back again.'

'Perhaps you are right, madame,' Julien said politely, 'although Lafayette has sent horsemen in all directions to find him.'

Eugénie knew Julien was an ardent royalist like her brother, but his voice was noncommittal as he spoke to Belle; he gave nothing away. *How can you be so lacking in feeling?* she thought.

There was a sudden, strange silence and she realized the bells had stopped.

'What am I doing, chattering?' exclaimed Belle. 'I must go to Fabrice! He'll be waiting for his costume.' She turned, ran into the workshop and came out with the red silk bag. 'Loulette, stay inside and keep the shutters closed until we're back.'

Julien stared at her. 'Madame, you're not thinking of going to the Tuileries?'

'Where else, monsieur? That's where the balloon demonstration is to take place.'

'There will be no demonstration today,' said Julien shortly. 'There's a crowd already collecting there.'

Belle nodded impatiently. 'They have come to see Fabrice.'

'I don't think you understand, madame . . .' Julien began, but Belle was not listening.

'And I am late for him!' she cried, and, turning on her heel, she picked up her skirts and began to hurry away from them, hatless as she was, down the empty street.

Julien put out his hand helplessly. 'Madame! Wait . . .'

He set off after her, flashing a dark, commanding glance behind him at Eugénie. 'You are to stay there, mademoiselle, do you hear?'

'How very ungentlemanly,' muttered Eugénie, taken aback by his vehemence. She felt immediately defiant, her earlier misgivings forgotten. 'Why should he order me around? Come, Manon. You know the way to the Tuileries, don't you?'

Manon's usually placid face was perturbed. 'Do you

think we should, mademoiselle?'

Loulette was looking at Eugénie with that curl of the lip Eugénie so disliked. Besides, she wanted to meet Guy again.

'Of course,' she said airily, not willing to lose face. 'I've always wanted to see a balloon demonstration and so have you, I know it.'

She brushed past Loulette and ran back inside to pick up the tickets from beside her half-finished dish of coffee. As she did so, she caught sight of her flushed, determined face in the workshop looking glass, rising above a sea of hats. For a second she hesitated, then caught up one of the new Liberty caps from its stand and settled it over her carefully curled hair. She had time to notice that it was most becoming before she hurried out again, the red ribbons fluttering around her cheeks.

It was the Liberty cap that saved her.

Eleven

They were only two streets away from the rue des Signes when they saw an angry group of people, armed with pickaxes, clustered around a house. They were shouting and aiming blows at the board hanging over its door. There was the sound of wood splintering and breaking. Then they began work on the shutters.

The old house began to shake. A powdery stream of plaster poured on to the street. A timber support cracked. Somewhere inside, a woman screamed: a piercing, helpless cry of terror. A man burst out of the house, gesticulated bravely and yelled a curse at the crowd. He was immediately knocked to the ground.

Eugénie had stopped involuntarily, the sweat trickling down her back turning icy. The man was now hidden from view by dark figures, moving against the sunlight, raising their axes. 'What are they doing?' she whispered to Manon.

Manon gripped Eugénie's arm. 'It's a notary's sign. The fleur-de-lis, the royal emblem. That's why they're destroying it. Quick, mademoiselle! This way.'

Too late.

The gaunt figure of a woman lurched jaggedly down the street towards them, her ragged clothes and bare feet covered in wood dust. She put an empty bottle to her lips, sucked, then in disgust threw it into the rubbish and dried sewage of the central gutter. Then, pointing a shaking finger at Eugénie, she leered in a thick, gutteral accent, 'Aristo! Royalist! Look at those fine clothes!' She turned back to those around the house and yelled, 'See what we have here!'

Manon spat out a ferocious volley of swear words that Eugénie had never heard before − Manon, who scarcely spoke. Eugénie was too petrified to be astonished. The woman staggered back from Manon's onslaught, her mouth open. The rest of the group, intent on destroying the traitors' house before them, had not heard her shout.

'And see,' Manon finished, a sturdy arm pointing in triumph at Eugénie, 'she wears a Liberty cap! She is a republican! She supports the constitution!'

Eugénie stared at the woman, too frightened to nod

her red ribbons. The woman gave her a bleary glance and backed off, parting her hands and shrugging.

Manon caught Eugénie's hand without a word and pulled her away. When Eugénie looked back, the woman was searching for her empty bottle of spirits in the filth of the gutter and swearing to herself.

Inside the house the screaming was cut off abruptly.

'She was from the provinces,' said Manon. 'They have no jobs. They come to look for work in Paris, but there are no jobs in Paris either.' Her voice was calm, matter-of-fact.

Eugénie looked at Manon's solid, unruffled bulk with a new respect; she was still shaken by what had happened. 'You were brave, Manon.'

She shook her head. 'I know people like her, Mademoiselle Eugénie. Every year when the harvest is bad, they plague my family on the outskirts of the city. They are dangerous when they are hungry and in a crowd, but if they are alone – pouf!' She snapped her fingers. 'They are cowards!'

As they came closer to the Tuileries Gardens and the maze of narrow lanes on its north side, they were forced to pass another crowd destroying an inn sign bearing the King's name. But this time they were ignored as they hurried past in the shadow of the leaning houses.

'I think we should return to the workshop, mademoiselle,' said Manon, once they were away.

Eugénie stood still. The trapped air of the streets was already turning humid, even out of the sunlight, but she was shivering. 'I can't,' she whispered. 'It will be just as dangerous to return now, Manon.'

Not far from the Place Louis XV they passed the old house belonging to her guardian, the great mansion shuttered and barred, wind-blown weeds already sprouting in its plaster. It would soon be derelict, like so many other mansions belonging to the aristocracy.

They reached the end of the lane she had walked down so often with Hortense, the one that led directly to the Tuileries Gardens. The gate opposite was open, leaning crookedly on its hinge; there were none of the fashionable women she remembered, who used to alight there from sedan-chairs, only a group of vulgar-looking men, barging through and shouting at each other. The long, raised terraces blocked her view of what was happening inside.

'There's no one collecting the tickets,' Manon said, frowning.

'We must be too late already!' said Eugénie in dismay, and a distant roar, as if from a crowd of people, confirmed her fear. They looked up to see the green balloon, but there was only the sun climbing an empty sky.

'Then it must be about to begin!' Eugénie thought of the cool shade of the horse-chestnut trees. 'Hurry, Manon!' she cried, and ran in eagerly between the embankments.

She stopped in shock before she reached the open expanse of the gardens. The walks were filled with people. She could tell from the noise they were making that they were not spectators, come to gaze admiringly at Fabrice's daring ascent.

'It's another insurrection!' she said in horror, as Manon came up behind her.

They stood close together, halfway up an embankment, not daring to move, while below them the crowds pushed on through the Tuileries to join the crush around the palace. Someone was hanging a placard on one of the gates.

'What does it say?' roared a man, with a deep, carrying voice.

The answer was passed back through the crowd, accompanied by guffaws of contemptuous laughter. '*Maison à louer*! House to let!'

The mood of the crowd suddenly changed. There was an air of festivity, a carefree, holiday atmosphere. Fathers swung tiny children up on their shoulders to see the grand palace, empty of its royal occupants, the few nervous guards pacing the dusty forecourt; women retreated to the shade of the trees, plumped themselves down and took out their knitting. A man climbed the gates, waving a tricolour flag.

Eugénie put her hand to her mouth. 'They've broken in! The guards have let them do it!'

She stood motionless, watching the invasion of the palace, while a strange chill passed through her despite the heat of the sun. She knew that something profoundly significant was happening. An invisible line that had divided and protected royalty from ordinary people for centuries was being destroyed in front of her eyes in a matter of moments.

The news that the gates were open passed rapidly from person to person. At once the crowd reformed, surging forward eagerly, like curious children given the chance at last to explore forbidden ground. The gardens were full of swarming figures beneath the dazzle of the sun.

Eugénie looked around wildly, clinging to Manon. 'Where can Fabrice be? And Belle? What's happened to the balloon?'

'We must move, mademoiselle, else we'll soon be crushed,' said Manon urgently. 'If we go further up on to the terrace, it will be easier to see.'

Eugénie saw a tall, lithe figure emerge from the rows of little trees as they reached the level ground above the gardens. 'Monsieur Deschamps!' she breathed, and thought she might faint with relief and delight.

Guy Deschamps bowed, his face concerned. 'Mademoiselle Eugénie! I never thought you'd venture here today!'

He was with three young men, unfamiliar to Eugénie, who had stout sticks in their hands. She found herself too overcome to curtsy: indeed, for a moment she thought she might weep. She wanted to fling herself against Guy's chest and feel his arms around her, protecting her. Not caring about the other young men, she gripped his arm imploringly.

'I am so thankful you are here to rescue us, monsieur! We have had such a time of it!'

Guy looked down at her, his eyes glinting beneath dark lashes. 'You are without an escort, mademoiselle? Where is Julien de Fortin?'

'I am not altogether sure,' said Eugénie. 'But I don't wish him to know I'm here!' She took a deep breath and calmed herself. 'He warned me against coming, you see.'

'I do indeed.' His mouth quirked with amusement. 'It was a trifle unwise.'

'I came to see the balloon demonstration,' she protested. 'I didn't realize what it would be like. I thought people would be pleased the King had left.'

Guy shook his head. His hat was under his arm, and

in the sun his rich auburn hair, tied back with a simple black ribbon, shone with coppery lights. A black, tight-fitting frock coat outlined his figure; a dress sword swung from his hip.

He is truly a most attractive man, thought Eugénie, and felt a strange flutter in her chest.

'The people feel they have been let down,' he said. 'Lafayette and Mayor Bailly have been trying to placate the crowds, but they have only become angrier. They suspect the Queen is behind the escape.' He looked about him carefully and lowered his voice. 'Your brother must be . . . surprised by such a turn of events. How has he reacted?'

'I don't know, monsieur,' said Eugénie. 'He couldn't come with me to the balloon demonstration. Perhaps he doesn't even know about the King's escape.'

'Oh, he must do. All Paris knows now.'

'But he is out of Paris, monsieur. I don't know where he is.'

'Indeed?' Guy paused, and said gently, 'No doubt he would be horrified to think of you here alone, Eugénie.'

He had used her first name, and how soft and pretty and entirely new it sounded.

She became flustered.

'But I am not alone, monsieur! I have Manon, my brave maid with me —' she gestured back at Manon, who was standing behind her, rocklike and disapproving '– and somewhere down there is Belle Fleurie, my landlady, and Fabrice le Brun, who is to rise into the sky.' She looked wildly, despairingly, at the mass of dark, unrecognizable figures below. 'But I do not know where they are!'

How childish he'll think me!

'I believe I see Julien,' said Guy. He pointed. 'See, over by the gate that leads to the Place Louis XV? He is persuading la Belle to leave at once, and also the aeronaut, who will not leave his balloon.' His eyes returned to hold her gaze. 'But I feel I should take you home, mademoiselle. You see, I know where you live.'

Eugénie looked back at him in surprise and some dismay.

He smiled teasingly. 'Your brother has plenty of friends to tell me! But a milliner's is scarcely suitable, I would have thought. What was Armand thinking of, I wonder, hiding you away in such a place when a society lady might have paraded you for our delight in the salons?'

'Madame Fleurie is most respectable, I do assure you, monsieur,' protested Eugénie, but she felt a blush rise to her cheeks at his words. She felt suddenly out of her depth.

Turning quickly away to hide her face and screwing

up her eyes against the sun, she suddenly glimpsed the vivid green of the balloon: deflated, spilling limply over the broken fence that surrounded it, while the incoming crowds surging through the gate from the Place Louis XV trampled on uncaringly, kicking the once lush folds out of their way.

'I see the balloon now, monsieur! Oh, may we go down?'

Guy had brought a pair of opera glasses from his pocket and put them to his eyes, quite as if he were at some musical entertainment. He gazed around, compressing his lips.

'Do you see them?' she asked eagerly. 'Julien, with my friends?'

He swivelled the glasses. 'I do, and I shall take you to them.' He smiled at Eugénie and tucked her arm into his. 'You'll be quite safe with me. This crowd is not interested in us, only in getting into the palace. Soon the National Guard will disperse them. My friends here will surround us and make sure we come to no harm.'

People parted to let them through, with sidelong glances at the sticks the young men carried. Guy and his friends were all dressed soberly, with tricolour cockades in their hats, and they took them for republicans. Their argument was with the King, and with his despicable nobles in their silks and satins and powdered wigs, not with a group of strong, healthy-looking youths escorting a young girl in a Liberty cap. Old men avoided them, and younger ones looked the other way, the poorest among them too aware of how weak the gnawing pain in their bellies made them, to shout a challenge.

The crowd thinned and they saw the group by the wrecked fence, trampled posters at their feet. Belle was wringing her hands and weeping. 'I cannot leave Fabrice!' she insisted hysterically to Julien, for what Eugénie judged from his scowling face must be the umpteenth time. He looked even more annoyed as he saw her approaching, her hand on Guy's arm.

Fabrice was inside the fence, trying to pull together the folds of the balloon. He looked purposeful and determined, but as if he would be there a long time.

Belle flung her arms around Eugénie. 'The King has spoilt everything for us! Fabrice's beautiful costume has gone too, the bag snatched from my arms.' She shook her fist at the unknown thief, skulking somewhere in the crowd, and tears rolled down her rouged cheeks. From somewhere Manon produced a spotless handkerchief, and Belle dabbed her eyes furiously.

There was the sound of horses' hooves. A warning

cry came from those around the gates that led out into the Place Louis XV. 'Beware the National Guard! Lafayette himself is coming!'

People began to scatter in all directions, except for those who had not heard, who were still around the palace gates, or milling into the courtyard in front of it, while Julien looked angrily at Eugénie.

'I told you to stay behind, mademoiselle. We must all go at once. It will be mayhem soon!'

Guy laid a placating hand on Julien's arm, looking beyond him, his eyes flicking over the panicked crowd. 'A word with Lafayette, *mon ami*,' he began, 'and we shall—'

A man brushed close to Julien; a knife flashed. Eugénie screamed, wrenching the skirts of Julien's coat, unbalancing him for a moment so that he lurched forward. He whirled around, but the man had vanished into the crowd.

'A madman,' said Julien, shrugging, but he was very pale. He straightened his hat with a hand that shook. 'A fanatic perhaps.'

He stared around again, then seemed to collect himself. He bowed stiffly to Eugénie. 'I am obliged to you, mademoiselle. I believe you saved my life.'

'What did you see, Mademoiselle Eugénie?' demanded Guy.

She shook her head; her legs felt weak. 'A man's arm, a knife . . .'

'Did you see the man's face?'

Eugénie shook her head again. She had been aware only of the weapon, shining in the sunlight; she had reacted instinctively.

'A premeditated attack, I think,' said Guy thoughtfully.

'You don't mean an assassin?' said Julien, trying to smile.

'I do indeed. Now why should someone want to kill you, Julien?'

'It could have been any of us,' said Julien lightly. 'We look like royalists, perhaps. All the more reason to leave.' He took Eugénie's arm almost forcibly. 'Come, mademoiselle, bring your maid. We shall leave the others to find their own way back.'

What an unfortunate manner he has! Eugénie thought resentfully. *I have just rescued him from certain death, yet he still treats me like a child for all that I am fourteen!*

'Why did you come today when I had warned you against it?' Julien asked her brusquely, as soon as they were out of earshot of the others and struggling through the crowds to the main gate.

'I felt like it,' she answered airily.

He glowered at her. 'It was most foolish of you.'

'You would be dead now if I had not been here,' she pointed out.

For answer he stuck his straight nose in the air and pulled her along even faster. His face still looked drained of colour in the sunlight, but she couldn't feel any sympathy: she'd not had a moment to bid Guy *au revoir*.

At last Julien secured a cab – battered and filthy, but by then Eugénie did not care – by giving the drunken driver a hefty bribe, and she and Manon settled back on the worn leather, profoundly relieved to be out of the mêlée. The cab swayed through the narrow streets, filled now with people singing the 'Ça Ira', but they were in celebratory mood and did not block the way. In a single morning they had managed to deface or destroy all the signs that might remotely hint of royalty.

Eugénie looked at Julien, sunk silently in his seat, his face morose. He was clearly not inclined to make polite conversation, but it struck her that he, if anyone, might know the whereabouts of her brother, and so she asked him directly.

'He rode out of Paris at first light this morning,' replied Julien shortly. 'Where he is now, I do not know.'

His eyes met hers, full of dark intensity in his white face.

Perhaps he wished to say more then, she was not

certain, but four days later, just before the King was arrested and brought back to Paris on the 25th June, Armand returned to the rue des Signes, exhausted, covered in dust and smelling strongly of horse dung.

TWELVE

Sébastien de Boncoeur, Eugénie's father, had once taken his little son and daughter with him to visit the court at the great royal palace in Versailles. Their mother had been dead for a year then – she had died giving birth to a stillborn child – and the official period of mourning was not yet over. However, the King had missed one of his favourite hunting and drinking companions – for Sébastien's courage in the saddle was almost as renowned as in the battlefield – and had summoned Sébastien back to court.

On arrival at the palace, Sébastien hurried off to the King's private chambers, leaving Armand and Eugénie, dressed in mourning black from head to foot, as their papa wished, huddled together on a chaise-longue in one of the anterooms.

For a few minutes they watched the coming and going about them, speechless and a little overawed. Then Eugénie grew bored and began to wriggle. Finally, she jumped up and skipped over to look at her reflection in the huge shining mirror opposite. She stuck her tongue out at herself and pulled faces while Armand looked on, aghast and ashamed.

Eventually he could bear it no longer, ran over and pulled her away, more roughly than he meant, so that she burst into loud sobs.

'Who are these two children?' said a woman's voice, young and musical, but with the trace of an accent.

'They are the son and daughter of the Marquis de Boncoeur, I believe, madame,' said another woman.

'Ah, yes, the poor little motherless ones! No wonder she cries!' The first woman knelt down to their level – with some difficulty, for Eugénie could see through her tears that she had a very fat tummy.

'How do you do, my pets?'

She put her arms around Eugénie, and Eugénie, startled, stopped crying immediately, and pulled away to stare at the stranger's face.

'Would you like some lemonade?'

They both nodded and Armand remembered just in time to bow.

The young woman rose to her feet and clapped her

hands merrily. 'Lemonade for these children, footman!'

The footman bowed deeply and hurried away.

The woman put her hand on Armand's shoulder and looked into his eyes with her very bright blue ones. She had skin like rose petals and short fair hair that reminded Armand of feathers. 'I believe you will be as brave as your father,' she whispered, and smiled down at him. 'I can see it in your eyes. To be brave in the face of adversity means the enemy will never triumph.' She squeezed his shoulder gently. 'Don't forget I said that, will you?'

Armand shook his head dumbly, though he did not understand what she meant. She was the most beautiful woman he had ever seen, and he would never forget her.

25 June 1791

Armand had never seen the Champs-Elysées so crowded that Saturday evening. People had climbed on to the roofs of the houses, and into the trees, the tricolour ribbons on their coats fluttering like blossom amongst the heavy summer foliage. There was a strange, confused silence as they waited, as if they could not decide what they felt about a king who had wanted to leave them to their own fate, but was at the same time the embodiment of their nation, and was now –

any moment, for the carriage with the royal family had already crossed the swivel-bridge over the river – returning to them.

The Tuileries was full of National Guards expecting trouble. Armand, adept at passing unnoticed through a crowd, squeezed himself into a gap by the iron gateway leading into the palace. He noticed that there were a number of deputies from the National Assembly waiting close by, and the King's own cousin, the Duc d'Orléans – which seemed tactless, to say the least.

The King is doomed now, thought Armand. *After this escape, he will never be able to persuade the people that he supports their constitution. Even if he signs it, they will suspect he has done so to save his skin. Soon they will want to be rid of him altogether.*

He could see the carriage containing the King and Queen and the two children approaching, surrounded by the National Guard, bayonets drawn in case of any disturbance by the crowd. But the crowd remained silent, even when the carriage stopped in front of the gates and the King climbed out, his clothes travel-stained, his linen dirty.

There was a strange dignity about his portly figure, Armand thought, for all that he looked even more like a butcher than ever with his double chin and borrowed coat of brown plush, heavily stained with sweat under the arms.

The Queen followed him from the carriage, dressed in a common, ill-fitting day dress, her fair skin flushed, though she held her head high. As soon as she put a foot to the ground, the crowd began to jeer and hurl lewd insults. Though she was used to scandalous allegations in the press, Marie-Antoinette tightened her mouth and paled; the wan, exhausted little Dauphin clung to her hand in bewilderment and fright.

Armand, in the gap by the gates, was directly in the Queen's path, though the King was surrounded by deputies as he went through into the courtyard. As she passed, little more than a hand's breadth away from Armand, she met his eyes with the direct blue gaze he remembered so well, now conveying a world of hurt and sorrow. He could see that the beautiful eyes were red-rimmed with fatigue and weeping, and felt an unbearable stab of pity.

She hesitated, almost as if she felt his emotion touch her.

She recognizes me! he thought. Then, unbelievably, he felt something brush his hand; his fingers closed around it instinctively and he hid it behind his thumb.

The gates were shut rapidly; the royal party climbed the steps into the palace, and were gone. As Armand slipped swiftly away too, he became aware that someone was following him. The sun was low, the cavernous narrow streets darkening in the shadow of the leaning houses. Among the crowds going home in the sultry heat, talking loudly now in contrast to their previous silence, he glimpsed a white coat, an indistinct pale face.

Had Le Fantôme been somewhere outside the palace, watching him, noticing the note pass to him from the Queen? Or was he following him for some other purpose?

Armand darted into a dark carriage entrance and pressed back against the stone, his face averted, his arms folded to hide the giveaway gleam of his hands. He sensed a strange but distinct chill as the pale figure passed by. A few moments later, when Armand was sure he was absolutely safe, he brought the tiny scrap of paper the Queen had passed to him out from behind his thumb.

Two words.

Save us.

Julien came in as he was burning the message in a candle flame, startling him so that he dropped the smouldering paper and nearly set fire to the waxed tablecloth.

'What are you doing?'

'Nothing.'

'It looks like it.' Julien picked up the scorched scrap. It became black crumbs in his fingers and he wiped them off on his breeches. 'A secret note, Armand? Something you do not want even your oldest friend to see? From a mistress, perhaps?'

But he was not smiling; his dark eyes burned. 'We cannot have secrets from each other now, Armand. It is too dangerous. You should have told me that you knew of von Fersen's plan.'

'I knew it would fail. I wanted to warn them they were being pursued. I guessed the route they'd take, tried to catch up . . .' Armand shook his head wearily and sat down on a rickety chair, running his fingers through his sweaty hair. 'If you must know,' he said abruptly, 'I was burning a message from the Queen.'

'The Queen!'

'She gave it to me as she went back into that prison, the Tuileries Palace. She'd written "Save us".'

Julien stared at him for a long moment, then he began to pace the stuffy room. Suddenly he whirled on Armand. 'No, no! We cannot save the whole royal family! It is too late now.'

'She gave it to me,' said Armand quietly. 'She asked it of me.'

'*You* cannot save the royal family then! You could not save them from their own folly this last week. Do you think you can in the future?' His voice softened. 'Don't you understand, Armand, she would have given it to anyone. She is desperate. She probably intended it for one of their spies amongst the National Guard, or a sympathetic deputy in the Assembly, anyone – but not you personally.'

'I think she knew who I was,' said Armand stubbornly.

Julien threw up his hands. 'You, a bankrupt marquis, who no longer possesses a title or estate, whose great schemes to save the monarchy have come to nothing!'

Armand flushed angrily. 'Be careful, Julien. Even old friends can be banished from our circle.'

'And then where would you be?' demanded Julien, firing up. His black hair seemed to stand on end with exasperation. 'You need me, Armand! You need me to pick holes in your hair-brained plots and think of better ones!'

'Do not flatter yourself,' said Armand cruelly. 'No one is irreplaceable. I could invite Guy to take your place, for instance.' He ignored Julien's sudden wary expression. 'We have plenty of good men, anyway. The Baron de Batz—'

Julien exploded again at the deliberate mention of the older man's name. 'A rogue who looks on the Revolution as a game! He would back any side if he thought he might do well out of it. I warned you about him, Armand. We have to restrain him, otherwise he'll lead us all into danger.'

'We're in danger, anyway,' retorted Armand. 'Each one of us. It was you that knife was intended for!'

Julien shrugged. 'I doubt it. He was just another starving lunatic.' He tried to speak calmly. 'I owe my life to your sister, and for that I shall be eternally grateful. But no, Armand, I cannot be persuaded by you to rescue the royal family *en masse*. This has been the first and last time such a caper could be tried.'

Armand thought of the Queen's proud, tragic face, and was silent, while Julien watched him, standing by the darkening window.

'Perhaps the people will let the King sign the constitution and it will all blow over,' Julien said at last.

'You do not believe that, and nor do I,' said Armand. 'The Revolution feeds on blood for its energy.'

There was another grim silence. Then Julien said gently, 'You do not need to prove yourself always, Armand. I know it is to do with your father, but he was a courageous man, as are you.'

Armand turned away at once. 'Don't speak of him. He brought disgrace on my family!'

'Then let us speak of Eugénie instead,' Julien said lightly, inwardly cursing his thoughtlessness. Why had he mentioned Armand's father again? 'If you are not careful, she will begin to suspect your mysterious disappearances, your secret meetings. It is high time you took her about instead of hiding her away. If you keep her amused, she will be less likely to get into scrapes.' He knew Armand had been appalled to hear of Eugénie's trip to the Tuileries.

Armand wiped his damp forehead with a handkerchief that still smelt of horse dung. 'But what of Le Fantôme?'

'He can do nothing until Eugénie is sixteen. Meanwhile, she has a brother who is adept with a small sword to protect her, as well as a most formidable maid, who sticks to her like salt. Introduce her to *le haut monde*, to high society, the opera, the Théâtre-Français, if it is not putting on revolutionary rubbish.'

He gave a twisted smile. 'Do it while you can, Armand. While civilization still holds sway in some corners of this benighted city.'

After Julien had left the room, Armand sat on alone.

'"Save us,"' he whispered, and the words flew away into the gathering shadows.

Thirteen

21 April 1792

Eugénie leant forward eagerly on the uncomfortable wooden bench, staring down at the long narrow room below the public gallery. She had persuaded Armand to take her to a sitting of the National Assembly in the *manège*, the old covered riding school near the Tuileries Palace, and now she sat in the narrow space between Armand and Manon, trying not to mind that her new costume *à l'amazone*, with its blue riding coat and striped tricolour skirt, would be most horribly crushed.

If only she could learn more about politics she would be able to converse more assuredly with Guy. He had been most attentive last week at Madame de Condorcet's salon, but it might have been that her *toilette*, fashioned by Belle in the Constitution Cut, with a skirt of red, white and blue posies, was particularly striking.

She had had to stand mute while Narbonne, Madame de Staël's lover, who had recently been given new military command – for war with the powers of Europe was almost certain – had been the centre of a circle of admirers, all asking intelligent questions.

'War will give the army new vigour,' Narbonne told them.

'And act as a stabilizing force,' added Madame de Staël, at his side, her eyes shining. 'Exactly what we need in domestic politics at the moment! It will unite radicals and moderates against a common enemy.'

And in the end war had been declared against Austria, and only the day before.

They had driven to the National Assembly through streets that seemed quiet and almost dazed by the news: the same streets that at the beginning of the year had shaken to the clamour of the mob protesting against the sugar shortage and violent attacks on grocery stores. But here the public gallery was agog and there was not a seat to spare.

Beyond the long windows set high in the walls, the spring day was warm and bright, shining rectangles of light on the intent faces within. Among the society benches the women in their bright tricolour costumes fanned themselves and cast sidelong glances at each other; the men, more sombrely dressed, shifted uncomfortably in the close atmosphere.

A central aisle ran the length of the chamber, and on either side of it rows of green leather seats ran up almost to the windows, so that the members of the Assembly faced each other. The speakers kept changing – it was most confusing, Eugénie thought – climbing up into a kind of pulpit to address the Assembly.

The present speaker was a small, slight man, perhaps in his early thirties, immaculately dressed in a green striped nankeen coat and blue waistcoat. Though it was now considered unpatriotic to powder because of the flour shortage, his hair was dressed in the old way, and stood out among the unpowdered heads in the chamber. Beneath the whitened hair, his face with its long, thin nose had a greenish pallor in the spring light. He had pushed his glasses up his forehead to avoid them becoming smeared with powder.

He spoke in a high squeaky voice and seemed much agitated – almost a figure of fun, Eugénie thought, though there was something compelling about the intensity of his fixed gaze.

'We are now embarked upon a course that will not in any way safeguard our revolution. War! As I have repeated many times before in this chamber, it can only lead to military dictatorship or total disaster. If we are defeated, the King will be restored to his former powers by foreign invaders, who even now have their collaborators at work amongst us.'

The speaker glared around as if able to identify spies amongst his audience. Few seemed to be listening, however; they continued to stroll about, talking. The President's bell rang continually; the ushers' cries of 'Chut! Chut!' were ignored.

'They have placed their own selfish interests above those of *la patrie*, our beloved country! What we need more than anything is the solid establishment of the constitution, yet everywhere I see enemies within and without, seeking to sabotage it. Invasion is imminent. Patriots, be warned, defend the nation and yourselves!'

Eugénie looked at Armand in alarm.

'Who is he?' she whispered.

'The public prosecutor. Robespierre, leader of the Jacobins.'

Eugénie knew the Jacobins were the left wing revolutionary party, and she had read some of Robespierre's pamphlets recently, as she tried to learn more. 'Robespierre is a visionary,' said Armand in a low voice. 'Paranoid, perhaps – but one day they will listen to him. Although he doesn't seem so now, he could be dangerous.'

'Order me to do what you will,' Robespierre was saying, leaning forward urgently over the edge of the pulpit, 'I would rather die myself before the death of liberty!'

As Robespierre climbed down, a young woman sitting among the tradespeople's benches, who had been sitting forward, listening intently, leant back.

The slight movement caught Eugénie's eye. Her heart leapt. She stared, and gripped Armand's arm again. He looked at her, irritated. 'What is it?'

'Hortense! Over there. I am certain it's her!'

Armand stared round, frowning, then shook his head. The young woman was now hidden by her neighbours. For a second Eugénie had been certain, though all she had seen was the dark brim of a hat shadowing an averted profile. For a fleeting moment the sharp cheekbones and pale olive skin had reminded her of Hortense. Her excitement was replaced by a cold little feeling of desolation.

All this time she had not heard from her. *Though why would I?* she thought. *Hortense has no idea where I am now.* But even during the six months she had been at the convent she had never received a single letter.

She tried to concentrate on the new speaker. The audience had fallen silent.

'. . . Trials of a prototype of Dr Guillotin's

157

decapitation machine have already been performed on fresh corpses, with satisfactory results. We know that Monsieur Robespierre is against the death penalty –' he nodded to where the last speaker was sitting alone, slumped on one of the benches, his head bowed '– but let me assure him again that this method is swift, practical and humane. The rope is pulled by the executioner, the blade falls, the head is severed from the body.'

He made a vigorous chopping movement with his closed fingers. 'A swish, a thud, and the man is dead –' he paused '– though we still have to find a way to prevent the onlookers from being drenched with blood.'

He gave a cold, ironic smile and looked around at his hushed audience.

'We must encourage the public to witness these executions, messieurs, to see for themselves the swift justice of the state. Only by keeping the death penalty under our own control can we prevent the people from exerting their own violent and lawless justice.'

A chill went through Eugénie, though she scarcely knew why. Was death by this machine not better than being strangled on the end of a rope, or broken on the wheel?

As the speaker came down from the pulpit to a buzz of talk, she looked over at the benches where she had seen the young woman. But now the gap between the two sturdy artisans had closed; some time during the last speech she must have left.

'We must leave at once,' Armand's voice said abruptly in her ear, startling her. 'Come, Eugénie!'

She was surprised at his urgency, but glad. The air in the gallery under the roof had grown clammy with so many bodies pressed together; besides, the present speaker was delivering a long dull speech on taxation.

His hand on her arm, Armand hurried her to the door, which led out on to a landing and a long flight of wooden stairs down to the exit.

There was an empty carriage waiting outside in the street, two horses pawing the ground, the driver slumped asleep in his seat. Armand began to lead her swiftly away. 'We must find a cab.'

A man dressed in white emerged from the exit behind them. He called out after them.

'Take no notice,' muttered Armand, without glancing behind him, his face grim. 'I know that man and do not wish to speak to him.'

'You cannot cut him, Armand,' protested Eugénie. 'What has he done?'

In any case, the man, who seemed to move exceedingly fast for his age, had now caught up with them.

'Marquis.' He bowed, smiling unpleasantly. 'But I forget. You have lost your title now.'

Armand inclined his head stiffly.

'And this must be your sister. Charming. So like you to look at.'

The man lifted his hat to Eugénie with black-gloved fingers, revealing powdered hair and a high, pale forehead that was strangely unlined for a man in middle age. It was not an attractive face; there was something repellent about the set of the thin lips and the cold eyes beneath heavy lids. She was not certain why he seemed familiar to her, but the feeling was disconcerting.

She dropped a small curtsy as his eyes examined her, scrutinizing her so closely that she felt as if she were an object he was about to purchase. His gaze rested on her so long she found herself blushing uncomfortably.

Armand stood frowning next to her; she sensed his uneasiness.

'What is it you want, monsieur?' he said abruptly. 'We wish to return home.'

The man inclined his head. 'It was a long session this morning. You must both be fatigued. Perhaps I can offer you a lift in my carriage.'

Armand gripped Eugénie's arm tighter, as if he thought she might accept the offer. 'No, monsieur, you cannot trap us that way,' he said shortly, almost rudely. 'Now tell me what this confrontation is about.'

'Trap? Confrontation, monsieur? What words! I saw you in the gallery and thought I might give you some news. News that I think you will be interested to hear.'

He took a step back and surveyed Armand in a leisurely way, a smile lurking at the corners of his thin lips. He looked as if he were savouring a long-awaited triumph. 'We are to be neighbours.'

'What do you mean?' demanded Armand. Eugénie felt his sudden fear.

'I have bought your guardian's estate. Haut-bois. Beyond its walls lies Chauvais, is that not so?'

'Impossible!' exclaimed Armand. 'Haut-bois has been in my guardian's family for generations. It is not for sale and never will be!'

Goullet looked mildly surprised. 'Your guardian has emigrated to Coblenz. Positively fashionable now among the aristocracy, is it not? At least he is too old to join the Prince de Condé's army like other aristocrats, but his name appears on "*La liste*" with those who have emigrated. His land has been confiscated as a result.'

'But the King vetoed such a thing happening!' said Armand furiously.

Goullet shook his head pityingly. 'The King? What power does he have now? I have friends in the government who believe that estates like Haut-bois should be in responsible hands. For too long the aristocrats have let them go to rack and ruin.'

'My guardian's steward would never allow such a thing!' declared Armand. 'He would care for Haut-bois until his old bones lay beneath its earth.'

Goullet brought an enamelled snuff box casually from his coat pocket and took a pinch of snuff before replying. He did not remove his black gloves, but pressed thumb and forefinger to each nostril and sniffed delicately.

'And the earth of Haut-bois is exactly where his bones are now. How naive you are, monsieur. I fear one cannot quarrel with the government.'

Armand went white. 'You have killed him?' He took a step towards Goullet, his hands clenched.

Goullet's eyes became ice. 'Oh, not me personally. The peasants who worked your guardian's estate were persuaded to do it. A bribe was all it took. You can achieve anything if you pay enough, including the purchase of Haut-bois.'

'Bought with scoundrel's money, made by cheating at gaming tables and Lord knows what other underhand schemes,' said Armand hotly.

Goullet's eyelids dropped down. 'Be very careful what you say. Your father was no stranger to the gaming table and his ill-gotten gains went into maintaining Chauvais – until he became bankrupt.'

Armand bit his lip and was silent.

Why does he not say something to defend Papa? thought Eugénie. She spoke up instead, unable to keep quiet. 'How dare you, monsieur?' she cried. 'You insult the dead and our family name!'

Goullet let out a short bark of laughter. 'I see your sister is no porcelain doll, monsieur, though she may look like one! I am glad of that. I look forward to furthering our acquaintance, mademoiselle. Meanwhile, have a care to your own estate, monsieur, or I may end up as the new owner of Chauvais as well.' He bowed briefly. 'Now, if I cannot offer you my carriage, I shall be on my way.'

They stared after him and Eugénie took Armand's arm. He was trembling with emotion; she could feel it through his coat. She held him close, protectively, but he began to stride along so fast in his rage that she could scarcely keep up.

'Who is that odious man, Armand? He is no gentleman! And he has no right to Haut-bois!'

'Raoul Goullet, known as Le Fantôme. He is in the pay of the government – a spy for the radicals – I am sure of it!'

'Hush, Armand!' Alarmed, she looked back to see Monsieur Goullet climbing into his carriage. The driver whipped up the horses, there was a ringing of hooves along the *pavé* of the narrow street and the carriage caught up with them, the horses kicking up mud and ordure so that they were forced to stand back beneath the low gables of the houses.

As the carriage passed, Eugénie saw that there was someone inside with him. A woman. Her head was turned away, but Eugénie saw the sharp cheekbones again and a lock of dark hair falling over the pale olive cheek.

This time she was sure.

It was Hortense.

They took a roundabout route, involving two different cabs, back to the rue des Signes; Eugénie did not know why.

Armand was tense, sitting on the edge of his seat.

'It was Hortense, Armand!'

'You are mistaken,' he said shortly, staring out and all around, almost as if he feared they were being followed.

She decided not to pursue it further at that moment, and after rattling along in silence for a while, she was startled when he suddenly said, 'I think I should find other lodgings for you, Eugénie.'

She stared at him in dismay. 'But why? I am happy at Belle's!'

He looked at her and appeared to capitulate. 'Very well then.' She sighed in relief, but after a few moments' silence he said, 'I believe I shall move into Belle's house with you, Eugénie. The rue Saint-Antoine is too dear, now that it is so difficult for my allowance to get through from Coblenz. I know that Belle will be glad of the rent and she has plenty of rooms.'

'That is good news indeed, Armand!' said Eugénie.

But secretly she was apprehensive. She had become used to her freedom, for Belle scarcely ever questioned where she was going and Armand had always been so busy with his friends. She had thought that she and Manon might return together to the National Assembly, in case Hortense came again.

To confirm her misgivings, Armand said, 'I don't think you should go to the National Assembly again, Eugénie. It is not an appropriate place for a young girl.'

Armand went to see Belle while Eugénie was out at the market with Manon.

'You know it could be dangerous,' he said quietly, 'for you to shelter two aristocrats. This war will inflame people's feelings against the aristocracy even more. Already they accuse the émigrés of joining the Prince de Condé's army to restore the King to power. We could go elsewhere, my sister and I.'

Loulette, twisting a ribbon at a corner of the worktable, listened without lifting her eyes from her work.

'You think I would let your sister go to some other lodging?' hissed Belle, her eyes wide and outraged. 'Why, she even helps in the kitchen now! She has learnt to make the best of it. She is a good girl. For her sake, I will take you in also, *mon petit* Marquis!'

Armand moved into Belle's house almost immediately.

He stopped Eugénie going to her piano and drawing lessons, to new exhibitions, from promenading with Manon in the Tuileries Gardens in the hope of seeing Guy Deschamps. In the space of a few months he turned from the easy-going brother, who had taken her on outings to the theatre and opera, into a tyrant who watched her movements day and night.

'Why are you behaving like this?' she cried.

'It is too dangerous in the streets now the Fédérés have arrived,' he said.

It was true that the Fédérés, National Guards, who had arrived from all over the country for the anniversary of the Fall of the Bastille and had stayed on to protect the city from invasion, were rough and uncouth radicals, but it was stifling indoors in the heat of summer and boring in the extreme.

Above all things, Eugénie hated to be bored.

She began to argue with him; sometimes she felt she hated him.

He was flushed with anger. 'Go to England if you don't like it, and cease being a worry to me!'

She did not want him to see how upset she was. She went to her room.

Oh, Armand. How you have changed.

FOURTEEN

July–early August 1792

During the time Eugénie had been at Belle's she had sensed that Loulette was softening towards her. From time to time she had offered her one of her dresses, or a sash or a hat, and they had been grudgingly accepted; she suspected Loulette sold them at once. Money was what Loulette needed, what they all needed.

Eugénie knew Armand worried about their finances. She had no idea how much money they had left, for the Comte's allowance had entirely stopped coming through; but he refused to discuss it with her.

During the dull, hot weeks cooped up indoors she helped Loulette make the tricolour cockades that people now had to wear to prove their patriotism; they were the only items from Belle's workshop still in demand.

She was shocked one day when, sitting side by side alone in the workshop, untangling ribbon, Loulette suddenly turned to her and said, 'You know they are hanging aristos in the streets again, don't you?' There was the old antagonistic expression on her pointed face. 'It's because those aristo émigrés have joined the foreign army that's going to give the King all his power back. If they knew I was sitting here with you, the mob would hang me too.'

Eugénie began to protest, but Loulette interrupted. This time there was a look of genuine fear on her face. 'They'd hang all of us – Manon, Belle and me.'

She picked up a red ribbon and pressed it against Eugénie's throat.

'And of course they'd hang *you* too. You and your aristo brother.'

Armand was going to Chauvais; he would not tell Eugénie his reason.

'Can't I come too?' Eugénie begged. She longed to see the estate again.

He shook his head. 'It is safest that you stay in Paris.'

But Paris did not seem safe at all.

France was now at war with Prussia as well as Austria, and had suffered a series of disastrous defeats. The Duke of Brunswick, commander of the joint armies, had threatened to raze Paris and torture anyone who resisted the re-establishment of the monarchy and the old regime. As the humid, airless days dragged by, the city rippled with rumour and panic. Eugénie worried about what Loulette had said: perhaps she and Armand should leave Belle's after all.

But then something happened that distracted her.

She received an invitation from Victoire to a supper party for the 9th August when Armand would still be away at Chauvais. She said nothing: she made Manon deliver her acceptance in secret. She was determined to go after these weeks of stifling boredom; only the sounding of the tocsin would stop her.

She was almost certain that Guy would be attending.

On the morning of his departure Armand was so very sweet to her that Eugénie felt exceedingly guilty and ashamed of her deception. She sat on his bed in his sweltering room while he packed his valise. Then he stopped, and came to sit beside her, taking her hand.

'Eugénie, it's for your own safety's sake that I've been so severe these past few weeks and kept you indoors. You must believe me.'

'I do, Armand,' she said meekly.

'I've been a monster, I know.' He shook his head, looking down at his hand covering hers. His knuckles looked raw, his fingernails were bitten to the quick. 'I wish I didn't have to go away, but I must. While I'm away, you should take care. There is great anger amongst the people from the radical Paris sections at the moment, and they are being goaded to it by the Fédérés. You know people gathered in the Champ de Mars yesterday – crowds of them – to demand the King's abdication?'

Eugénie shook her head. She knew nothing, immured in the house.

'Some kind of insurrection may happen soon. Meanwhile, the streets are dangerous. Be careful. Promise me?'

She felt a rush of love for him, with his furrowed brow and anxious eyes. 'I promise.'

All the same, she still intended to attend Victoire's supper party.

Belle took a pin from between her lips and deftly pierced it into the hem of Eugénie's new dress.

'I should not be going against your brother's wishes,' she said, sighing. 'But I cannot keep you a prisoner in my own house!' She glanced over her shoulder at Manon. 'It must be a secret between us women, eh, *chéries*?'

She sighed again. 'I do this for my own poor idle hands as much as for you, Mademoiselle Eugénie. I kept this last roll of silk for a special occasion. There will be dancing, surely?'

Eugénie imagined having Guy as her partner, brushing close to him as he looked into her eyes. 'I hope so.'

The atmosphere in the workshop was sombre these days. Most of Belle's old customers had emigrated, and those that were left had little money now that their tenants were no longer forced to pay them dues.

Belle had had to sell most of her stock. But she had her pride. She stuffed a few dozen sacks with straw, wrapped them in pretty paper and placed them on the workshop shelves. From where she stood being fitted, Eugénie could read some of the labels, beautifully written out in Belle's flowing hand: *Holland, Embroidered Caps, Tiffany and Gauzes, Velvet Ribbon, Flowers with Pins, Sprigged Lawn.*

'A little trickery, *mes amies*. It's the only way to survive,' Belle had declared defiantly, hands on hips, as she surveyed her well-stocked workshop. While all around her shops were empty, it appeared that Madame Fleurie was running an impressively prosperous business.

But Belle's large expressive eyes were sad these days and her face looked starved, not only from lack of food. Fabrice had not visited for nearly a year, neither had he written.

'If it were not for your brother's money, I do not know what would become of us,' said Belle as she checked Eugénie's hem was even. 'We would be scrabbling in the gutter or begging in the Palais-Royal.' Her eyes grew more tragic still, at the prospect. 'But then, who has money to give beggars now? We are all paupers, and there are even aristocrats selling off their chateau furniture in the rue Saint-Honoré!'

She gave Eugénie's blue skirts a final shake. 'There! One or two stitches still to put in, that's all.'

'Pretend you are dancing now, Mademoiselle Eugénie,' said Manon. Eugénie detected a wistful note in her voice, as if she longed to go dancing herself, in a sky-blue dress made especially for the occasion.

Manon is young; she must want these things, too, thought Eugénie. *Attending as my chaperone tomorrow is not the same at all.* It occurred to her that she had never considered a maid's feelings before.

So Eugénie held out her skirts, curtsied to her invisible partner and in the cramped space around the table began to dance. Her feet grew swifter and lighter with the joyous freedom of dancing, faster and faster, until she seemed to be flying round the table, her face fixed in a crazy smile of delight.

Then the door from the street burst open, and the wild dance was over.

It was Julien de Fortin, hatless, dishevelled, without apologies.

Eugénie stopped abruptly, breathless and blushing, clutching hold of the table to steady herself, as the late sunlight lit them all. Julien looked at her in a puzzled way, as if for a moment he did not recognize her. She saw that his face was chalk-white, that his black coat seemed wet. Belle and Manon stood up to curtsy, but he ignored them. He was breathing fast, as if he had been running, and his voice shook when he spoke, addressing Eugénie without ceremony.

'Where's your brother? Where's Armand?'

'Monsieur, he has left for Chauvais,' Eugénie said, bewildered by his urgency. 'Did you not know?'

'I hoped to catch him before he left.' Julien sank down and covered his face.

Belle let out a cry: bright scarlet glistened on the dark cloth of his sleeves.

'Monsieur, you are hurt!' she exclaimed in alarm.

Julien shook his head. His hair was plastered to his scalp with sweat. 'It is not my blood.'

'Not yours?' repeated Eugénie stupidly.

'Jean-Paul. He was coming to see me, with François.' His voice broke.

'Is he wounded then?' said Eugénie, her mouth dry. Armand's friend, Jean-Paul, who lived just up the rue des Signes. François, another of Armand's circle. 'We should go to them! Where are they?'

'Wait, Eugénie,' said Belle, putting a hand on her arm.

Julien blinked rapidly and licked his lips; he seemed numb with shock. Manon slipped out of the room and came back with a jug of thin wine and a cup. She poured some for him and he drank deeply, the cup shaking in his bloodstained hand, while they all stared at him. When he spoke again, his voice was stronger.

'I heard commotion outside and went down to the front door. I had to use all my strength to open it. Jean-Paul and François were lying against it. They had been stabbed many times. There was nothing I could do.' He shuddered, and whispered, 'So much blood.'

'They'd been murdered?' said Eugénie in blank horror. 'But why?'

He turned on her a look of such contempt she shrank back.

'Don't you realize we're all in danger – anyone who believes in both king and constitution? There are republican radicals who would assassinate us all.' He leant towards her, dark eyes flashing in his white face above the horribly bloody coat.

'I tell you, mademoiselle, you should leave this country. Go to England! Go before it's too late!'

FIFTEEN

9 August 1792

It was Victoire's party a few days later. Eugénie knew she should not be attending when such a sad and terrible thing had happened so recently; she could not stop thinking of poor Jean-Paul and François, and the quantity of blood soaking Julien's coat. *But it has been so very dull imprisoned indoors*, she told herself. *Besides, I am sure I am not important enough to be assassinated.*

It was still light as Manon helped her dress, and she held a little looking glass to her face critically. Belle had given her a pot of powdered mother-of-pearl to dust over her bare shoulders and catch the candlelight, and some rouge for her cheeks and lips. Her dress matched the blue of her eyes, and Manon had dressed her hair in loose curls about her shoulders. Altogether she was decidedly pleased with her appearance.

The driver of the hired carriage was late, and when he arrived, his cab took up most of the width of the narrow rue des Signes. Dusk was falling and clouds of moths were flitting around the hanging lanterns.

It was weeks since Eugénie had been any distance from Belle's house. She peered through the dusty windows of the cab as it bumped away, anticipation of the night to come mixed with apprehension making her pulse flutter. It was no cooler, and she pressed a *papier poudre* to her perspiring upper lip.

Manon, clutching the edges of the little tip-up seat opposite, looked at her admiringly. 'You look beautiful, mademoiselle.' There was no jealousy in her voice.

Eugénie looked at Manon's own plain but open face, and was filled with gratitude for her steadfastness.

'Thank you, Manon.' She added gently, lowering her voice so the driver should not hear, 'Now we all have to be less formal with each other for the sake of l'Égalité, you needn't call me "mademoiselle" any more, you know.' As Manon began to protest, she shook her head, smiling. 'Besides, in the streets it's safest not to show one has a maid. We're all equal citizens now. Isn't that what the Revolution—' She broke off nervously. 'What's that noise?'

There was the sound of raucous singing somewhere ahead.

Manon pursed her lips. 'The Fédérés, mademoiselle – Eugénie – singing their war song. People call it "La Marseillaise". It's everywhere now, in the market place and cafés and theatres.'

Eugénie listened, and a chill ran through her. The singing grew louder. *They are coming . . . to butcher your sons and wives!* Stirring, dramatic, sinister words, howled out through the twilit streets: a bloodthirsty call to arms to the people of Paris against the foreign invaders.

The coach swayed faster as the driver whipped up the horses. But the Fédérés, with their red caps, the *bonnets rouges*, and naked, brawny arms, were all around the cab, their song growing ragged as some of them began to shout, 'Aristos! Aristos!'

An animal roar went up, drowning the words, as if they had spotted their prey.

'*À la lanterne!*' someone yelled out, flourishing a rope, and the cry was taken up. 'String 'em up! Hang the aristos!'

Eugénie gasped and shrank back against the seat. Then she realized that the shout was not for her.

A group of men had entered from a side alley, innocently enough it seemed, except that they did not wear the tricolour cockade in their hats. At once they were set on and felled to the ground. The coach gathered momentum, shaking wildly from side to side and scattering the remaining Fédérés. Some shook their fists after it, yelling insults and threats, before turning back to their victims, now dark shapes hanging in the air beneath the lamplight.

Eugénie's heart was beating wildly. It was a while before she let go of the leather fob.

'They pick a quarrel with anyone – guards, *sans culottes* or those they call aristos,' said Manon in disgust. 'And to think they stayed in Paris to protect us from the invader!'

There were groups of *sans culottes* in grubby red-and-white striped trousers clustered about on street corners, watching sourly as the coach passed and muttering to each other. Glowering peasants lolled against the walls, armed with staves and pikes, their sunburnt faces shining with sweat in the lantern light; drunks staggered in the shadows. There was an air of conspiracy and expectation in the humid night, as if they all waited for a signal.

'They would not dare murder the King in the Tuileries Palace, surely?' said Eugénie, staring out wide-eyed. 'He has the Swiss Guard to protect him!'

Manon shrugged. 'How long could they last?'

'But it's Mayor Pétion's duty to prevent disorder!'

'The Mayor's been made a prisoner in case he interferes, did you not know, mademoiselle?'

Eugénie shook her head. They gazed out silently as the carriage drove along the rue Saint-Honoré, where more crowds were gathering. The trees were black skeletons, their leaves already shrivelled by the relentless temperatures of that summer. 'They say the King will not last long now the leaves have fallen,' said Manon dourly.

From somewhere came the dull sound of drumbeats. Armand was right. *I should not have come tonight*, thought Eugénie. The Marais was grave-quiet, though, the streets deserted. Most of the old walled houses were shut up. She looked through the imposing entrances as they passed, and glimpsed the occasional brightly lit house in the courtyard within, its white stone shining as a pair of brave retainers stood to attention with blazing torches, guarding the doors. Others were in total darkness, their aristocratic owners long fled.

She shivered despite the heat.

When they arrived at Victoire's, the guests were assembled in the great salon, beneath a brilliant forest of chandeliers. The candles only seemed to make it hotter. The men had red, perspiring faces and fiddled with their cravats as if they found it hard to breathe; the women trilled with nervous laughter and fanned themselves vigorously.

All the guests were wearing the tricolour, and were introduced as 'Citizen' by Victoire with great emphasis, whatever their old title. Eugénie began to feel a little uncomfortable. She looked around desperately for Guy, but he was not there. Sadly disappointed, she retreated to the chairs set against the wall, with Manon beside her.

Then a kind, elderly gentleman coaxed her up, asking her about her journey there. Eugénie recounted her brush with the Fédérés, and soon she had a circle of male admirers, though all of them were old. She noticed that Victoire looked quite put out to see her the centre of attention; her face was drawn above her tricolour costume, although she was heavily rouged.

'We must enjoy ourselves while we may, if Paris is to be invaded,' she cried tipsily, an empty glass in her hand that was hastily refilled by a footman. 'Eat, drink, my friends!'

The little chamber orchestra at the end of the salon began to play the 'Ça Ira'; it had been turned into a quadrille. Eugénie's elderly gentleman bowed to her. 'May I have the pleasure, mademoiselle?'

Eugénie tried to speak as the dreadful tune filled the

room. She felt herself break into a cold sweat; at once she had thought of the night she escaped the convent.

'You look pale, my dear,' said the elderly man. 'Are you feeling faint?'

'It is very hot. I am obliged to you, but I think I will sit this one out, monsieur.'

Some of the guests were already dancing. The women whirled in their red, white and blue skirts, heads back, laughing hysterically, sweat running down their painted faces.

Victoire herself came over with a glass of lemonade for Eugénie, her manner most friendly and confiding, though somewhat slurred. 'We have not seen enough of you lately, dear Eugénie. I do believe Armand has been hiding you away!'

Eugénie gave a weak smile. The music had changed to one of Monsieur Mozart's tunes. 'He tries to protect me, madame.'

Victoire shook her head. 'What times we are living through! When shall we be able to hold our weekly salons again, our balls? What sacrifices we have made for the sake of the constitution!'

She lowered her voice.

'And some of our friends have made greater sacrifices than others. Why, it is quite extraordinary what one can pick up for nothing now in that pawnshop in the rue

Saint-Honoré! The pawnbroker runs a thriving business, derived from the misfortunes of the nobility, I am sure, though I do not enquire too closely.' She waved a languid hand. 'I bought that ormolu console from him only yesterday.'

Eugénie glanced at it briefly. It was similar to one that stood in the salon at Chauvais, with gilded fretwork around the top.

'Exquisite, madame, you have an excellent eye,' she said, as was expected of her, though she had little interest in furniture at that precise moment. While Victoire teetered off on her heels to confide her new purchase to someone else, she sat on disconsolately beside Manon, hiding her face behind her fan.

'Mademoiselle Eugénie! I thought I recognized those two neat little feet, though I see you are doing your utmost to hide the rest of your charms from me.'

She looked up over her fan with a leap of her heart as she recognized Guy's voice, and saw him bowing low to her. His frockcoat of dark-green silk was without a crease; he looked cool and relaxed. At once the party was dull no longer, but full of promise.

'Monsieur Deschamps!' she cried, unable to conceal her delight.

'Guy, if you please. Surely we know each other well enough now, and besides, we are all citizens together these days, are we not?' He took her hand and kissed it, his greenish eyes sparkling at her. 'Ah, that is better. It is a pity to hide such a pretty face.'

Eugénie withdrew her hand from his grasp and in her confusion hid behind her fan again, gazing at him over the top. She was aware of Manon tactfully looking away, as if something was interesting her on the other side of the room.

'Oh, Guy, I am so pleased to see you! That is – I mean . . .' She stopped, blushing, then recovered herself. 'It is always good to see a friend.'

'And it is all too long since we last met, is it not? Where have you been? I have been quite desolated to find you absent from any gatherings for weeks!'

'Armand thought it safest that I remain at home.'

'I've not seen enough of Armand either. Is he not here tonight?'

'Armand has gone to Chauvais.'

'Indeed?' He looked at her, his face suddenly serious. 'So you are here alone?'

'I came with my maid.' Anxiety seized her. 'But please, Guy, say nothing of seeing me to Armand. He didn't know I was coming.' Her voice wavered. 'I don't think he would approve.'

'He would be right,' said Guy gravely. 'It is an

unpredictable time in the streets.'

'I came with my maid and shall return in the same cab. It's waiting outside. Please – you will keep silent, won't you?'

'How can I resist those eyes? I shall say nothing. Besides, it means I have you all to myself. Can I tempt you to dance, though I vow the night seems almost tropical?'

They danced. As they passed, and twirled, and passed again, Eugénie was conscious of Guy's gaze on her alone. She knew that her bare shoulders gleamed in the brilliant candlelight and that her eyes shone; she was looking her best, although perhaps a trifle flushed with the heat. She could not help admiring the moulding of Guy's taut thighs in their buckskin breeches as he nimbly executed the turns.

But it was far too hot to dance for long.

They stopped, and Guy suggested refreshment. He glanced at Manon, still sitting stolidly, then back at Eugénie. 'Let us wander through to the supper room. A long cool drink is in order, I think. Will you take my arm?'

'I shall return shortly, Manon,' Eugénie said quickly, seeing her half rise.

'She is like your shadow, is she not?' said Guy,

amused, as they left the room. 'But I am glad she is not with us. I want you all to myself.'

Her heart began to flutter.

They sat together in a little card room off the dining area. The door was open, the curtain drawn back, and she could see couples eating in the other rooms and hear the chamber orchestra playing Monsieur Handel's music now. Guy let her eat, while he chatted in a charming way of trivial things: the hot weather, how she must miss Chauvais, his time at law school before Armand. She began to relax. She found she was famished after eating frugally in the rue des Signes for so long; she had not seen such a magnificent feast for an age.

At last she put her plate down with a sigh. Hours seemed to have gone by as if in a single minute. Her dress now felt uncomfortably tight. Her head swam with the heat, and with the unaccustomed food and champagne, for the footmen had been most attentive.

Guy had been watching her with a half-smile, the candlelight shining on his dark auburn hair. He leant forward in his chair, his handsome head bent towards her.

'I am very glad you are here tonight, Eugénie. There is no one else I would rather be with.'

She fluttered her fan coyly. 'I do believe that is because the most of the ladies present are somewhat older, monsieur!'

He shook his head. 'I protest! It is true that you have youth and beauty on your side, which is a little unfair on the others, but you know full well I have admired you a good while.'

Eugénie opened her eyes very wide. 'Have you, monsieur?'

He laid his hand on hers. 'And I believe you feel the same about me,' he said softly. 'Is that not true?'

Eugénie felt a little faint. Whether it was his slanting green eyes now looking intensely into hers, or the press of his hand on her helpless fingers, or the heat of the small, windowless room, she did not know.

In a rush she rose to her feet, and his grasp loosened. 'Forgive me, monsieur. This room – it is so very close in here . . .'

He rose too, as courteous as ever. 'Of course, how foolish of me! Let us go out on to the balcony and take the night air.' He took her arm and laid it on his.

They stepped through the curtains together on to a wide stone balcony that ran the length of the first-floor withdrawing-room. The air was no cooler and still heavy with humidity, but at least did not smell of food, candlewax and perfume.

Eugénie went across to the stone balustrade and looked out. There was no view of Paris and little to see save for the darkened street below, for the area of the Marais had been built on low-lying marshland; but above them the stars were beginning to fade and the sky to lighten in the far distance with streaks of pink.

'It will be sunrise before long,' she said in surprise. 'I had no notion it was so late!'

'Nor I,' said Guy, taking out his watch. 'Close on three-thirty in the morning! How time passes when one is enjoying oneself.'

'It is tomorrow then. I should go home.'

But she did not want to go. She wanted to stay beside him on the deserted balcony for ever, looking at the night sky. He was standing very close to her, his hands resting on the balustrade beside hers. She wanted him to move his fingers over hers again. She looked up at the stars.

'So far from the Revolution,' she murmured. 'How beautiful they are!'

'Not as beautiful to me as my companion,' whispered Guy.

He took her gently by the shoulders and turned her to him. She could see the outline of his face, but not his expression in the darkness. He bent his head to hers.

He is going to kiss me! The thudding of her heart

almost overwhelmed her. She raised her face and felt his lips touch hers for a second.

Then suddenly, shockingly, the night was filled with clamour. All around them the church bells were ringing out wildly, the clanging taken up by distant churches so that the whole of Paris shook with sound.

They jerked apart. 'Devil take it, the tocsin!' said Guy.

'What can have happened?' cried Eugénie, frightened.

He swung round to the room behind them, taking her hand. 'Come, let us find out!'

He strode inside, with Eugénie almost running at his side. Everywhere guests were scattering in panic, the women scarcely stopping for their hats and wraps, the men shouting as they hurried down the marble staircase, the older ones clutching their wigs. The members of the orchestra had stopped playing: they ran with their instruments, coat tails and music sheets flying.

Eugénie looked back and saw Victoire's face, white with terror; she was standing at the top of the stairs, wringing her hands.

A breathless, sweating footman ran into the hall. 'They are marching on the Tuileries Palace, thousands of people, from all over the city!'

The outer doors were jammed with guests struggling

to leave. Eugénie looked round wildly for Manon as Guy pulled her outside into the courtyard. In the light of the burning torches there were dark figures everywhere, fleeing to the waiting carriages, the horses pawing the ground nervously at the agitation around them.

'Manon – I must find her!' Eugénie gasped.

'No time,' Guy said. 'We cannot afford to wait! Here's my carriage. I'll take you home.' He almost pushed her up the steps and rapped on the partition at once. The driver flicked his whip and the carriage began to move.

'But you've not told the driver where I live!' cried Eugénie.

The carriage came to a sudden halt in the confusion of vehicles at the gates. The door was wrenched open from the outside. Manon stood there. Someone was with her.

'Eugénie, get out!' said Julien de Fortin, without ceremony.

'But I—' The next moment he had leapt into the carriage and lifted her forcibly into his arms. She hit him with her fan. 'Let go!'

'You heard what Mademoiselle de Boncoeur said,' said Guy, grim about the mouth in the carriage light.

Ignoring both Guy and the vigorous buffeting from

Eugénie, Julien set her down on the ground and put his hand to the hilt of his dress sword. 'I demand satisfaction, monsieur!'

'And I am damned if I will give it to you!' said Guy. 'You have the lady, monsieur. Is that not enough?' His expression changed; he gave an easy laugh. 'Dammit, man, we are friends, are we not? We do not wish to duel! I was merely escorting Eugénie to safety.'

'She will be safer with me and her maid,' said Julien through gritted teeth. He was gripping Eugénie by the arm. 'It was fortunate that I also had an invitation for tonight. I've a carriage waiting in the street outside, mademoiselle. Come!'

Manon laid a hand on her other arm. 'Please, Mademoiselle Eugénie.'

They could hear cannon fire outside the rocking carriage as the driver drove the horses as fast as he dared through the back streets towards the rue des Signes.

Eugénie huddled silently in a corner. She vowed to herself that as long as she lived, she would never speak to Julien de Fortin again.

SIXTEEN

August–October 1792

Later that same morning, the 10th August, the royal family were escorted to the National Assembly for their safety, where for three sweltering days they remained in the minute-writer's cramped box by the President's chair. Then they were imprisoned in the Temple. After the King left the Tuileries Palace, its staff – footmen, pages, cooks and maids – and over six hundred of the Swiss Guards who had tried to defend him, were hacked to pieces by the invading mob.

On the 21st September the monarchy was formally abolished.

On his hasty return from Chauvais, Armand de Boncoeur, with Eugénie and the faithful Manon, moved out of Belle's house. Armand had found them lodgings in a poorer district close by: top-floor rooms in a house in the rue des Trois Chats that reeked of damp and decay, and where the concierge was perpetually drunk.

He told Eugénie that the revolutionaries were hunting down any aristocrats remaining in Paris; even the constitutional monarchists in the National Assembly were not safe. It was true, but not the whole truth. He did not tell her that he also wanted to hide her from Le Fantôme, for before long she would be sixteen.

'You must tell no one where we live, Eugénie. Belle will need to know, but no one else – none of the acquaintances you had in your old life. You do understand?' He looked at her earnestly. 'It could put me – both of us – in terrible danger.'

She nodded miserably, knowing this meant she could not see Guy. She could not risk endangering Armand.

Late in September, Armand went secretly to Belle's to see if he had any letters. One had just come from his uncle, Thomas Coveney, in Deal. The next day, when Julien came to visit him in the rue des Trois Chats, he was reading it again.

I have heard the dreadful news about the royal
family's imprisonment and the slaughter that

has taken place in the Paris prisons. The English ambassador has returned, telling of horrors. It cannot be long before our two countries are at war, and then it will be impossible for you to travel here. I entreat you to reconsider.

Armand, you are responsible for your sister, now that your guardian has emigrated. It is your duty to bring her as safely as you can to us in England. It is a dangerous journey, and she cannot travel alone. I urge you to do so without further delay.

Armand, sitting at the rickety table, put his head in his hands and groaned. The letter fell from his fingers and fluttered to the floor, where Julien picked it up silently, smoothed it and put it on the table. They were in Armand's cramped little room under the low eaves.

'What am I to do, Julien? Rescue the King from the Temple, or accompany Eugénie to England, as is my duty – as my uncle so helpfully points out?'

'Take Eugénie to England before it's too late,' Julien said promptly. 'Don't be a fool, Armand! There's been one attempt on your life already.'

'We don't know for certain that Jean-Paul's murderer was after me.'

'Jean-Paul was wearing the coat you left behind after one of our meetings,' Julien pointed out patiently, 'and he was fair-headed, like you.'

'But if I leave the country that scoundrel Goullet will declare Chauvais forfeit and claim it for himself!'

'Better that than have him claim Eugénie. She will be sixteen shortly, and if you wait any longer it will be impossible to leave Paris.'

Armand groaned again. 'But what of our plans for the King if I do that?'

Julien looked at him in exasperation. 'What about love, Armand? You love your sister. Surely that counts for more than rescuing a king, whom you do not know and therefore cannot care about, who allowed his country to become bankrupt and disintegrate into turmoil?'

Armand stared at him, his blue eyes widening in shock. 'How can you speak like that? You sound as radical as a Fédéré, you who've been such an inspiration to our cause!'

Julien sighed with irritation. 'You know that's not true. I'm simply being realistic. France is now officially a republic anyway, declared so by the Convention. We are in Year One of the new France and must call each other "Citizen", or have you forgotten? The King has no role. They will have to decide what to do with him.'

'He will be guillotined, I am sure of it,' said Armand despairingly.

Julien shook his head. 'They would have to bring him to trial first. They will never do that. They'll depose him instead, or persuade him to abdicate. We're not like the English, who executed their king. We are still the most civilized country in Europe.'

'You think so?' said Armand bitterly. 'Think of the prisoners massacred last month, over twelve hundred of them, mostly ordinary people, not even aristocrats. Danton just stood by and let it happen. Danton, the Minister for Justice! Some justice!'

'It was feared there were traitors among them, counter-revolutionaries who'd hand the city over to the Prussians. People panicked.'

'You think that justifies mass murder?'

Julien flushed angrily. 'No, of course I don't, as well you know.'

They were silent, Armand pacing the dirty floorboards, Julien staring out of the window at the rain. After a moment Armand said gloomily, 'There is bloodlust in Paris now. I don't believe anyone will escape it, not even the King. Can we allow that to happen and do nothing?'

'What you must do is take your sister to England,' said Julien shortly. 'I will put my poor brains to puzzling out how to rescue the King. Besides . . .' He lowered his voice in case Eugénie should hear through the thin walls. '. . . Even if Jean-Paul's assassin wasn't out to murder you, you know there are revolutionary agents after you – anti-monarchists – who would denounce you to Robespierre.'

'And what about that attack on your own life? I'd understand if you wanted to leave us, Julien.'

'You need me,' said Julien shortly. 'I'm the only one who can stand up to the Baron and demolish his wild ideas. Without me, you'll all be killed. Travel to England while you can, Armand. You may even be able to raise help for the King there.'

Armand brightened at once, as Julien had known he would. 'I have another uncle, Thomas's brother, who is a Member of the English Parliament. Perhaps through him . . .'

'Indeed.' Julien nodded thankfully. 'Now I must plan how to get you and Eugénie out of Paris. You can't travel under your own names.'

'It will be dangerous, presumably?'

'For a young aristocrat and his sister, yes – quite apart from the fact that you are suspected of being a counter-revolutionary.'

'How ironic that is,' said Armand bitterly. 'A counter-revolutionary! I, who fought so hard for a revolution, for an end to the old regime, for a fair constitution! I believe I even lost my soul to it. Now I hate the violence and bloodshed the Revolution has brought. All I can do is struggle to save the royal family from it.'

'All?' said Julien sarcastically. 'If you manage that, it will be a miracle!'

'I owe it to the Queen,' said Armand miserably. 'She trusted me to save them.'

'And now they are in the Temple it is impossible. How can you break through a prison that's an old fortress, through a succession of locked doors?'

'Julien, you have to think of something before they all go to the guillotine – the King, the Queen, the little Dauphin and his sister. For that will surely happen unless we can rescue them.'

'It may not be possible until they leave the Temple.'

'You mean . . .'

'Until their future is decided – one way or the other.'

Armand thought again of that pale face, the desperate plea on the note: 'Save us'. But then he thought of Eugénie. He must get her out of these dank, squalid rooms, to safety.

'Julien, I pass my leadership to you. I'll take no part in any plans, except as an observer. I'll take Eugénie to England as soon as it's possible.'

* * *

Around five o'clock Armand and Eugénie ate their last meal of the day together as usual. Food was getting even sparser and more expensive. Today they had some pottage Manon had made, without bread to accompany it: there had been no bread at the baker's that morning.

Armand was silent, his expression distracted in the light of the single candle on the table.

'What is it, Armand?' Eugénie said gently, setting down her empty bowl. She still felt hungry, but there was nothing else to eat. Draughts eddied round their feet; she pulled her shawl more closely round her shoulders, shivering.

'I have had another letter from our uncle in Deal, inviting us to stay. I think we should take up his offer.'

'You'll come with me?' said Eugénie in delight.

He nodded.

She pressed further. 'And not return to Paris?'

'I'll return to Chauvais.' He saw her disappointed face in the guttering candlelight and tried to sound reasonable, not impatient. 'I can't remain with you in England, Eugénie. You must understand. Unless I return to Chauvais, we could lose it to the revolutionaries.'

'But that will happen anyway, surely?' she said in dismay. 'Oh, Armand, it will be too dangerous for you to return to France, even to Chauvais. They will accuse you of being a spy and put you in prison!'

'They cannot do that,' he said stubbornly. 'They have no proof. And I do not intend to give it to them.' He stretched his hand towards her. 'When things are safer – more settled – I'll send for you to join me at Chauvais.'

But he hated lying to her; she could never return while Goullet lived.

'Manon,' Eugénie whispered in the darkness, when they had blown out the candle that night and were lying in bed, huddled together beneath the thin blankets, their cold feet touching the brick that Manon had warmed in the oven. 'Manon, we must leave for England soon, my brother and I. Will you come with us?'

There was a long pause. She waited tensely for Manon's answer, yet she knew what it would be.

'I cannot, Mademoiselle Eugénie.' The habit of service since childhood meant that despite the equality advocated so vigorously by the new republic, Manon had never managed to call Eugénie by her first name, though they now slept in the same bed and were even at this moment wrapped together for warmth. 'I can't leave my family – my poor mother, my father. I must return to them in Montparnasse and help. You do understand, mademoiselle?'

Tears sprang into Eugénie's eyes. How would she manage without Manon's solid, comforting presence? Manon, who was now almost as dear to her as a sister, whose particular smell of sweat, garlic and something indefinably animal she knew after all these nights so intimately; Manon, who had never questioned or complained when their circumstances changed, but had remained loyally with her even though she was associating with a despised aristocrat and, if discovered, would be accused of being a traitor to the Republic.

After a moment she managed to whisper, 'I'm sorry, Manon. I should not have asked you. It was selfish of me.'

Manon's strong, warm arms crept around her and her hot breath, smelling of the pottage they had all eaten earlier, stirred the hair on the back of Eugénie's neck. 'Do not upset yourself, mademoiselle. We shall meet again, I am sure of it. But I wish you were not going to such an unfriendly, cold place. You must be sure to take *tisane de menthe* for your digestion, for the English eat nothing but roast beef, the bloodier the better.'

'Are you sure?' said Eugénie, the tears drying on her cheeks.

'Yes, indeed. The more they can cram in at one sitting, the better, I have heard. Even a whole cow.'

'Really?' said Eugénie in amazement, and they both

began to giggle, until the bed shook and the lodger on the floor beneath hammered angrily on the ceiling with his stick for silence.

The next morning Manon came back from shopping accompanied by Belle. Manon had evidently told her the news, for she looked tearstained already. She swept Eugénie into her arms mournfully.

'*Ma pauvre!* You are to go to England, that terrible cold country where it is always raining!'

'Hush, Belle!' Eugénie said, her voice muffled by Belle's bony silk shoulder. 'It is meant to be a secret.'

'You would have gone without telling me?' Belle said reproachfully, letting her go.

'Of course not. But I mean to return as soon as possible.' Eugénie smiled cheerfully as she said this, but Belle's expression remained doubtful.

'At least you will be safe,' said Belle. 'Rose Bertin, my great rival, has a business there, in London, you know. Of course, it is easy to make a name for yourself when you have been *modiste* to Marie-Antoinette.' She shrugged disparagingly. 'But their fortunes are so closely tied together soon she will have to leave her shop in the rue de Richelieu altogether. They say she encouraged the Queen's extravagances.' She looked wistful suddenly. 'I suppose you will go to Madame Bertin for your *toilettes* now.'

Eugénie laughed. 'I do not think so, Belle, even if I could afford them. Deal is a long way from London. Besides, I have all my pretty costumes waiting for my return!'

Belle nodded, mollified, then looked around the smoky little room, wrinkling her nose. 'I am glad you have not brought them to this filthy place, *ma petite*.'

Manon bristled. 'I keep it as clean as I can, madame. I cannot stop the fire smoking or the walls dripping.'

Belle ignored her. 'When are you to leave, mademoiselle?'

'As soon as the paperwork is done,' said Eugénie. 'We need passports, my brother and I. We need new names.'

'Shall you go in disguise?' said Belle, her eyes widening.

'I am not sure yet,' said Eugénie slowly. 'But I have an idea. Indeed, Belle, you have just given it to me.'

SEVENTEEN

November 1792

Julien had stopped going to the law school. He had long left the rooms he had once shared with Armand in the rue Saint-Antoine, and moved to a secret address that even his friends did not know. But he could not bear to hide away there; he roamed the tangled heart of the city, wearing a plain dark greatcoat and carrying, as many did now, a 'Hercules' club, a heavy blackthorn stick, in case he was attacked.

Sometimes he would attend the National Convention, which had been elected in September to write a constitution. He wore a hat pulled well over his face, and listened, as the radical Jacobins, Robespierre and Danton among them, demanded the trial of the King.

One day he came face to face with Guy as he descended the narrow stairwell. Both young men bowed their heads to each other in a semblance of good manners, although the gesture was no longer considered necessary nowadays. Julien made to brush by.

'Julien! Wait a moment, please.' Guy, polite as always, spoke evenly. 'I hope we can forget our misunderstanding.'

'I do not consider it a misunderstanding, citizen,' said Julien curtly.

'You told Armand?'

Julien nodded, reflecting bitterly that when he had said to Armand that he believed Guy had had dishonourable intentions towards Eugénie that night, Armand had flatly refused to believe him. *Guy?* A good and loyal friend, whom he respected so much!

Guy climbed up a step closer and lowered his voice. 'I have not seen Armand for a while. I assume he has gone into hiding?' His face was grave, his eyes anxious. 'It would be best for him – and for his sister.'

Julien nodded again, coldly.

Guy hesitated. 'I should like to see Mademoiselle Eugénie again. I feel I must apologize – in case she misinterpreted my actions that night. Do you know where I may find her now?'

Julien put his hat back on: an ancient, round felt hat, its cockade bedraggled. He rammed its crown down with finality. 'I fear I cannot help you, citizen. Good day to you.'

* * *

Loulette still came to Belle's out of habit each day, though there was little pay nowadays. Early one morning she was walking down the rue des Signes when a tall figure detached itself from beneath the overhanging gable of the neighbouring house and approached her.

'Oh, *citoyen*, you made me jump!' said Loulette half flirtatiously, for he was a young man, expensively dressed, though properly sober as the Revolution demanded.

'Perhaps you can tell me, *citoyenne*,' the young man said civilly, in the tones of a gentleman, 'whether a certain Eugénie de Boncoeur still lives at this address?'

Was this good-looking young man Eugénie's sweetheart? How fortunate Eugénie was; she had everything.

'No, *citoyen*, she does not, and I am afraid I do not know where she lives now.'

But as the young man turned away Loulette thought she heard him jingle the coins in his pocket.

She added hastily, 'All I do know, is that she will not be in the country for much longer: she is bound for England with her brother.' Belle had told her they were leaving, and there was no harm in passing it on, surely?

'Do you know when?'

'No, *citoyen*. I know nothing – yet.' She lingered on the last word, looking at him out of the corner of her eye.

The young man brought a handful of coins out of his breeches pocket and counted out fifteen sous. Loulette stood looking at them breathlessly. She had not seen so much money for a long time.

'Thank you,' he said, and he took her hand in his gloved one, turned it over and poured the coins into her rough red palm. 'There will be more for you if you find out anything else. But it is to be a secret between us, you understand? I wish to surprise her – a final goodbye.'

'I understand, monsieur,' said Loulette.

All through the next few weeks Loulette's new acquaintance would turn up now and again outside the workshop. It was as if he knew when Belle was out. He would tap on the closed shutters with his cane and then Loulette would skip outside and give him whatever new information she had. He learnt a good deal, for Belle had never been good at keeping secrets, and Loulette's rewards grew larger.

He knew now that Eugénie and Armand were leaving Paris at the end of November under assumed names; he knew that they were sailing for Deal on the south coast of England, though he did not know the details of their journey; and he knew the name of the relation with whom they would be staying. It would not take him long to discover the other details, he thought, with some satisfaction.

But Loulette was unexpectedly discreet when it came to finding out where Eugénie and Armand were living now; she had begun to suspect that the young man was not a disconsolate suitor at all. 'I cannot tell you that, *citoyen* –' she opened her eyes very wide '– for we do not know. But,' she added, ever hopeful of further reward, 'if you give me your name, then I can make enquiries for you.'

He looked angry. 'I thought I told you this was a secret between us. I want them to know nothing, do you understand?'

Loulette nodded, frightened. She realized now that this stranger was most likely a government spy who was after Monsieur de Boncoeur. What had she said? She had not meant to betray him.

So she shook her head, pretending ignorance when questioned further, and after a while to her great relief the stranger stopped coming to the workshop in the rue des Signes.

But Le Scalpel did not give up immediately. He followed the unsuspecting Loulette to the market place for Belle's shopping, and all the way to the Croix-Rouge

– where, unknown to him, Loulette's father was a furniture-maker – cursing beneath his breath as he was splattered with mud and horse dung, only to lose her among the cavernous streets.

Le Scalpel passed on what he knew to Le Fantôme, and Le Fantôme went to see Robespierre.

'De Boncoeur has disappeared, citizen,' Le Fantôme admitted.

They faced each other, Robespierre immaculately dressed, despite the Republic's fashion for less showy clothes; Le Fantôme, conceding to it by dressing entirely in black.

Le Fantôme looked down at his hands, their horror disguised so artfully by the smooth softness of the leather gloves. 'If we are to find them, it means searching every stinking hell-hole in Paris, unless of course you arrest the milliner and the young seamstress on charges of conspiracy. They will soon break under questioning and reveal anything they know.'

Robespierre sucked in his cheeks thoughtfully as he looked at his chief agent. Sometimes his face looked feline, as it did at this moment. 'But if they do not know de Boncoeur's whereabouts then I would have to let them go. I must show that there is proper justice in our new republic, Goullet. Besides word might reach de

Boncoeur and warn him. No, the best time to arrest de Boncoeur and his sister is when they show themselves at the city gates next month. If you can issue me with descriptions, I will inform the guards to be particularly vigilant during that time.'

'Not the girl, citizen. She is innocent. She knows nothing of her brother's traitorous schemes.'

Robespierre took off his glasses and his pale, weak eyes squinted at Le Fantôme with curiosity. 'What is this? You are protecting an aristocrat?'

'There is a long-standing arrangement for marriage between us, citizen. A contract was drawn up some years ago, signed by her guardian and myself. We are to be married next year when *la petite* Boncoeur turns sixteen.' He smiled grimly. 'If she is not republican now, I can vouch that she will be by her wedding night.'

The hint of a smile touched Robespierre's thin lips. 'I understand, Goullet. I am not inhuman. When we arrest de Boncoeur, we shall take the girl in for questioning, as is normal procedure. Then, if she appears innocent, we shall deliver her into your safe keeping.'

Julien went to the rue des Trois Chats late and under cover of darkness. He took the usual precautions to avoid being followed, but the narrow little streets in the area were deserted and unlit.

He crept up the stairs, past the tenant on the floor below, to Armand's room, and slipped in without knocking. The room smelt of the single oil lamp, of damp, and stale food. Surrounded by darkness, Armand was sitting at the rickety table from which the early evening meal had been cleared; in the circle of meagre yellow light he was gazing into space, dreaming and half drowsing, his mouth turned down in profile, but he spun round when he heard Julien.

'Don't creep in like that!'

'I didn't want to rouse anyone, Armand – we must be careful if you're to remain safe until you've left France. I've brought the papers for you and Eugénie.'

Julien took them out of his bag and laid them down on the table. 'I don't like her plan, I have to tell you – I think these particular identities are risky and foolish.'

'For God's sake don't tell her so! I don't want anything to put her off leaving Paris.'

'You think anything I'd say would have any influence over her?'

Armand stared glumly at the papers. 'How did you manage it?'

'I know one or two people in the right departments,' Julien said vaguely. He did not elaborate, and Armand did not question him further. Julien's contacts were wide-ranging and mysterious. It was better not to know.

'Have you brought a newspaper?' Armand asked longingly. 'That's what I miss most with this incarceration – not having the freedom to move through the streets of Paris, to learn at first hand how the Revolution progresses.'

'I've brought a rag, that's all. *Le Père Duchesne.* Hébert's written his usual inflammatory stuff. But I'd rather tell you the news myself.' He looked sombre. 'I warn you, it's not good.'

'What is it? What has happened?'

Julien hesitated. 'They have found incriminating documents in the Tuileries Palace.'

'Incriminating?'

'Letters from the King denouncing the constitution, showing that he has never had any true intention of accepting it, others written to the Austrian royal family begging them to declare war on France. They were found in an iron safe hidden behind some panelling in a passage.'

'They must be forged, put there deliberately by his enemies!'

'No, Armand,' said Julien gently. 'The documents are genuine. And it means that the King is certain to be brought to trial. They have been arguing about it for weeks anyway. Now they have good reason to do it.'

Armand looked at him in horror. 'But you

know what that means? The trial may well go against him.'

Julien nodded sombrely. 'If it does, he may face the death penalty. This discovery alters everything, Armand. Now his enemies have the proof they need that he is not fit to be king and has betrayed his own country.'

Armand sat silent, stunned. After a while he said, almost to himself, 'Who can tell what a man may do *in extremis*? And God knows, he has had cause to be frightened, for himself and for his family! No doubt he was thinking of the Queen's safety, of the little Dauphin who should be king after him, and what was in the best interest for France.'

'No doubt,' said Julien drily. 'And no doubt the Queen influenced him.'

Armand was not listening. He continued passionately, 'This does not alter anything, do you not see? It means that we must act quickly. We must try to save them before the worst happens.'

'It's impossible now, Armand. The Temple is too secure a prison and the guards will be watching them like hawks. We have to wait for the outcome of the trial. All may be well, after all.'

'But if the trial goes against the King . . .'

'Then we can only act when he has left the Temple.'

'You mean . . .'

'Exactly,' said Julien grimly. 'When he is on his way to the guillotine.'

'Then we have to plan for that eventuality.'

Julien looked at Armand's desperate face and said gently, 'You mustn't let this alter your own plans for departure, even if you leave before the outcome of the trial.'

Armand shook his head violently. 'You need me. If the King is condemned, his rescue will be the biggest thing we've ever planned. We don't have enough men in our little group. We'll need a large number on horseback, armed, taking them by surprise. We'll have to bring in the Baron de Batz and his contacts. You must persuade the Baron to come here secretly, Julien, so we can talk to him. There is a cellar room we can use for meetings. It's cold and filthy, but at least no one will hear us.'

Julien sighed. 'I don't like including him, but I agree we need his contacts. We can plan the King's rescue now if we must, but Armand, you must leave whatever happens. You can't jeopardize Eugénie's safety.'

Armand dropped his head. 'I know, I know. But I can't leave until I know the outcome of the trial and we have finalized every last detail of the plan. You must understand that.'

'I don't,' said Julien shortly. 'You are putting your

own and Eugénie's life in danger for the sake of your obsession, Armand!'

'I don't have any choice,' said Armand quietly. 'The Queen gave it to *me*, that message. I have to do my best and if it means delaying our departure by a month, then that is what I have to do.'

The days and nights dragged on. Eugénie was not sleeping well; outside the night echoed with dreadful sound as *sans culottes*, armed to the teeth, roamed the streets bawling out, 'Execute the traitor king, execute Louis Capet!'

She seemed always to be listening fearfully in the darkness, for soldiers come to arrest Armand, or for revolutionaries surging triumphantly up the stairs to murder herself and Armand, the hated aristocrats, as they lay in bed. They would be discovered one day soon, she was certain of that.

Julien had been to see Armand several times since they had left Belle's.

She shifted uncomfortably in bed as she thought of the thin intense face dominated by those arched black brows and the clever dark eyes that always managed to ruffle her with their gaze. What did he think of her? Not that she cared. She disliked him intensely. He had no manners, he was no gentleman.

Each tiny noise now – the sharp scuttle and gnaw of rats in the rafters, the dry clicking of cockroaches across the floorboards, ash falling from the dying fire – frightened her. Even Manon's heavy, regular breathing next to her was no comfort any more.

Then one night she heard an unmistakable click as the latch on Armand's door was lifted and released. She sat up in bed immediately, listening. Footsteps crossed the landing, quietly, stealthily. Then the stairs creaked. Was he going to the privy at the back? Or was he – could he be – going out into the street?

Moonlight striped the floor between the shutters giving her some light, but it was bitterly cold. Shivering, she fumbled hastily for her house slippers and drew a coverlet from the bed to wrap around her nightgown. Nothing would wake Manon, but she did not want to alert Armand yet. She eased the door latch up as quietly as she could and crept out on to the tiny landing.

It was pitch dark here, but far below she saw the glow of an oil lamp. Armand was already at the front door, sliding back the bolts to open it. In desperation she was about to call his name and stop him, not caring if the other tenants were woken – the concierge, drunk as usual, would be asleep in the kitchen – when a gush of damp, wintry air reached her and sudden moonlight outlined two dark figures entering the narrow hall. She recognized the slighter one as Julien's. She heard whispers, then a deep fruity guffaw that could not be silenced.

She knew that laugh. It filled her with unease. She had heard it before, but could not place it.

The figures moved down the hall. She was not certain where they were going, then she heard a door scrape open over the floorboards and a faint but disgusting smell of mould and wet rot reached her. It was the old cellar under the house, oozing with mud and piled with mouldering empty barrels, more of a cave dug into the foundations than a room; she had once opened the door by mistake and peered down the ladder in horrified curiosity.

The light wavered and it was dark again, the whispers fading with the footsteps.

She went back to bed and lay as cold and heavy as stone. It was the Baron's voice she had heard; she remembered it now. Julien must have brought him here. She hated Julien for that. What was the Baron plotting now, this very minute, down in that dismal cellar room, which would involve and implicate her brother? Whatever it was, it would surely end in disaster.

Eighteen

November 1792–January 1793

Eugénie had a chance to confront Julien the very
next day. He brought Belle to see her, as a rainy
dusk was falling in the late afternoon. Manon ushered
them into the drab, shadowy room as if it were
Versailles itself.

'Madame Belle and Monsieur de Fortin to see you,
mademoiselle,' she announced in a loud whisper,
shutting the door smartly on any eavesdroppers that
might be lurking in the stairwell.

Julien bowed to Eugénie. She nodded back stiffly,
without greeting him. His black hair glistened with
raindrops, but she did not invite him to the fire.
Instead she embraced Belle, who was wearing a
drenched cloak, a hood hiding her face. While Manon
hastened Belle to the guttering fire and helped her

off with her wet cloak, she remained by the door.

Julien was forced to stand where he was, facing her awkwardly. Water ran from his hair down his face, but he did not wipe it away.

'So we are still to leave Paris, then, my brother and I?' Eugénie demanded.

'Of course,' he said in surprise, or perhaps feigning it, she did not know.

Belle and Manon were talking together and did not look up, but all the same she dropped her voice. Her words came out in a hiss.

'In spite of whatever mad plan you are now concocting to save the King? Oh, don't look so shocked. I know what influence you have over Armand, and how dearly he desires to be the hero who rescues Louis XVI from the guillotine! I saw you bring your friend the Baron here last night—'

'Let me speak, Eugénie. First, the Baron is not my friend—'

'Not a friend?' It was difficult to sound sarcastic when whispering. 'Then is it wise to trust him with such secret plans? And it was you who brought him here, to this house of hiding that no stranger is meant to know of! He could betray us all. And why is Armand involved at all if we are about to leave?'

Julien bit his lip. His wet face was pinched with the

cold and damp. 'Eugénie, hasn't he told you? You're not to leave Paris for a month or more.'

She stared at him in horror. 'But . . .'

Julien shook his head. 'He'll take no part in any action, I do assure you, but you know how fervently royalist he is. He could not bear to be left out of the planning. He wants to know the outcome of the trial before you leave.'

As Manon led Belle behind the screen to find a towel to wipe her face, Eugénie clenched her hands.

'You have encouraged him all along! Why couldn't you stop him – you, the clever scholarship boy?' She stepped closer to him, looking up through narrowed eyes. 'I've been watching you. You're not a true royalist! I know your heart is not in it. You are using Armand to disguise your own cowardice.'

She had gone too far. Julien stepped back as if she had hit him. His face grew tighter still. Eugénie ploughed on regardless.

'We're now in hiding because of it, in this hideous rat-infested place! It's too late to rescue the King now. Soon it will be too late for us to leave Paris!'

Julien shook his head. 'I have the paperwork ready and signed,' he said coldly. 'I have to make the last arrangements for your journey out of the city, that is all. You and Armand can be safely away by the time any plan is put into action.'

He stared at her for a moment in freezing silence, then turned and stalked out of the room.

A few days before Christmas, the King was brought to trial before the Convention. Armand was sunk in gloom and could not raise any interest in their departure plans. Eugénie tried to talk to him, but it seemed that all he wanted to do was to read the newspapers.

'Shall we ever leave Paris, Armand?' cried Eugénie.

Armand looked up from his newspaper with irritation. 'Of course.'

'When, then?'

'When I know the outcome of the trial.'

He threatened to go to the Convention and listen to the proceedings in disguise.

'Let me go,' said Eugénie. Perhaps she could contrive to meet Guy; she had pined for him, reliving and reliving the night of Victoire's party. But Armand said it was not safe.

However, as the King's trial continued, Armand grew careless himself. In the night now the noise from the hall would alert Eugénie, if she had not already heard the footsteps in the street. More and more were coming to meet in the cellar room. *How many are involved?* she thought. Sooner or later someone would be indiscreet, and their plans would be betrayed to the authorities.

Christmas was miserable. Manon was away, visiting her family in Montparnasse, the day was dark with drizzle and their quarters on the top floor of the ancient building seemed meaner and damper than ever. There was little to eat but stale bread and cheese, and certainly nothing to celebrate.

'It is my doing that we are in this sorry state,' said Armand, as they tried to warm themselves at the fitful fire. The wood was damp like everything else, and spat and hissed at them. 'What would Maman say if she were still alive?'

He looked so unexpectedly full of compunction that Eugénie rose from her chair and put her arms about him as if he were a small boy. She leant her head against his.

'It is enough that we are together,' she whispered. 'And safe for the moment. But don't do anything foolish before we leave, dearest brother, I beg you.'

But she did not trust him. In the afternoon twilight she put on her outdoor clothes, hastily pinning the tricolour cockade on a bonnet that hid most of her face behind its brim, and went creeping through the drizzle alone to the dark little church a street away. Most of its treasures had been stolen, but the Madonna still stared at the few kneeling supplicants with a patient benevolence on her painted face.

Eugénie tried to pray, but the words would not come. She stared up helplessly at the varnished blue eyes; there was a chip in one of them, she noticed, as if someone had tried to smash the statue in a fit of fury. But as no feelings of comfort came to her, she grew frustrated with the unchanging face above her that seemed to accept so placidly the raging turmoil of the city. She returned dismally to the house, only to find Julien had arrived and was closeted with Armand.

She could not wish Julien a happy Christmas. It seemed to her now that he was the cause of all their troubles.

As the King's trial continued, it looked certain that he would be found guilty. The voices behind Armand's door held a renewed urgency. And then, when Manon was out at the market, Armand suddenly announced to Eugénie that their departure was planned for five days' time.

Eugénie flung her arms around him. 'Thank you, Armand!' Up until this moment she had not been truly sure that they would ever leave the city.

'Do not thank me,' he said coolly, disengaging himself from her embrace. 'Thank Julien instead, for it is he who has made all the arrangements for our journey.'

She stepped back, compressing her lips. She could never thank Julien for anything.

That afternoon Julien brought Belle to see Eugénie for the last time.

'In case you are questioned on the journey you should go over everything with Belle again,' he said to Eugénie.

She tossed her head. 'You think I am too foolish to remember what I am to say?'

He did not meet her eyes, and she knew that was exactly what he did think. She turned her back on him angrily and hugged Belle.

'No matter!' she said gaily. 'I am always glad of the chance to see you, *ma chère* Belle!'

Eugénie and Belle spent a very happy hour together until at last Belle grew too hoarse to speak. 'You do not look well,' said Eugénie in concern.

'It is nothing. A *petite maladie*. This weather . . .' She mopped her reddened nose. 'Now, you understand everything I have told you, *ma petite*. This, then, is *adieu* – goodbye – for us two.'

'No, Belle, it is only *au revoir*,' said Eugénie. 'I shall see you again. I shall return to Paris and you in turn shall come to Chauvais.'

But now she could not speak as confidently as she once had. Her voice died, and they clung together.

Nineteen

Early–mid–January 1793

Eugénie began to feel ill a few days before they were due to leave. Her bones ached, she felt hot yet shivery; she had a headache and, like Belle, could scarcely speak for her sore throat.

'I shall be well soon,' she croaked. 'I will! I must be!'

Armand put his cold hand on her burning forehead, and she shuddered and pulled the coverlet back over her that she had only just pushed away. In desperation to keep her warm, he and Manon threw an old chair to join the few damp spluttering logs on the fire, and moved the bed closer to the grate.

'She is not fit to travel, monsieur,' said Manon in a low voice.

'I can see that,' he said miserably. 'She should be seen by a doctor, but it is too dangerous to bring a stranger here. Oh, Manon, what are we to do?'

'You can do nothing except wait,' she said, sensible as always. 'The fever will take its course. Belle is better now.'

Armand ran his fingers through his thick fair hair. 'But how will Eugénie recover in this foul place? She needs good food and wine, but I must keep all the money we have for the journey.' He thought for a moment, then abruptly pulled a gold ring from his finger. 'Here, take this to the pawnbroker's in the rue Saint-Honoré. See how many assignats it will raise. It is not safe for me to wear such a thing any longer, anyway.'

Manon looked doubtfully at the ring lying heavy in her palm. The shining gold was engraved with the de Boncoeur crest: a stag's head surrounded by a circlet of ivy leaves.

'They will think me a thief, monsieur!'

He shook his head. 'No one asks questions any more. And I have been to that particular pawnshop many times.'

He did not elaborate, and Manon was trained not to ask questions, even if she had suspected the purpose behind his urgent summer visit to Chauvais – and perhaps other journeys before it. 'The pawnbroker will recognize the ring, but he is discreet. He has often asked me if I would like to sell it. But if you are worried, you can say I gave it to you in lieu of wages –' he gave her a charming, rueful smile '– and I only wish that were true, Manon.'

'I will go at once, monsieur.'

'Do not forget to sign for it,' he said gaily. 'I intend to buy it back one day!'

But his smile faded as he looked down at Eugénie tossing and muttering in a fevered sleep.

Later that day, after Manon had left the gold signet ring in return for a paltry amount of paper notes, the pawnbroker, who had grown rich on the proceeds of impoverished aristocrats, sent his new young assistant to fetch Le Fantôme.

Le Fantôme's black-gloved fingers pushed a wad of assignats over the counter and he waited impatiently while the pawnbroker brought the ring out from a desk drawer. The gold glimmered in the darkness of the shop as Le Fantôme turned it this way and that, scrutinizing the crest with his cold, pale eyes. Then he nodded in satisfaction.

'You have done well. You have his signature?'

'Here, *citoyen*.' Eagerly the pawnbroker pulled several sheets of paper, each with a few lines of writing upon it, from the same drawer. This client looked rich; there was the prospect of further sales. 'I noted down all the items as the young man brought them in. He put his signature to each document. We still have several of his pieces unsold, if you are interested.'

Le Fantôme took the top sheet, which gave the details of an ormolu console. Beneath the pawnbroker's cramped handwriting was a large boyish signature, decorated with loops and flourishes. 'Armand de Boncoeur.'

'May I keep this?'

'I fear that bureau has already been sold, *citoyen*.' The pawnbroker cleared his throat delicately. 'I can give you details of the purchaser, if you wish.'

'That won't be necessary. You have no information as to this young man's whereabouts? It is important.' Le Fantôme leant across the counter and lowered his voice grimly as the pawnbroker's eyes widened. 'Robespierre himself would be interested to know. Need I say more?'

The pawnbroker paled and shook his head in alarm. 'No, I know nothing, monsieur. If I could tell you more, I would, I swear it! But the girl who brought the ring – she told me in passing that she had left his employ months ago.' He wrung his hands. 'I am a republican, monsieur. I detest these aristocrats who have betrayed *la patrie*. Long may they suffer!'

Le Fantôme regarded him through narrowed eyes. 'If he ever comes in here again, you are to send your boy for me immediately. There will be good money for you if de Boncoeur is still here when I come. But . . .' he paused ominously '. . . if you let him go, you will have abetted a traitor and Robespierre will not look kindly upon that. Do you understand?'

The pawnbroker nodded his head vigorously and his voice trembled. 'I understand, monsieur.'

Eugénie's fever had gone, though she was pale and low in spirits. *If I can only leave this place*, she thought, *then I will recover properly.*

She ignored the trembling in her legs and began to walk about the room, desperate to grow stronger, while Manon plied her with tempting titbits, bought with the ring's assignats, and bullied her until she had eaten properly.

But as she recovered, she was aware of Armand's restlessness. Each day she heard him pacing his own room. At night she heard his voice and Julien's through her wall, agitated, exasperated, apprehensive. She knew that after weeks of wrangling and tumult in the Convention the King had finally been condemned to death by execution and would soon face the guillotine, but she had no desire to read about it in the newspapers that Manon brought her. Everything had narrowed down to this room, her prison – and her desire to escape it.

Then one morning Armand said to her, 'I

believe tomorrow may be our last chance to leave for England, Eugénie.'

She had been staring listlessly out of the window at the rain, shivering in the chill draught that came through the cracks in the glass, but she turned at that and stared at him. In the last few months his face had become drawn, though his blue eyes could still shine with his old enthusiasm and ardour. At this moment they merely looked anxious. 'Are you well enough, Eugénie?'

'Of course I am! Why, I feel fit as a fiddle!'

He smiled at that, and his eyes lit up at last.

Julien, visiting Armand later that morning, shook his head gravely when he heard the news.

'Armand, it's utter folly! To leave tomorrow of all days!'

Armand rose from his chair and resumed his restless pacing, looking intently at Julien. 'Listen to me. If our rescue plan fails and the King is executed tomorrow, the English will declare war on France. They will have no other option. If they don't, they will appear to sanction the execution of kings. As you know, they've rebels in their own country who support republicanism and would do much to rid the country of King George III. Once war is declared, it will be impossible to travel to England.'

Julien was still looking at him doubtfully.

'Nothing else need change,' said Armand. He was aware a pleading note had crept into his voice, and despised himself for it. Why did he always want Julien's approval for every decision he made, simply because Julien was older and had a reputation for being clever?

'Our rescue plan must go ahead,' he continued firmly. 'Everything we have worked on over these last few weeks will – must – be put into action tomorrow. And while it is going on, Eugénie and I will melt away into thin air.'

Julien frowned. 'The crowds will be out to view the execution. Is it wise to leave at such a time?'

Armand shrugged, trying to appear careless. 'That may work in our favour. Everyone will be intent upon the guillotine, not on two fleeing aristocrats.'

'The gates will be manned with extra guards.'

'But you have produced such convincing papers we should not rouse any suspicion.'

It seemed that he had persuaded Julien, for at last he gave his crooked smile and shrugged.

They discussed the last-minute details for the next day: for Armand and Eugénie's departure and for the rescue of the King. Then Julien came over to Armand and looked into his eyes.

'Then this, my friend, is my last visit,' he said

carefully, as if he could not trust his voice. 'It is time to say farewell.'

Armand shook his head. '*Au revoir*, that is all,' he said, unaware that Eugénie had said the same to Belle days before. 'We shall meet again.'

'In a happier time, I trust,' said Julien, oddly formal.

Armand kissed him on both cheeks. Tears glinted in his eyes. '*Bon chance*, old friend,' he whispered.

'And to you.' Julien put out his hand, and Armand grasped it.

'Until the death, *mon comrade*,' said Julien steadily. He looked down at their clasped hands. 'We hold each other's lives between our palms, do we not? We shall never betray each other.'

'Never.'

Manon woke Eugénie at six the following morning, the 21st. It was bitterly cold and still dark outside when they opened the shutters a crack and peered out. The window was wet with rain and the light from the hanging lanterns below furred by mist. They could not see the outline of the houses opposite. Eugénie was aware of the silence in the street; it was unusual, even on a raw morning in January.

She washed her face first, breaking the ice in the bowl as usual, then dressed in the light of a single log burning in the grate. It was all they had left in the way of firewood, and gave out no heat but a little precious light. She put on her own clean shift, petticoats and bodice, and then, with some distaste, Loulette's work jacket and skirt, which smelt overpoweringly of sweat, old fat and garlic, though the jacket elbows were neatly patched. She wrapped the thick shawl around her shoulders – it was warm, at least – and put Loulette's hat on over her hair, the tricolour cockade stuck in at a jaunty angle. Belle had given Loulette a set of clothes from the workshop to wear to work instead, telling her that her assistant should be well dressed.

'I am Loulette Cartaret,' Eugénie murmured to herself, mimicking Loulette's accent, but her voice wavered and held no conviction. She was trembling now that the longed-for departure had come at last, and her palms were damp although it was so cold. Manon nodded her head in encouragement, gazing at her expectantly.

'I am Loulette Cartaret,' Eugénie repeated more strongly. 'I am a milliner's assistant, working for Madame Fleurie. She is sending me to England to take samples to Monsieur Coveney's wife and other wealthy clients in London. Monsieur Coveney has been doing business in Paris and is accompanying me to England.'

Manon brought her a hand mirror, though it was too

dark in the room to glimpse any more of her reflection than her large, scared eyes. Then Armand came in with a candle, in his old dark greatcoat.

They drank yesterday's coffee reheated by Manon, and the last of the stale bread. Armand ate nothing, and his hands trembled on his bowl of coffee. He saw that Eugénie had noticed. 'I do not fear for us, but for the King,' he whispered.

The King! Hard crumbs stuck in Eugénie's throat. He would be having his last breakfast now, saying his last prayers, bidding his weeping wife and children a last farewell. Then they would bring the coach for him that would take him to the Place de la Revolution, as the Place Louis XV was now called, and death under the blade of the guillotine.

'So now we leave this district and go on foot to my old tailor's house in the rue Saint-Honoré,' Armand said quietly. 'There we wait until the gates of the city are reopened and we can leave by coach.'

'Will that be after the King's execution?' asked Eugénie.

Armand compressed his lips and nodded.

Eugénie was taking a small valise, into which Manon had packed a nightgown, an extra shawl and a pair of house slippers, as well as a brush and comb and Eugénie's *toilette* box, which she could not bear to leave.

She had an attaché case that contained official papers in the name of Loulette Cartaret, a sheaf of fake invoices carefully written out by Belle to addresses in London dictated by Armand, several fashion dolls and an inventory of the materials with which she was supposed to be travelling. Both the cases had already been sent ahead to the tailor's house, as had Armand's luggage. When they left their lodgings they did not want to be seen carrying anything that would arouse suspicion.

'Come,' said Armand, who had brought out his watch for the hundredth time and was peering at its face in the semi-darkness, 'We must go.'

Silently, Eugénie hugged Manon to her. 'Send word to me when you reach England, mademoiselle,' said Manon anxiously. 'You have my parents' address – near the catacombs in Montparnasse?'

Eugénie nodded; she could not speak.

'One day we hope to repay you for everything, Manon,' said Armand, and taking her broad, rough hand, he kissed it. Overcome and speechless, Manon shook her head and dipped him a curtsy. While Eugénie still hovered in the doorway, she turned and began to strip the bed as if she had nothing else on her mind but clearing the room ruthlessly of all traces of its recent incumbents.

PART TWO

Pursued

21 – end January 1793

TWENTY

The streets around the rue des Trois Chats were deserted. Dank air hung in the narrow alleyways through which they passed, absorbing their footsteps on the glistening cobbles. They walked as fast as they could through the mist of fine rain. Above them, the shutters were closed for the day by order of the Commune.

It was eerily quiet.

They came into the wider, once more prosperous, streets near the rue Saint-Honoré, where before the Revolution fine new buildings had been begun and never completed. The mist floated up through gaping holes in the old decaying houses that had once belonged to aristocrats, giving them a wide-mouthed, famished look. The shops were closed, their shutters pulled down; the streets empty of carts and carriages; the lanterns put out at first light, so that they walked through a grey gloom so silent they might have been two ghosts in a city of the dead.

Then Armand put a finger to lips, slowing his pace.

The sound of marching came to Eugénie through the mist. It was a contingent of the National Guard. She could see the blue coats and red sashes flashing in the distance, the only colour in that grey world, as it passed the end of the street in which she and Armand stood. The sound of heavy boots striking the *pavé* seemed to go on and on. They shrank back against the houses, but they need not have worried.

They were not alone any longer. People were coming out of the houses. A crowd was collecting at the end of the street to watch the National Guard go by, as if that was the signal they had been waiting for. But they were silent.

Do they feel any regret at what is to happen to the King? Eugénie wondered. *Do they blame him for all their ills, or are some of them still loyal to the ancien régime?*

Soon years of history would be destroyed in a single moment: the flashing slice of the guillotine's blade, the fountains of blood, then in the tumbril amongst a pile of other corpses, the headless body that might belong to anyone; and the divine right of kings would be over for ever. Even the children, pale and thin after a bitter winter of rising food prices, were dumb as they clutched their parents' hands, as if they knew something momentous was about to happen.

The soldiers were lining up four deep along the sides of the rue Saint-Honoré, people pressed back behind them against the houses, craning over each others' shoulders, so that Armand and Eugénie were able to slip unnoticed into the cobbled courtyard behind the tailor's. The hired coach was there already; soon the coachman would bring the horses.

Armand knocked quietly three times on the back door, and they heard the sound of heavy bolts being drawn back. The tailor ushered them in silently. He had been waiting, peering out through the spyhole.

Monsieur Marchand was a small, obsequious man with thin black hair and a pockmarked face. He bolted the door again behind them, then turned and clutched Eugénie's right hand in both of his somewhat clammy ones and brought it to his lips.

'Mademoiselle,' he whispered, bowing low.

He is exceedingly nervous and no wonder, she thought. *His head will be under that blade if it is discovered he has helped us.*

Monsieur Marchand showed her into an upstairs room overlooking the street, and took Armand away. When her brother reappeared, he wore a frockcoat, waistcoat and breeches cut in the English style, and over them, a heavy greatcoat with a caped collar. She darted around him, admiring the quality of the cloth and the sheen of his new knee boots.

'You look a true Englishman indeed, Monsieur Coveney!'

Armand gave a rueful smile. 'Except that when I open my mouth I have a French accent!'

Eugénie shrugged. 'No one will know unless they are English themselves.'

They waited. The tailor appeared and reappeared, rubbing his hands together, starting at every sound. He offered them a dish of coffee, which they refused politely.

Eugénie opened the shutter a crack and saw the mist was lifting, though the drizzle still meandered down from a grey sky. Below her were rows of people, the gaudy red, white and blue of the tricolour cockade stuck into hats and lapels. From outside came the sound of the soldiers' marching feet, a swell of footsteps on the *pavé*, as more and more people gathered silently.

Armand crouched in an armchair by the fire, playing nervously with a crumpled ball of paper. *The Queen begged me to save them*, he thought. *Yet I have done nothing. It is Julien who will take the glory, if this succeeds.*

He strained his ears for the musket fire, which

would mean the rescue was going according to plan. But instead he heard a distant throbbing, coming closer and closer.

'What is that sound?' said Eugénie.

'Drums,' said Armand, as the slow beat was taken up by drummers in the street below.

Eugénie rushed to the window again and opened it. At once the drumbeats, louder, ominous, vibrated through the room. Armand put his hands over his ears and did not move from the fire.

A squadron of cavalry trotted by. The people craned to see, pushing and shoving each other behind the massed lines of soldiers either side of the street. The Mayor's large green coach was rolling along in the midst of the mass of armed horsemen. The curtains were drawn at the windows, but the movement of the coach made them swing backwards and forwards, so that Eugénie caught a glimpse of the man inside and recognized the King's plump, white face; he was wearing a hat but no overcoat, and a priest was sitting beside him. He looked composed and calm as the coach passed the silent crowds who had once been his subjects.

Then the moment had gone. The coach rolled on, the drums below fell silent.

Armand was listening intently, his head cocked. 'The last chance,' he breathed, and clenched his hands.

In the distance the drums were still beating. Then abruptly they stopped. For a moment or two there was complete silence all over Paris; then the drums rolled out once more.

Armand dropped his head. 'It's over,' he said dully. The distant drums had stopped.

When he raised his head, tears glinted in his eyes. 'We've failed.'

'But what of Julien and the others?' Eugénie faltered. 'What can have happened?'

Below, the crowds were already coming to life, cheering, slapping each other on the back, as if they had just won a great victory.

'I don't know.' He wrung his hands. 'I should have been there.' He looked at her and there was no love in his glance. She was certain he was thinking, *If I had not had to escort you to England* . . .

A pain shot into her heart. She bit her lip, then pulled herself together. Rough cries of '*Vive la Nation!*' '*Vive la République!*' filled the air.

'We have to think of each other now. We have to survive this, both of us, Armand.' She put a hand on his arm and tried to speak firmly. 'Come, we'll be able to leave soon. They'll be opening the city gates. We should check the boxes on the carriage before we leave.'

* * *

The tailor fussed around as they opened the boxes on the back of the carriage. 'Madame Fleurie sent everything over by cart yesterday,' he said, rubbing his hands anxiously. 'I hope it is in order.'

The bolts of material that filled the bottom box looked remarkably convincing as long as they were not inspected too closely. Each one was wrapped around a sack stuffed with straw, Belle's old trick from the workshop. The top box contained a portmanteau of clothes supposedly belonging to Armand, the English country gentleman. They were Monsieur Marchand's display pieces, from the days when *le style anglais* was popular in Paris.

'I cannot thank you enough for your generosity, monsieur,' Armand said to the tailor. 'I hope to be able to repay you one day.'

Monsieur Marchand's eyes filled. 'Let us pray those days return, monsieur,' he whispered. 'I do not recognize Paris now. I have served gentlemen all my life and they have made me a rich man. What am I to do without them?'

His apprentice came running in to the courtyard. 'They are opening the city gates, *citoyens*!'

Beyond the courtyard, farmers' carts clanked past and the occasional carriage rolled by. People sauntered, arm in arm, talking and laughing, as if today were a holiday. The strange, heightened moment of festival that seemed to come almost as a reaction after events of great revolutionary violence had come again now. Paris was returning to life.

'Where is the coachman with the horses?' said Armand apprehensively, pulling out his watch. It was a little after ten-thirty.

'He will be here in a moment, monsieur,' said Monsieur Marchand. 'I know Duplé. He is reliable.'

'He had better be,' said Armand grimly.

'Here he is,' said Eugénie with relief, as a figure appeared at the courtyard gates and the apprentice rushed to open them. But the figure was on foot; there were no horses to be seen.

She stared. 'It's Julien!' Julien, with an old hat pulled well down and a filthy greatcoat.

Armand rushed forward. Julien's face was white and strained and his lips bleeding where he had bitten them.

'The Baron's contacts never turned up,' he said bitterly.

Armand stared. 'What none of them?' he demanded in disbelief. 'None of the five hundred royalists he promised us?'

Julien shook his head; he was trembling. 'We stood on that embankment by the rue de Cléry, but we were too few to sweep the King's carriage away.'

Shocked, Armand repeated, 'None of them?'

'We did our best,' said Julien brokenly. 'We charged the guards around the carriage, but there were too many of them. I lost my musket in the confusion.'

'But the Baron? What happened to him?' said Armand. He still looked dazed. He could not believe that his great hero, in whom he had placed all his trust, had let him down.

'De Batz escaped, needless to say. Some of us didn't. They were arrested. They'll make them confess. They'll be hunting me now. They saw my face.' He looked round wildly.

Monsieur Marchand wrung his hands. 'I cannot hide you, monsieur, I am sorry. I will be in enough trouble as it is, if it is found I have helped Monsieur le Marquis.'

Armand seemed to snap out of his daze. 'Take my papers,' he said abruptly to Julien. 'Escort Eugénie to Deal instead of me.'

TWENTY-ONE

Eugénie gasped. 'Armand?'

'Take my place,' repeated Armand, as Julien stood dumbfounded. 'I have not been involved in this directly. They do not know what I look like.'

Julien and Eugénie began to protest at the same time. Armand silenced them with a wave of his hand. 'Keep your voices down, for God's sake! Monsieur Marchand, would you let my friend seek refuge in your workshop for five minutes while I talk to my sister? It is a matter of the greatest importance.'

The tailor nodded reluctantly.

'What are you thinking of, Armand?' demanded Eugénie as soon as they were alone in the courtyard. 'If you stay in Paris, you will be discovered!'

Armand shook his head. 'They cannot connect me with this. I have been careful to cover my traces. And after all, I was not even there today.' He came closer to her, whispering urgently. 'Eugénie, I have to do this for Julien, do you understand? He is my dearest friend. I cannot see him guillotined as a traitor! I know you wish me to come with you, but I assure you that Julien will be an entirely trustworthy escort.'

'I am not thinking of my virtue!' she snapped. *Least of all with that callow youth!* 'Can we not hide him in one of the luggage boxes, then you can still come with me?' she suggested desperately.

Armand shook his head. 'They may look into all the boxes being taken out of Paris.'

Eugénie stared at him and her heart sank. She could see that his mind was set on the exchange.

'But how in the world will Julien succeed in escaping even if he takes your place?' she said. 'They will have his description already.'

Armand spread his hands helplessly. 'I don't know. I don't know what to do. It is too much to ask of you, I know, Eugénie. It will endanger you too if he is found out. They will accuse you of being a conspirator.'

She could never refuse Armand, and now he was relying on her. 'I suppose they will not expect him to be disguised as an Englishman,' she said at last, reluctantly, 'and at least the papers are in order. I will do the talking for him. If we are questioned, I will explain that his French is poor.'

Before she could change her mind, he had grasped her hands with a brilliant smile. 'Thank you, dearest sister!'

'You must change into my clothes and I shall wear my old ones,' declared Armand in the workshop.

'But my English is not fluent like yours,' said Julien. 'I shall never be taken for an Englishman!'

'Then keep your mouth shut.'

'But, Armand,' said Eugénie desperately. 'What will happen to you? Where will you go? When shall I see you again?'

He shrugged. She could see that already his mind was on the future. His eyes had their old brightness; he sparked with excitement. 'I shall lie low until this has blown over,' he said. 'Don't fear for me, Eugénie. I'll join you in Deal as soon as I can.'

A lump rose in her throat. It was hard to speak without weeping. 'Promise me you won't dream up any other schemes,' she whispered.

He put his arms around her. 'I'll send a message to you through Belle. Now, let me help you into the cab outside. The coachman will be here in a minute, and Julien must be ready.'

* * *

Julien! she thought fiercely, as she sat against the upholstery, watching the coachman harness up the two horses he had brought with him.

It was for Julien that Armand was risking his life, and Julien, the coward, was allowing him to do so. She could not even weep now at being parted from Armand; she was too angry with both of them.

Her anger somehow prevented her from being apprehensive. Her only thought was how bored she was going to be with Julien's company on the long journey to Crozier Saint-Clement, the fishing village near Calais where they hoped to board a boat to take them to England.

Armand did not reappear. When Julien climbed in to sit opposite her, she did not meet his eyes. The clothes looked wrong, hanging and bagging on his slight frame. He had tied his black hair back in a neat *queue*, but somehow his face – bony and dark-eyed – did not look English. His cheeks were drained of colour; he looked as if he was still in shock. It gave her an idea.

'You must pretend you have been suffering from a *maladie*,' she said, her anger still bubbling, as the cab clattered through the courtyard. She did not look back at the tailor's house; she knew she would not see Armand again now. 'That is why you have lost weight, so that your clothes no longer fit you.'

She leant forward, keeping her voice low so that the coachman should not hear – though there was scant chance of that, with all the noise the crowds were making beyond the gates. 'This is what you must do. Feign illness, cough, hold a handkerchief to your face to hide it. It would be better if you did not speak at all.'

'Then that means that you must speak for me,' said Julien. He took a handkerchief from his pocket with a hand that still trembled, as the coach emerged into the street. 'You will have to face the guards alone, Eugénie.'

The hackney cab took them, as planned, to board the *diligence*, the public stagecoach, at the nearest stop. Julien had thought this method of travel would draw less attention to them.

In the office they bought their tickets from the surly-looking booking agent. The agent was only interested in selling two more tickets, not in the travellers before him. Business was bad, now that the exodus of aristocrats was over: people were too frightened to go anywhere unless they had to.

Scarcely glancing at them, he took the money proffered by Julien without thanks and passed over two tickets.

* * *

Their luggage was loaded by a porter into the boxes on the back of the *diligence*, and they climbed in to join the other passengers – two men who might be farmers, three thin, dirty youths, a couple of old women bundled up in layers of clothing. They inspected Eugénie and Julien avidly, but their faces were surly and suspicious. Although Eugénie smiled and nodded, no one responded.

Julien huddled into the only remaining corner seat and looked out of the window; Eugénie sat away from him, staring down at her lap to avoid the lustful glances of the three youths. The old women tutted, pinching up their mouths and shaking their heads at each other.

Eugénie could feel a blush stealing up her cheeks. She had never been in a public conveyance before; the interior of the *diligence* was cold and draughty, and smelt overpoweringly of stale sweat and vomit. It was a huge, cumbersome vehicle that lurched and bumped heavily over the cobbles and *pavé* of Paris until it drew up with a jerk that almost made her slide off the seat.

With a sinking heart she saw that they were outside a tall forbidding gateway, and had joined a group of farm carts waiting to pass through the barrier.

Someone rapped at the window, making all the passengers jump. 'Your papers!' demanded a voice.

She looked over with a sinking heart and saw the

unshaven face of a National Guardsman. There were others standing around outside the guardhouse or lolling against its walls, but though their manner was slovenly, their eyes were sharp. She wondered if they knew there had been a rescue attempt on the King before his execution and were already looking out for the fleeing conspirators: there was no way of knowing.

The coachman collected the papers. Eugénie passed hers over and prayed silently. All she could do was wait. Through the open door she saw the soldier slouch off to the guardhouse, riffling carelessly through the papers as he went. Chill, damp air came into the interior of the *diligence* and she tried not to shiver in case it seemed like fear. The clanking of the farm carts came to her, as they passed through the barrier without a problem.

Out of the corner of her eye she noticed that Julien was holding his handkerchief over his mouth.

Perhaps it draws attention to him, she thought anxiously. *They could not have brought a description of him here so fast, could they? Surely he won't be recognized in this part of Paris?*

She sat tensely, waiting for his name to be called.

But in the end it was her own name she heard.

TWENTY-TWO

'Citoyenne Cartaret?'

The guard in charge lounged over a desk in the small, dark room that stank of alcohol and tobacco. Behind him his subordinates eyed her lasciviously, their muskets propped against the wall. Empty bottles littered the dirt floor.

'Yes, *citoyen*.' She kept her eyes lowered.

'You travel to England?'

'Yes, *citoyen*, on business.' In time she remembered to talk with Loulette's accent, but her voice shook.

'Alone?'

She shook her head. 'Monsieur Coveney – you have his papers there – has requested me to return with him to make clothes for his wife. I am also to go to London to do business for my employer, a milliner.' She

255

looked up at him with her most dazzling, wide-eyed glance. 'Madame Isobelle Fleurie. Perhaps you know her by repute?'

The guard snorted sourly, still looking down at the papers so that the glance was wasted. 'I see you are to travel on, yes. You have samples with you?'

Eugénie gestured at her attaché case. 'In here, *citoyen*.'

'Let me see.'

He scrutinized the sample books as if he thought they might contain secret messages to the English. Then, pursing his lips, he examined the book of advance orders that Belle had so meticulously made up for Eugénie, with fictitious names and addresses in London. She stood uncomfortably, aware that the other soldiers were grinning at each other drunkenly.

The guard in charge jerked his head at the youngest soldier, a youth of about fourteen who had also been gazing at Eugénie, a look of admiration lighting his heavy features. 'You, boy! Go and check her baggage.'

The boy dragged his eyes away from Eugénie reluctantly and sloped off. The one in charge growled another question.

'Why is the Englishman travelling on public transport? Are they not all rich aristocrats?' He spat into a corner.

Eugénie thought rapidly. 'He is not well, *citoyen*. He had to delay his travel plans until now.' She paused, 'And it was not a good morning to find a private carriage in Paris, as I am sure you understand.' She touched the tricolour rosette in her hat meaningfully and added for good measure. *'Vive la République!'*

'Vive la République!' echoed the guards dutifully, though they nudged each other as they did so. 'Silence!' rapped out the man in charge.

The boy came back. All eyes went to him. Eugénie waited to be denounced, her heart beating heavily.

'Nothing to report, *citoyen*.' He stared down at the floor, perhaps overcome by so much attention. 'Her baggage is all in order.'

His eyes slid to Eugénie. She felt the blood rush back into her face. Had he discovered the fake bolts of material? Surely, if he had, he would not risk protecting her? Or perhaps he had been taken in by them: he certainly looked witless enough.

But even as relief filled her, the guard in charge snapped another question. 'You are very young to be given so much responsibility. Why does the milliner not travel to England herself, as is usual, rather than employing a chit of a girl to do her business?'

Eugénie hesitated. She could not say Belle was too busy to go herself, since everyone knew there was little work for milliners now.

'Yes?' The guard was impatient and watching her with renewed suspicion.

She lowered her eyes. 'Monsieur Coveney is a valued customer of Madame Fleurie. He has visited France before. This time he particularly asked for me to go with him when he returned to England.' She paused, put on a coy expression. 'He was alone, in a foreign city – you know how it is. And he speaks little French. He has come to depend on me.' She spread her hands and fluttered her eyelashes bashfully, aware of tipsy sniggers breaking out behind her.

The guard frowned. 'I see. Did Citoyenne Fleurie know of the relationship between you both?'

Eugénie looked wide-eyed again. 'He is a rich customer, *citoyen*, and times are hard. Citoyenne Fleurie did not want to offend him. Besides . . .' She wanted to give the impression that she was struggling to maintain her dignity, which was true to a point, since the sniggers behind her were now lecherous guffaws. She stuck her chin in the air.

'Besides, Citoyenne Fleurie has absolute confidence in me. I am an excellent seamstress. Ask me about the most appropriate stitch and thread for each material, *citoyen*, and I can tell you the answer in detail.'

'That will not be necessary,' said the guard irritably.

It was clear he was not interested in her any longer. There was nothing suspicious about her papers, after all. The sour look on his face told her that he had been hoping to make an arrest to increase his standing with the authorities. Instead, he had mistakenly picked a little fortune-hunter. He had seen it all before.

His lip curled as he stamped the papers, refolding her passport. 'You can go.' Escorted by two smirking soldiers and with her face burning, Eugénie went back to the *diligence*.

The other passengers, sitting silent and frozen, with the door still open on the dank air, looked amazed to see her return; they had already given her up to the guillotine. Julien did not meet her eyes as she climbed in. He had been biting his lip; it was bleeding again.

She sat down, the door was slammed, and the barrier raised at last. The driver whipped up the horses and the heavy coach rumbled through.

Eugénie suddenly felt very weak. She was glad she was sitting down. It took a long time for her heart beat to slow.

No one spoke in the *diligence*, but the relief was palatable among all the passengers as they emerged into open countryside. She darted a look at Julien, but he was staring out of the window at the wet fields, his face set.

As she recovered, her mind churned with resentment.

I have risked my life for you, Julien, and I have endured the insults of those appalling men. She glared at him, willing him to turn and receive the full hatred of her gaze, but he remained motionless. *But I'll not do it a second time.*

Next time we will both end up under the blade.

The pawnbroker was counting his takings early that afternoon when the door of the shop opened, and he heard the clatter of boots on the step down into the interior.

Startled, he looked up to see the sinister figure of Monsieur Goullet. Behind him were two members of the National Guard, armed with muskets. His hand began to tremble as he closed his cash box, but he tried to keep his voice steady.

'Citoyen Goullet? The ring? Was it not satisfactory?'

Monsieur Goullet came closer, his pale eyes shining with a strange light of their own in the gloom of the shop. His face too was drained of colour, the parchment skin strained tightly over the cheekbones above the black cravat, the dark age-spots standing out. It was an unpleasant face, an evil face, the pawnbroker thought, not for the first time, and his fear grew.

'You lied to me,' his visitor hissed. 'You said you did not know the whereabouts of Monsieur le Marquis.'

The pawnbroker wrung his hands. 'It is true, *citoyen*.'

Monsieur Goullet jerked his head at the two soldiers. 'Search that drawer.'

The papers were pulled out roughly and the drawer flung on the floor. Citoyen Goullet scattered them over the desktop and scrutinized each one, while the pawnbroker stood aghast and shaken.

'They all have his signature, but no address,' snapped Goullet.

'That is what I told you, *citoyen*,' whispered the pawnbroker.

'But he brought these articles in himself?'

The pawnbroker nodded. 'Apart from the ring, yes.'

'And he gave you no information at all?' He brought his bloodless face close to the pawnbroker, while the two soldiers fingered their muskets. 'Did he never speak?' He hissed the last word.

The pawnbroker searched his memory frantically. He knew his life depended on producing some small nugget that would satisfy Monsieur Goullet. In other circumstances he would never betray that charming young Marquis, who was always grateful, though he must have been almost penniless, judging by the shabbiness of his clothes . . .

At once a chance remark the young Marquis had made when he last saw him flashed into his mind. It would do no harm to mention it, surely?

'The last time he came he did confide ...' he began.

'Yes?'

'... that what I gave him would pay his tailor.' He began to stutter apologetically on seeing the pale man's impatient frown. 'I remember it particularly because new clothes seem an odd extravagance in these times, though to be sure he needed—'

'When was this?'

'More than a week ago. He came late one evening. He seemed –' the pawnbroker paused and looked anxiously at Citoyen Goullet '– almost desperate for the money.'

'And that was the last time he came?'

'Yes, *citoyen*. The maid with the ring came later, only two days ago.'

'The maid came for him because he dared not come himself,' said Goullet between his teeth. 'She was under his instruction and knew very well where he was. Give me the paperwork for the ring!'

'But *citoyen*, there is no address on it,' said the pawnbroker, peering at his own cramped writing. 'I remember I did not write it down because she said she hoped to return for the ring one day if it had not been sold.'

'Seize him!' Goullet said furiously to the two soldiers. 'He is under arrest.'

The pawnbroker began to shake violently and would have fallen to his knees had they not grabbed him by the arms.

'*Citoyen*, I beg you, what have I done?'

'You have over a period aided an aristocrat who happens to be a traitor.' Goullet curled his lip as if the trembling man before him was beneath his notice. 'Take him away.'

'You have been to Belle Fleurie's workshop?' demanded Le Fantôme.

Le Scalpel nodded. 'I have, but there is no one there. The shop is locked up. I could not see through the shutters, but no doubt any stock was removed by cart at night. The neighbours, of course, are saying nothing, though I shouted all manner of threats up at their windows.'

Le Fantôme sucked on his thin lower lip in frustration. 'Now, when we have grounds to arrest de Boncoeur, we cannot trace him, nor find anyone who can!'

He flexed his fingers, the bones cracking inside the gloves, as if he would dearly like to place them around de Boncoeur's neck. Le Scalpel watched, and felt a slight tremor. One day it might be my neck those fingers squeeze to the death, he thought.

But Le Fantôme had control of himself swiftly. He turned towards his cabinets filled with porcelain. As if to calm himself, he picked out a fragile figurine, gazing at it through half-closed eyes, his mouth grim. In the candlelight its colours were delicately pretty in his black-gloved fingers.

'What do we know, *mon petit* Scalpel? We know de Boncoeur was still in Paris a week ago. We know for certain he was one of the ringleaders in today's failed rescue and we assume he took part. We know he has had a new set of clothes made. And we know he intends to flee to Deal on the south coast of England, with his sister.' He placed the figurine back and gently locked the glass door on it. 'Perhaps these clothes are to wear on his journey. Could they be part of a disguise, perhaps?'

'Perhaps he wishes to be taken for an *English* gentleman,' said Le Scalpel thoughtfully.

Le Fantôme's pale eyes gleamed suddenly and he smacked a clenched fist into his other hand. 'Exactly, *mon ami*! That is our answer. You have today's lists from the guardhouses? Let me see those from the barriers to the north and west of the city.'

Le Scalpel nodded and began to sort through the lists he had brought. 'But would de Boncoeur choose today of all days? Too dangerous, surely?'

Le Fantôme laughed grimly and seized the handful of papers that Le Scalpel was proffering. 'You think that after all this time I do not know how his mind works? It is an ideal day for escape, Le Scalpel! All Paris has been agog with the execution of Louis Capet and the excitement of *la nouvelle République*. They are drinking themselves silly in the guardhouses. They could have let anyone through.'

And so it proved. In a certain *diligence* there was listed as passenger one Thomas Coveney, Englishman, returning to Deal, England, after completing business in Paris.

'And who is this in the very same *diligence*?' demanded Le Fantôme. ' "Loulette Cartaret, milliner's assistant", to undertake business for her employer in Deal, Kent, and in London.'

'The assistant I met would never be sent on such a mission,' declared Le Scalpel contemptuously. 'She's a street girl, cannot even write. Surely de Boncoeur has not recruited her as a spy?' He frowned. 'Unless . . .'

Their eyes met. 'Unless that is my fiancée in disguise,' said Le Fantôme softly.

Le Scalpel nodded. He spread his hands, slim,

youthful hands with manicured nails. Once they might have been taken for the hands of a gentleman, but there were no gentlemen left in Paris. 'What should we do? Pursue them? If they have escaped from Paris, they may succeed in—'

'Not a chance,' said Le Fantôme abruptly. 'I tell you, de Boncoeur will not leave this country alive. We will discover where they are bound, have all the ports watched. There are barriers along all the routes to the coast. They will be stopped, perhaps even at the next guardhouse, if we send word ahead. There is no chance they can escape.'

Le Scalpel tapped the list. 'Would you like me to question those guards?'

'I shall come with you. We'll take the cabriolet. I shall drive it myself.'

Le Fantôme was at the door before him. For a middle-aged man he was swift and light on his feet. But that was not surprising, since he was an assassin. He bared yellow teeth at the younger man. 'I believe we are on the trail, *mon petit* Scalpel. Soon we shall have de Boncoeur beneath the blade.'

'Why do you hate him so much?' asked Le Scalpel curiously.

Le Fantôme barked a sarcastic laugh over his shoulder. He was in a rare good mood. Le Scalpel knew there was nothing he liked better than being on a blood trail that would end in the certain death of the hunted.

'He is a scheming royalist aristocrat, a counter-revolutionary and threat to our government. And now he has stolen my bride. Is that not enough?'

Yet there was another reason, Le Scalpel was sure, a reason that lurked somewhere in the darkness of Le Fantôme's past. To find it had become an obsession with him. Once waiting for Le Fantôme to return to his rooms, he had ransacked a desk in the deserted apartment, desperate to find some clue to the mystery of his master's personality.

He had found bills and receipts, neatly folded and tied with black ribbon. There were accounts from some of the best-known gaming-houses in Paris and Europe. He knew already that Le Fantôme's winnings had helped rebuild his fortune. Any secret government papers would be locked away in the safe, any documents dealing with stocks and shares. He did not expect to find those, not did they interest him. But to his immense frustration, there had been no letters, nothing personal at all.

Except that at the very bottom of one drawer he had found a miniature of a man's face and shoulders.

It was a cheap copy, poorly executed, of a section of a full-length portrait, with a surround of fake jewels, the sort of thing you'd pick up at the Palais-Royal in the old days for next to nothing. The man was in military uniform, medals on his breast. What was odd about the miniature was that it had been almost destroyed. It looked as if it had been stamped on – viciously.

Yet it had been kept.

TWENTY-THREE

That first day seemed to last for ever.

At the start of the journey, outside Paris, where all the great roads converged, the going was good and the surface of the road smooth. There was no throng of carriages as Eugénie expected; the stretch of road before them was empty. Her pulse began to slow at last as she stared out at the leafless trees of the great forest of Chantilly, catching a glimpse between them of the ruins of the chateau, once so imposing when lived in by the Prince de Condé, but now devastated by revolutionaries; there was little left, either, of the stables, where once he had kept over two hundred English horses.

Out of the forest, the road began to deteriorate. Once it had been paved, but it had not been recently repaired. Shortly after the outbreak of revolution the hated *Corvée* had been suspended, so villagers were no longer forced by law to maintain their local stretch of road. Now the surface lay in broken chunks that the coachman had to avoid.

Elsewhere the surface was thick with mud and deeply rutted, the ruts full of black water and hidden stones that could unhinge a wheel and send a vehicle crashing on to its side. Like other coachmen before him, the driver did his best to avoid the ruts by swerving further and further out, so that the road was now so wide it seemed to have no boundaries at all, but simply meandered off into the fields on either side. Once or twice, over the hills above Liancourt, the passengers had to get out and walk, to ease the load for the horses. Though her boots were soon clogged with mud and her clothes damp, Eugénie was glad of the fresh air, for the *diligence* bucked and swayed like a ship at sea, and inside it the passengers clung grimly and silently to the straps.

I will not be sick! Eugénie told herself, and fortunately, just as she thought she could not bear the lurching movement any longer, the next coaching inn would appear in the misty distance almost exactly an hour after the last break, and they would stop to change horses.

Once a post-chaise drawn by four horses careered towards them from the opposite direction, then swerved away in a storm of grit and mud. But otherwise there was almost no traffic: a few farm carts, peasants riding donkeys. In the old days there would have been crested *berlines* drawn by six horses, like her guardian's, carrying rich aristocrats, thought Eugénie, but not any more. Now few dared travel about in the old way for fear of causing suspicion, and most aristocrats had fled abroad if they were not languishing in prison. For everyone else, travel, unless it was vital, had become too much of a nuisance and anxiety, with the constant checkpoints outside every town, especially now that there was a shortage of horses because of the war.

We have left it too late, thought Eugénie, staring out at the bare vines twisting up the grey slopes to either side. They looked dead in the fading light of a bitter winter's day – as if they would never return to new green life.

It was five o'clock and Monsieur Marchand, the tailor, was having supper with his wife, when a loud knock sounded on the door. His wife paled.

On the step outside were two men, one middle-aged, one young. Out of long habit the tailor glanced with a professional eye at their clothes before their faces, and in the misty yellow light of the overhead lantern saw that both the heavy greatcoats were well made and of good thick material. He realized that he knew the younger man – perhaps had even made clothes for him in the past – though he did not show any sign of wanting to greet him now. Indeed, he was standing over him in the most intimidating fashion. The tailor thought of his wife alone inside.

'What can I do for you, *citoyens*?' he said nervously.

He was shocked when the older man demanded abruptly, rudely, 'You know Armand de Boncoeur?'

The tailor's heartbeat quickened.

'I have made clothes for him in the past, yes, *citoyen*.'

'Have you seen him recently?'

'No, no, *citoyen*,' he lied, 'I have not.'

'Indeed?' The older man with the unpleasant face feigned surprise. 'But I gather you have made a new set of clothes for him and been paid handsomely for it.'

Mon Dieu! How had he learnt that? The tailor began to bluster. 'Yes, yes, that is true. A little while back, *citoyen*.' He spread his hands. 'I am a tailor. It is how I make my living. I do not enquire too closely about my customers so long as they pay their bills.' He tried to smile.

'New clothes? Extravagant, surely, for an impoverished aristocrat. Can you tell us anything more?'

The tailor looked at the pale face looming above him, mouth set thinly, and decided he had better tell the truth – or part of it. 'He wanted clothes cut in the

English style, *citoyen*. He intended to go to England, you understand.'

'Another émigré losing his estate.' The older man shook his head in mock sadness, then brought his face close to the tailor's, the freckles standing out darkly on the yellow flesh of his cheeks. 'Did he tell you when he was planning to leave?'

The tailor thought of the young man who put the Marquis in danger by taking his place, who had worn those new clothes that had not been made for his figure and to whom he owed no loyalty at all. He would set a false trail after the Marquis, and then these two threatening strangers would leave him and his dear wife in peace.

'I believe he was leaving – today, *citoyen*.'

'Which port was he embarking from?'

The tailor shook his head.

'Did he say anything else about his journey?' demanded the pale man irritably. 'We have reason to understand he was taking his sister with him.'

The beautiful young girl, whose cheap clothes made her look like a shop girl, but whose colouring was so like that of the Marquis and who had been so distraught to leave him behind – he'd not betray her either. 'He did not mention a sister, *citoyen*,' he said truthfully, 'nor, indeed, anything about his journey.'

'If you are lying, it will be the worst for you,' hissed the pale man. 'The Republic does not forgive traitors!'

The tailor shook his head again vigorously. He felt his knees go weak.

The two men did not thank him for the information; they looked at each other in silence and then they were gone into the darkness, swiftly, as if they shared one mind, one purpose. Somewhere close by a whip cracked and horses' hooves clipped the cobbles at a swift trot, but by then the tailor had returned thankfully indoors to reassure his wife that the strangers had left and all was well.

He did not expect them to return.

There were checkpoints manned by the National Guard every few miles and outside every town. Each time the *diligence* stopped and their papers were handed over, Eugénie felt her heart first freeze and then beat rapidly. But today the guards seemed more interested in gossiping about the news from Paris and pestering the driver for more information, than examining each passenger's papers for anything suspicious.

Once, when they stopped outside a village, a grinning guard stuck his head in through the open door and waved a handkerchief triumphantly under Eugénie's nose.

'See this? Given it by a passenger in a chaise. He went to Capet's execution this morning. Bled like a pig, apparently. They were wallowing in it, soaking their handkerchiefs in it – rags, anything they'd got.'

The handkerchief was red-brown and stuck with dry blood.

'*Vive la République*,' Eugénie said, through stiff lips.

'A king bleeds just the same as the rest of us, eh? Liberty, equality, fraternity, eh? Let all the nobility bleed, I say.' He looked round the other passengers for confirmation, his grin wider.

Julien glowered at him, black eyes burning in his white face.

'Is a king not still a human being?' he burst out in perfect French.

The passengers began to murmur uneasily, edging away from Julien as the guard stared at him, his eyes suddenly alert and suspicious.

'You must excuse my travelling companion, *citoyen*,' put in Eugénie hastily. 'He is English. He knows nothing of our politics.' She dimpled up at the guard disarmingly. 'Anyway, he is a fine one to talk. They executed their own king, the English!'

The passengers nodded and began to mutter to each other, 'Hypocrite! The Englishman is a hypocrite!' while Julien sat frozen-faced in his corner.

The guard slapped his thigh and guffawed. 'And yet they have a king back on the throne again! Where is their republic now, poor fools?'

Eugénie joined in, tinkling merrily and praying that Julien would stay silent. 'You are right, *citoyen*! We shall not be so careless with ours, shall we?'

The guard gestured at Julien, while keeping fascinated eyes on Eugénie. He spoke as if Julien could hear nothing. 'Why do you travel with such a fool as this Englishman?'

Eugénie clicked open her attaché case with alacrity and produced her papers. 'As you see, *citoyen*, I go to measure his wife for new gowns.' She put a hand to her face and whispered behind it, 'And no doubt she is as big a fool as he, and gross of figure too, like all English women! I hope my tape measure will stretch!' She pouted. 'But if there is money in it, what do I care?'

The guard's face grew bitter. 'Ah, money. That is what we all want, eh? Give us a share of the aristos' money. They had it too long while we starved to death.' He dragged his eyes away from her and gave the papers a cursory glance. '*Bon chance*, then, *ma belle*.'

He gave them back and his eyes flickered over her figure a last time. 'A pity you cannot stop for longer.'

'Another time perhaps, *citoyen*,' said Eugénie,

dropping her eyes modestly, but with the hint of promise in her smile.

She did not look at Julien as the *diligence* pulled away.

When Le Fantôme guided the horse over the cobbles and the cabriolet glided to a halt beneath the flaring torches, the guards at the Paris gate had been celebrating the birth of the Republic for some hours. They struggled to pull themselves to attention.

'*Vive la République!*'

Le Fantôme cast a contemptuous glance over them, and without ceremony pointed to two names on his list. 'Describe them,' he commanded. 'I ask on behalf of the government.'

'But we have let so many through, *citoyen!*' stuttered the soldier in charge.

'Let me refresh your memory,' said Le Fantôme. 'A pretty young girl, scarce sixteen, with an Englishman: she a milliner's apprentice, he a young gentleman returning to his country. A handsome couple. I am quite certain –' his voice held threat '– you would have noticed them.'

'Ah, yes,' said the guard with relief, his face clearing. He spoke slowly, trying not to slur his words. 'We questioned the girl. A young thing, lovely fair hair. She was the mistress of the Englishman.'

'I think not,' said Le Fantôme tightly.

'And the Englishman,' said Le Scalpel. 'Can you describe him?'

'My subordinate saw him,' said the guard. He beckoned him over. 'This Monsieur Coveney these citizens are asking about. You remember? The Englishman in the *diligence* this morning? What did he look like?'

The subordinate's eyes were glazed with drink. He shook his head. 'They were all farmers apart from the girl.'

'There was a young man among them, an Englishman,' said Le Fantôme irritably, pointing at the name on the list.

The guard puckered his brow. His eyes focused. 'Ah! A dark young man, who said nothing.'

'Dark?' said Le Scalpel, frowning at Le Fantôme. They stared at each other.

'A disguise, possibly,' said Le Fantôme thoughtfully.

'Dark-haired, he was, *citoyens*,' said the guard. He nodded with heavy, drunken emphasis. 'Hair black as coal under his hat. Nasty surly-looking fellow. Those English think they own the world – arrogant rogues whether they be aristocrats or not. Should have questioned him instead.'

Le Scalpel turned to Le Fantôme and murmured,

'There is a distinct possibility that Armand de Boncoeur may still be in Paris.'

'Then who was in the coach?'

'If I am not mistaken it sounds like our friend Julien de Fortin, counter-revolutionary and master plotter, responsible for today's attempted rescue of the King!'

'And whom we have tried to assassinate before as an enemy of the state.' Le Fantôme's eyes gleamed with a triumphant, fanatical light. 'Then, if we are clever, we will catch both of them. Two birds with one stone.' He paused. 'That stone will be you, *mon petit* Scalpel.'

The tailor and his wife were asleep when the thunderous knocking came again. The tailor lit a candle with a trembling hand, pulled on his beautiful silk dressing gown and stumbled downstairs to face his now terrifyingly familiar visitors.

Though this time he gave the address of the Marquis's most recent lodgings, they did not spare him. The soldiers that had come with the two men took him away, handcuffing and marching him off, elderly as he was, inappropriately clothed and shuddering with cold and fear, into the darkness.

His wife never knew what happened to him.

* * *

It was early in the morning the following day and still dark when the same loud knocking on the door of the house in the rue des Trois Chats roused the concierge from his warm bed. Grumbling and hungover, he staggered downstairs only to step back in horror as the soft, rotting wood of the front door was kicked in by a soldier's boot.

A tall man with a cadaverous face the colour of candlewax stepped in gingerly, narrowing pale eyes to see in the gloom of the hallway. His nostrils quivered at the stink of decay and damp. But it was no worse than most of the houses in Paris. A young man followed him, well-groomed, debonair.

Their clothes were plain but beautifully cut, expensive. The trembling concierge could not think why such men should be visiting him, and with soldiers! He looked at the ruined door and began to have terrible misgivings.

'You have rooms vacant, vacant since yesterday.' It was not a question.

'Yes, *citoyen.*'

'Who were the tenants?'

'I do not know, *citoyen.*' The concierge shrank back against the cracked plaster at the look of cold anger on the visitor's face. 'That is the truth, *citoyen*! They always paid their rent on time to the landlord when he visited.

It is not my business to ask questions.'

'You should, especially with enemies of the Republic all about us,' said the young man grimly. 'These tenants were a young man and a girl?'

'Yes, *citoyen*, and a maid.'

'Ah,' said the pale man, adding with sarcasm, 'And I suppose you do not know where they were going?'

'The young girl and the maid, no.' The concierge shook his head. 'But, *citoyen*, the young man is still here,' he added, desperate to please.

'*What?* Why did you not say so before?'

The concierge stuttered, 'He came ba—'

A soldier seized his shoulder roughly.

'Where is he?' said the pale man quietly as the concierge began to sob in terror.

'Do not arrest me, I beg you! I know nothing more, believe me! I acted in good faith.'

'Just tell me where the youth is hiding,' hissed the pale man.

'He wanted my cheapest room, he said,' said the concierge wildly. 'He showed me what he wanted. It has never been rented out before – it is not suitable . . .'

'Show us,' said the pale man through gritted teeth.

And so the concierge led them to the cellar door.

Twenty-Four

As darkness fell, the coach stopped at an inn in the little town of Clermont, lying in a dale between wooded hills.

The inn was beamed, with heavy, dusty tapestries hanging on the walls. Eugénie was shown to her bedchamber, which she found to her dismay she was sharing with three unknown women. There were four beds with plain iron bedsteads crammed into the dingy room, and no parlour off it in which to seek refuge and partake of a quiet supper; and it seemed they all had to share the same washing bowl, which had not even been placed behind a screen for modesty's sake. She looked for a bell to summon the *fille* to bring a jug of hot water but there was no bell, so she was forced to wash her face and hands, grimed with the day's journey, with cold water in the dirty bowl.

While she did so, the three women stared at her silently with open curiosity, tinged, she fancied, with some jealousy, for the three of them were old and plain, and round as dumplings.

Just as if I were some curiosity at the Palais-Royal! she thought indignantly, and swept out past them, her head held high, as soon as she had dried herself on the single grubby cloth. She was careful to take her attaché case with her, though no doubt they would soon be going through the clothes in her valise. She could still hear them clucking to each other in heavy disapproval, not even bothering to lower their voices, 'Hoity-toity! Gives herself airs, doesn't she?' when she was halfway down the passage.

Julien was sitting on an oak bench in the shadowy corner of the smoke-filled taproom. Rough tables – boards set on crossbars – had been pulled back to allow the warmth of the open fire to reach the nooks and crannies, but every time the outer door was opened a freezing draught combined with billowing smoke blew round the room; the walls were stained black to the ceiling beams with centuries of smoke, grime and burning oil from the lamps.

The old days of crowded inns, noisy with travellers and their valets, were over; there were few people staying tonight and most of these were men. Though Eugénie tried to be as inconspicuous as possible and avoided the light, they all looked up as she came in.

After so many hours in the *diligence* it was difficult to walk straight. Someone had the audacity to reach out to her skirts as if she were some common slut. She weaved her way across to Julien and pulled up a rush-bottomed chair, turning her back on the room and the staring eyes.

She was ravenously hungry and could not speak until Julien had shouted for the sulky-looking serving *fille*, and the food had been brought – coarse barley bread, meat burnt almost to a cinder, a hard lump of yellow cheese – thumped down before them with no grace, but at least the plates were set on clean linen and the jug of rough wine was warming.

They looked at each other.

It is hard to look at Julien, Eugénie thought. *Those dark eyes burn so. I do believe he hates me.*

'You draw too much attention to yourself,' said Julien in a low voice. 'In the *diligence* and now here.'

Eugénie felt outrage rise in her chest. 'You think I do it on purpose?' she whispered fiercely. 'Consider your own behaviour today, if you will. You are meant to be an Englishman, yet you speak in French. You take no care in what you say, but make pronouncements that arouse the suspicions of every National Guard. You forget to hold your handkerchief before your face to hide it when we are stopped. It is a miracle we have got as far as we have without being arrested!' She pushed her plate away. 'And I have six more days of this to endure!'

'I admit there have been times when I've behaved thoughtlessly today,' said Julien stiffly. 'But you should have a care as to your own behaviour. I watched you flirting with those guards. They will remember you.'

Eugénie flushed with anger. 'I did it to divert their attention from you! You think I enjoyed it, like some street girl? Why, I had to undergo the most appalling humiliation when they questioned me this morning! No girl of my class and position should have to suffer such indignity.'

'And you blame me for it,' said Julien coldly. 'You think that if Armand had been in my place, he could have saved you?'

Eugénie knew that no one could have saved her, but all the same she retorted, 'Armand protects me always!'

'No doubt he has always had to do so.'

'And what does that mean precisely?'

'You have a propensity for getting into scrapes, Eugénie, and you do not take kindly to guidance.'

He was insufferably pompous. She felt hot with fury. 'What? You're lecturing me now? How dare you? You, of all people! If your foolish plan had not failed this morning—'

He leant across the table urgently. 'Hush, Eugénie! You know we must not speak of that.'

'Then we shall not speak of anything,' she said, and sat fuming against the uncomfortable straight-backed chair. With enormous effort she compressed her lips for at least a minute before she burst out, 'I have no desire to converse with such an ungrateful, irritating youth in any case.'

She was even more annoyed when Julien did not say anything, but merely lifted a supercilious black eyebrow. For another strained minute they both remained silent.

'This journey is fraught enough as it is,' said Julien at last. 'I know you do not like me and resent my taking your brother's place, but at least let us try to remain civil to each other until we reach Calais.'

'I have no intention of being anything but civil,' said Eugénie haughtily. 'I have been properly brought up.' She rose to her feet with dignity. 'And now, monsieur, I bid you goodnight.'

In the night her old nightmare came back. She tossed and whimpered, and ran through the burning convent from an unknown pursuer. She awoke with a start to find a hand smoothing back her hair.

'Manon,' she muttered with sleepy joy, 'Oh, Manon, is that you?'

'Who is Manon?' a voice murmured. 'A friend, perhaps? A sister or cousin?'

In alarm she tried to shrink away, aware of a bulky shape bending over her that was not Manon at all.

'There, there, *ma petite*,' the voice said, and a hand stroked the hair from her damp brow.

The shutters were closed, and the room in darkness. It was one of the old women, but it was impossible to make out her features. She felt drugged with weariness and could scarcely make sense of the woman's next words.

'Who are you, *ma jolie*?'

'What?' Eugénie muttered.

'You are not what you appear, but rather what you seem, aren't you?'

'I don't understand.' The dream was closing round her again, or perhaps another dream. She was not sure what was real and what not.

'I know what you are, but don't worry your pretty head.' The hand went on stroking and stroking her hair and the voice went on whispering, 'Don't worry, I won't tell.'

'Go away.'

Her eyelids were too heavy to stay open and so

Eugénie gave up the fight. Immediately she was drawn down into a deep pool of sleep and forgetfulness.

Beyond Clermont the land became flat and chalky, a few grey fields buffeted by the freezing wind. The passengers in the *diligence* pulled their overcoats and shawls up around their faces and huddled back against their seats, as the windows rattled and the bitter air leaked in.

They had the same passengers as yesterday, with two additions. One was one of the women who had been sharing with Eugénie at the inn. Eugénie stared at her when she climbed in, suddenly remembering the voice whispering in the night. The woman had a round, plain, unremarkable face; she nodded at Eugénie briefly, as if in recognition that they had shared a bedchamber, and then looked away as she settled into her seat. She did not look at Eugénie again. The man with her, some relative perhaps, his heavy redingote straining around his middle, was equally unremarkable.

With two extra passengers there was less room in the *diligence*, and Eugénie found herself squashed in the corner next to Julien. She thought she could feel his leg against hers. Blushing, she tried to press herself back against the window, only to have icy draughts down her neck. She glanced at him involuntarily and saw he was gazing fixedly ahead. Turning away from him as far as she could, she stared out of the window.

When the concierge opened the cellar door they could see nothing save a line of rickety steps leading down into darkness.

'Bring a lamp,' ordered the pale man.

The concierge brought an oil lamp and held it up. It swung in his shaking hands, so Le Fantôme seized it in exasperation and held it high over his head. The young man with him craned to see over his shoulder. The dank, deathly breath of the cellar seeped up to them.

A pair of eyes shone in the darkness. A figure was crouching on a straw pallet amongst the filth, the stub of an unlit candle in a dish beside him.

Le Fantôme had been waiting for this moment a long time. He almost laughed. There was the terrified boy, literally at his feet. It was so easy in the end.

'Armand de Boncoeur,' he shouted down. 'Armand de Boncoeur, you are under arrest as a traitor to the Republic!'

All day the dreadful, heart-stopping routine of having their papers inspected continued. They changed horses every hour at coaching inns, where innkeepers and ostlers would pester them for news from Paris, but passed few villages in the flat grey landscape.

There were lonely farm buildings dotted along the road, mostly thatched mud cabins, with smoke streaming away from a hole in the roof in the wind. Occasionally they passed donkeys pulling dung carts, led by a peasant wrapped in rags. Some trudged along in wooden shoes, most were barefoot.

Eugénie noticed that the women had hitched up their skirts shockingly high to avoid the mud, and did not seem to care that their bare filthy thighs were exposed. Their worn faces had never seen rouge, their hair had never been powdered and primped; they were all bent with toil, as gnarled as the few trees that dotted the landscape, and it was impossible to tell what age they were.

How can one live like that? She felt suddenly ashamed. This was true poverty, not the kind of genteel privations she had suffered while staying in the rue des Trois Chats. She stared out and thought, *This is why we needed a revolution! It was to save these people from starvation and squalor.*

But the Revolution had done nothing for them, it seemed. They were still slaves to the soil, and the price of bread was ever higher. As for equality and fraternity, who in the National Convention would regard one of these peasants as his brother?

At last she fell asleep, with the leather fob tickling her face, only to dream she was a small girl again, ordering the groom to saddle her pony, Magie. '*Vite*, Georges! I wish to ride now!'

She must have spoken the words out loud, for they woke her immediately, and as she opened her eyes she found her head had fallen against Julien's shoulder and that the whole carriage was gazing at her.

She sat up in embarrassment, drawing away from Julien immediately.

What did I say? she thought frantically, as she reverted to looking out of the window again, for already the dream had vanished.

She was aware of two things.

The first was that Julien had not removed her head from his shoulder while she slept, and that made her feel hot all over. The second was that the woman from the inn had not stopped staring at her, and there was now unmistakable suspicion in her look.

It was the last stop for changing horses before Breteuil, where they were to spend the night.

As the *diligence* clattered into the courtyard of the coaching inn, Eugénie saw that a post-chaise was already there, the postilion unbuckling the sweating horses from their harnesses in the light of torches set in brackets in the old brick of the walls. Already the daylight was beginning to fade.

'The chaise will take the freshest horses now,' Julien muttered wryly in Eugénie's ear, taking advantage of the general din as the doors of the *diligence* were opened and the courtyard rang with the shouts of ostlers and the innkeeper's loud invitation to all and sundry to partake of his hospitality. Some of the passengers in the *diligence* were already climbing out into the dusk, including the woman from the inn and her travelling companion.

'I need some air, Julien,' said Eugénie in a low voice. 'Will you accompany me?'

They stepped down on to the cobbles. She walked quickly away from the hubbub, gesturing that he should follow. They stood away from the lights, in the shadow of an outhouse packed with bundles of straw.

'That woman,' said Eugénie, gesturing surreptitiously. 'She suspects me. I am certain of it.'

Julien glanced over his shoulder to where the woman stood talking with her companion some distance from them. Then she walked away towards the open door of the inn. After a moment the man followed.

'She's going to tell him about me,' whispered Eugénie. 'She knows I am in disguise!'

'I think she goes to relieve herself,' said Julien

in a matter-of-fact way, raising an eyebrow at Eugénie's expression.

How coarse he is, she thought with distaste, but with an effort pulled herself together. 'The privies are in the yard,' she pointed out frostily. 'Inns such as this poor example do not house their closets inside.'

'Then she goes to refresh herself with the local beer.'

'I think not. Julien, you must believe me. If we cannot trust each other's instincts, then we'll not survive.'

He looked at her and saw she was serious. 'Let me think what's best to do.'

'There's not time,' Eugénie said impatiently. 'I have thought it out already. We must travel on in the chaise. They will be leaving before the *diligence*, and in any case it will take a while before she can get a message to the next guardhouse.' She paused, and added urgently, 'But have we the money for our fares?'

He nodded. 'But we've no tickets. We'll not be allowed on.'

'Then we must board at the last moment, before the steps are pulled in and the passengers have a chance to complain.'

Julien looked dubious. 'I do not think this a sensible plan, Eugénie.'

'This is not the time for sense!' she retorted. 'What else can we do?'

He nodded reluctantly.

They walked swiftly across to the chaise. The new postilion was walking the fresh horses across the yard under the streaming light.

'We must collect our luggage from the *diligence* while he is engaged,' said Eugénie urgently.

The back of the *diligence* was in shadow, but those passengers from the *diligence* who chanced to see Julien slinging the valises into the boxes on the back of the chaise would think nothing of it; many travellers changed their mode of travel between stops.

As the ostler helped with the harnessing of the horses, two passengers climbed back into the chaise; then a third. Eugénie and Julien watched them, standing to one side as if conversing.

They looked altogether a better class of passenger, thought Eugénie, as you might expect of those travelling in a privately hired post-chaise – the couple were the owner of a factory and his wife, perhaps, for they looked prosperous in good, warm clothing; the lone man, equally rotund, could be in the same business.

The chaise was now ready to go, its lights burning inside and out, the postilion already mounting the lead horse. She nipped up the steps so that Julien was forced to follow her, and smiled a tentative, sweetly pleading smile.

'I do hope you don't mind us joining you, *citoyens*, but this gentleman is English and unwell, unused as he is to the hardship of our *diligences*.' She shrugged, as if it were an English weakness that any Frenchman would take in his stride. 'Would you take pity on him for the next stretch of your journey?'

'We understood there were to be but the three of us,' began the wife, looking to her husband for support. 'The price we paid in Paris reflected that.'

The husband – the bluff, prosperous owner of a woollen factory, for Eugénie had guessed correctly – was touched by the charms of the pretty, anxious girl before him and her obvious concern for the dark-haired young gentleman, who was looking so unhappy. He looked forward to pondering upon their relationship.

He patted his wife on the knee. 'Hush, my dear. Let us be charitable.'

'But we may catch some English malady . . .' the wife protested in a loud whisper, as Julien covered his face with his handkerchief and coughed into it.

'We do good trade with England,' her husband rebuked her, 'or did before the Treaty of Commerce. You have no objection to the young lady and gentleman joining us for the last lap tonight, do you, brother?'

The other man shook his head.

'Please, *citoyenne*, take a seat,' the husband said to

Eugénie. 'And your companion. We have plenty of room.' His wife dug him in the ribs. 'We can come to some private arrangement as far as expenses are concerned,' he added hastily. 'But we are travelling on to Amiens tonight. If you are fatigued . . .'

Eugénie shook her head decisively. 'Speaking for myself, I am not weary in the slightest, and my companion will sleep. He speaks little French.'

Julien nodded and frowned as if he understood little of what she was saying but was an amenable gentleman, anxious to please. He resigned himself to shutting his eyes, which at another less fraught moment would have been very welcome, but now he was forced to see through half-closed lids, for as the steps were being pushed in, the coachman had inevitably noticed he had two extra passengers. Julien was so tense that it was difficult to appear either unconcerned or uncomprehending. He did his best.

'Who are these people?' the coachman demanded. 'I have but three names on my list.'

'We have made a private arrangement,' the factory owner said. 'Do not concern yourself. I'm sure your papers are in order, are they not, *ma petite*?' he added, looking at Eugénie. She nodded quickly, touching her attaché case, and the factory owner looked at the driver and nodded in turn.

'*Allons-y!* Drive on! We are all ready.'

In the yard the driver of the *diligence* had begun to protest vociferously that there were no fresh horses left to pull the *diligence* to Breteuil. The driver of the chaise, anxious not to lose his advantage, climbed up on to his seat on the front box with alacrity and took up the reins.

The innkeeper, who had come back into the yard to see off the chaise with its wealthier customers, wrung his hands apologetically.

'There is a shortage of horses, *citoyens*. Because of the war, you understand. They took away all but a few. What could I do?' His eyes brightened. 'But your passengers are most welcome to spend the night here.'

The chaise began to move. Eugénie risked a quick look out of the rear window and saw that the woman from the inn in Clermont had come into the yard with her companion and both were looking after them and pointing, shouting something she could not hear.

The chaise gathered speed. They were already moving faster than the *diligence* could manage. Soon the inn and its frail, flaring lights were lost behind them in the night.

TWENTY-FIVE

The inn in Amiens stood by the thirteenth-century cathedral, and as the chaise turned into the courtyard, Eugénie could see the cathedral rising through the sky, seeming to float upwards like a great ship into the darkness from the misty ground, as weightless and insubstantial as one of Fabrice's balloons.

Scarcely able to speak for weariness, she thanked the factory owner, Pierre Rougier, for his kindness.

'It was a pleasure, mademoiselle,' he said jovially, his good humour undiminished by the lateness of the hour and the fatigue of the journey. 'Tomorrow you may travel on with my brother, who has business in Boulogne. Now, shall I see about some rooms for you, since the English gentleman is not familiar with our language?'

'You are most kind, *citoyen*.' Impulsively she clasped his hands; he looked quite overcome.

He managed to secure Eugénie a bedchamber to herself, for which she was profoundly thankful. Behind a screen there was a flowered jug and bowl on a white-painted stand, and a porcelain bidet; behind another, a canopied bed. She rang the bell and the willing *fille* took the jug and filled it with hot water, and later brought her soup, bread and wine, which she laid out for Eugénie on a little table covered with spotless linen.

She had no dreams that night, and if the bells of the cathedral rang for midnight mass, she did not hear them.

Julien joined her in her chamber for breakfast early the next morning, while the *fille* waited on them. It was still dark, a dismal January morning outside, with the wind blowing against the opened shutters, rattling the glass and bringing the ragged sound of bells into the room.

'You slept, I trust, mademoiselle?' he enquired politely in a low voice, breaking the bread on his plate and not looking at her. It seemed oddly intimate to sit either side of the little table in the candlelight, merely the two of them and the maid standing apart, and they were both aware of it.

Eugénie, who felt much refreshed, nodded, and glanced at the *fille*, but she was standing by the door with downcast eyes.

There was an awkward silence between them.

'What are we to do?' she asked directly at last, keeping her voice low and making a clatter with her bowl of coffee. 'Have we funds enough to travel on to Boulogne in the chaise?'

'I have money of my own, which I think we should use as well,' he said. 'The chaise is so much faster than the *diligence*. We may yet outrun any pursuit.' He sounded gloomy, rather than optimistic. 'Besides, the route via St Omer, Lille and Péronne is slower, and I've heard that they are very particular in their searches at Péronne, the old frontier town.' He glanced at the window as another gust threw rain against the glass. 'I hope we will not be delayed in Calais because of bad weather.'

The *fille* vanished swiftly to fetch them fresh coffee. Eugénie leant across the table.

'Julien,' she whispered urgently. 'You must give me half the money. You should not keep it all!'

He looked taken aback. 'It is best I deal with money matters,' he said stiffly.

'No, it is not. Think of it. What if we were to become separated, or you arrested? How would I manage on my own? And some of it is mine anyway, or rather, Armand's!'

To her indignation, she saw that he was looking most uncomfortable. 'I do not like to think of you handling money,' he muttered. 'It is not—'

'What?' she countered in exasperation. 'Not appropriate for a girl from my refined background? Oh, come, Julien, have we not already forgone the conventions, travelling together as we are? Or did you mean inappropriate in the hands of a mere female?' She shook her head at him crossly. 'Has the Revolution not taught you that women are far more capable, rational beings than you men believe us to be? Why, it would have ground to a halt if it had not been for women!'

He looked unconvinced still, biting his lip.

'You believe me to be some empty-headed, untrustworthy little spendthrift, is that it?'

'No, no,' he said, but she was sure it was so, even when, with some reluctance, he took from his purse a bundle of assignats, passing them to her behind the edge of the tablecloth as the *fille* came back into the room.

Though Eugenie slipped the money into her attaché case at once, she was not placated and resolved to convey her feelings to him by refusing any more breakfast. It was a pity, since the *fille* had brought them some hot sugared brioche that looked exceedingly delicious.

Julien, however, devoured it all.

They travelled the fifteen miles to Flixecourt without the necessity of conversing with the factory owner's brother, Jacques Rougier.

Unlike his jovial sibling, he appeared to have an earnest, reclusive disposition. He sat studying the papers he had with him and sticking his short plump legs out to counter the rocking of the chaise. It was a gentler motion altogether than that of the *diligence*, higher slung and better sprung; the interior richly upholstered and the seats padded with horsehair, with a top squab of goosedown. Because they were riding in a chaise, beggars swarmed round them at every stop, though the guards would yell and kick them away, and hasten the chaise on its way with a brusque gesture after a merely cursory glance at their papers.

It was poor, flat countryside, the roads lined with straggles of poplars; beneath them, ragged women gathered winter grass and weeds to feed their cows, stuffing handful of the rank green mess into their apron pockets.

They reached the coaching inn at Flixecourt by noon, and Jacques suggested a pause for luncheon. They were forced to comply for politeness's sake, though they both cast apprehensive glances at each other. But though there were other travellers eating and drinking in the main room, there was no one they recognized from the *diligence*, nor did any bunch of soldiers burst in and arrest them, as Eugénie half expected.

'We have been exceptionally fortunate so far,' said Julien as they came out into the yard.

'Do not speak of it, even,' whispered Eugénie.

She looked with anxious eyes at the chaise, but all was normal, the postilion bringing out the new lead horse from the stables, the ostler harnessing up the three other fresh horses, the coachman downing a mug of small beer and pacing the cobbles to keep warm in the icy wind.

Julien helped her up the steps, and followed her. They sat down, closing the door against the cold, and waited for Jacques Rougier, who had not eaten with them, despite their invitation. When he did appear, his round, solemn face was graver still. After her misgivings, Eugénie quite expected some calamity, but he only enquired if they would mind taking on an extra passenger.

'It appears that a poor young lady is in need of our aid,' he said. 'She was forced to travel alone from Paris through difficult personal circumstances, and has endured the unwanted attentions of a certain gentleman on the *diligence* in which she was travelling. Yesterday afternoon it broke a chassis and now her only desire is to escape the inn –' he gestured back across the yard '– where this gentleman and the other passengers are staying before they can travel on.'

He has as kind a heart as his brother, Eugénie thought. 'We have no objection,' she said at once. 'You have already generously allowed us to share with you. We shall be a carriage full of lame ducks!'

They heard the sound of baggage being loaded into one of the boxes on the back, then the young woman climbed in, her head bent shyly as she bade them, '*Bon après midi*' in a murmur, and sat on the same side as Eugénie and Julien, by the far window. Jacques pulled the steps up on to the carriage floor, the horses were whipped up and they were off again.

Eugénie was decidedly intrigued to see a woman who had excited the attentions of a male admirer on her journey, for surely she must be very beautiful; but she was awkwardly seated and it looked somewhat rude to peer sideways past Julien. When she did so surreptitiously, the woman's face was turned away from her to look out of the window; she could only see the back of a large black hat with a conical crown.

Jacques settled back to his papers and the carriage

was silent, save for the creaking of the wheels as they spun over the road.

It was dreary countryside: flat still, with great stretches of wood on either side of the rough road, the bent trees as withered and grey as the dying afternoon.

They stopped to change horses in Abbeville. The town with its old wooden houses and narrow dirty streets was poorly lit; the guards at the check on the way out surly and taciturn, glowering at the papers handed them.

'I believe a few coins may encourage the process,' said Jacques, a sly gleam in his eye that took Eugénie by surprise. He fished a handful of money from his pocket. Suddenly there were no more guards around the chaise.

As the chaise gathered speed towards Bernay, where they were to spend the night, the young woman spoke. '*Bravo, citoyen!*'

Jacques smiled self-consciously. 'I know from experience that occasionally a bribe can expedite matters, mademoiselle.'

'You travel a good deal?'

'Mostly in Flanders and Picardy, on business. I would not venture as far as Paris at such a time as this. A long journey is made even more tedious with so many checks.'

'It is indeed, monsieur.'

Her voice was not aristocratic, yet it was cultured and softly modulated. It sounded familiar, very familiar to Eugénie, who had known it in all its highs and lows, its political passion, its calm, logical reasoning.

Hortense – here in the carriage with them.

TWENTY-SIX

Eugénie felt hot, then cold. All this time she had longed to see Hortense, but now was the worst time of all to be reunited, for how on greeting her could Hortense not give her away unknowingly to Monsieur Rougier?

She stole a look down the carriage. She would know that profile anywhere; its oval shape, its olive smoothness, the wisps of dark hair that always fell down beneath her hat. She pressed back in her seat, her heart beating, pulled her own hat down and her shawl up around her face and turned to the window, feigning sleep.

Darkness was falling now and fortunately they had not yet lit the lamps inside the chaise; but how would she avoid Hortense recognizing her at the inn at

Bernay, where they were to spend the night? And how could she warn Julien?

Already she could hear Jacques, turned unusually gregarious by Hortense's presence, introducing them both in a low, confidential voice. 'The young mademoiselle asleep in the corner is Loulette Cartaret, and this gentleman here is English, Monsieur Coveney.'

There was a slight pause. Eugénie imagined Julien nodding at Hortense, doffing his hat, taking in those lustrous black eyes. They were much the same age.

An odd feeling stirred in her.

'Monsieur Coveney?' Hortense spoke.

'How do you do, mademoiselle . . .?' At least he could manage that phrase in English.

'Mademoiselle Thierry, monsieur.' But that, surely, was not Hortense's surname? It had been Tati when she worked for the Comte. Or had she somehow muddled the names in her memory?

'*Enchanté*, Mademoiselle Thierry.' He had never said such a thing to her, Eugénie.

The conversation went on for a while, dealing in pleasantries and dodging around the difficult subject of the Revolution, for it was never polite to discuss politics in a chaise or ask too many personal questions of your fellow passengers. Julien had reverted to French, though he was clearly trying to make it halting and ungrammatical.

Eugénie sighed into her shawl. Once Jacques had retired to his rooms at the inn, she could explain everything to Hortense and it would all be so much easier.

But Jacques did not leave them. When they arrived at Bernais, Hortense was the first to disappear into the inn. Jacques gallantly helped Eugénie down the steps of the chaise, and insisted on inspecting her chamber upstairs.

'My dear, I know this inn of old. It is notorious for its rooms, and for its appalling food and wine.' He patted his stomach ruefully. 'Alas, we have no choice but to rest here tonight.'

Eugénie glanced around the dark little chamber. At that moment she could not have cared less about its smell and the moth-eaten curtains around the bed that looked as if they had hung there for a hundred years.

'Thank you, monsieur, but it is perfectly adequate.'

She wanted to push him from the room, but at last achieved his departure with much smiling and reassurance. Then she performed a hasty *toilette* and went to the door.

She must find Hortense and speak to her. Or should she warn Julien first?

Oh, she did not know what to do for the best. It was all such a muddle.

* * *

In fact, Julien and Hortense were already in conversation, and had been for the last few minutes.

Hortense had been speaking to the innkeeper, a corpulent, red-faced man whose eyes, though half hidden by the flesh of his cheeks, still managed to look sharp and sly. Julien, who instinctively did not like the look of him, had managed to avoid conversing with him so far and had been shown to his bedchamber by the single *fille* in attendance. It was when he came downstairs that he saw Hortense walking towards the staircase with her mouth downturned.

'You look unhappy, Citoyenne Thierry.'

She hesitated. He pressed her, suddenly curious to know more about this beautiful young woman who travelled on her own and had such intelligent eyes. Without thinking he spoke in French. 'Is your room not to your satisfaction?'

For a moment she paused again, as if wondering whether it was proper to answer him, alone in the passageway as they were, then she seemed to seize on his question with relief. She shook her head.

'Because I had to change my travel arrangements, it seems I must share with the *fille* under the roof. There is no other guest chamber left.'

'That is too bad.' He thought for a moment. 'It may

be possible for you to share with my travelling companion, Citoyenne Cartaret. I think she will have no objection.'

Oh, yes she would. He thought of Eugénie's furious face. He would have to cajole her, but he could not let this woman, bourgeois but clearly refined, sleep with the *fille* in an attic, filthy no doubt and crawling with lice and spiders.

'That would be most kind, *citoyen*,' said Mademoiselle Thierry.

She came closer. She was wearing a perfume: mimosa, he thought. It was the summer scent of the chateau gardens he had known as a child.

He stared at her, and the brilliant eyes, fringed with black lashes, did not look down demurely, but met his with a direct gaze. 'You speak French most excellent well for an Englishman, monsieur.'

Damn, he had forgotten again. He inclined his head. 'You are most generous, mademoiselle.'

'And your travelling companion? You both go to England?'

He nodded, and tried to sound convincing. 'She goes to do business there, with my wife first, and then on to London.'

'Oh?'

'She is a milliner's assistant, you understand.' He

repeated it, horribly aware now of how unbelievable it sounded: 'Assistant to a renowned milliner, who once worked for Rose Bertin.'

'And yet she is so very young,' she answered drily. 'I could see she was no more than sixteen years, although she hid her face. Her employer must have great faith in her. Responsibility, indeed! And you, Monsieur Coveney?'

Her voice was so soft, her perfume so enticing. 'I am returning to England.'

Suddenly she spoke in English, sharply. 'That is interesting, monsieur. I did not know Monsieur Coveney had another brother, but I am certain he will be pleased to see you.'

'*Comment?*' Julien said, bewildered but aware of danger. 'What did you say, mademoiselle?'

'It is strange to meet an Englishman who cannot speak his own language,' she said in French.

Julien thought quickly. 'I was brought up here in France,' he said truthfully. 'Indeed, you could say that French is my mother tongue, and not English.'

'That is doubtless true, but it is not the whole story. You see,' she added very gently, 'I have worked for Monsieur Coveney. I was governess to his daughter in Deal. He shares no looks with you. Indeed, there is not the slightest resemblance. For that matter I have also met his brother.' She added with emphasis, 'His *only* brother. They both speak English because they are English, unlike you, *citoyen*, who are French.' She narrowed her eyes and her face hardened. 'You are an impostor!'

This was the most damnable and extraordinary bad luck. Was she a revolutionary, or might she be sympathetic? Whatever he did, he must protect Eugénie.

'Come,' he said, stepping closer and lowering his voice, trying to behave calmly. 'Let us sort this out like two civilized beings. I am sure you will understand, mademoiselle, once I have explained my circumstance.' He looked around quickly, conscious that any moment Eugénie would be tripping down the stairs to join him. 'I see a quiet parlour before us. Let us go in there and discuss this.'

She looked at him, and for a moment he believed he saw the shiny black eyes soften as she nodded.

In the shadows at the top of the staircase, Eugénie hesitated. She saw Julien and Hortense with their backs towards her, she saw Julien place his hand above Hortense's elbow and steer her away down the passage. Her mouth opened in outrage. She began to descend.

Then all at once there was commotion.

Four armed guards burst in from a side entrance,

accompanied by the landlord. Julien turned in shock and stood rooted. The light cast by the oil lamps trembled as the narrow passageway was suddenly filled with uniformed figures bearing muskets. Heavy boots trod over the floorboards; the air crackled with potential violence.

The landlord pointed at Julien, his face redder than ever with bewilderment and alarm.

'That is the man you asked for, *citoyens* – Monsieur Coveney! He arrived at my inn scarce half an hour ago. I know nothing of him, I can assure you!'

'We received a message that he had arrived,' said a guard abruptly, in the strong local accent. He turned to Julien. 'You are under arrest!'

Hortense stepped back as the guards pushed by. Julien did not look at her. He found himself flanked by a guard on either side, his arms seized. A musket was pointed at his chest. There was no point in struggling. He tried to bluster.

'What is it you want with me? I am an English gentleman! Is this how you treat innocent travellers in France?'

The guards ignored him, if anything holding his arms tighter.

At the top of the stairs Eugénie was transfixed with horror, staring down at Julien in the grip of two soldiers, as the landlord of the inn gabbled on, desperate to redeem himself.

'I knew nothing of this man before today. I would not harbour traitors under my roof wittingly! I am a loyal servant of the Republic, I do assure you!'

'We have information about another name also,' said the guard abruptly. 'A young girl who goes under the name of Loulette Cartaret.'

Eugénie's stomach gave a lurch of fear. Wild thoughts of escape rushed through her head. Could she hide in another chamber? In a closet somewhere? In the attics?

But she could not leave Julien to his fate alone. They must hold fast together, the two of them.

She walked down the stairs. 'I am Loulette Cartaret,' she said, her mouth dry.

'We have reason to believe you are travelling under a false name,' said the guard.

Standing in the doorway of the parlour, Hortense let out a little sound. Eugénie turned and their eyes met. Immediately Hortense looked down. A faint flush had come into her cheeks.

She looks guilty, thought Eugénie with sudden chilling understanding. *It is she who has betrayed us!*

'You are under arrest, *citoyenne*,' snarled the guard in charge.

'Do not hurt her!' cried Julien, as another guard advanced, his hand on his musket.

'I will come with you willingly,' said Eugénie. She held her head high. 'There is no need to hold my arm in such an uncouth way, I do assure you.'

The guard in question ignored her. She could feel his musket pressing against her side. He was squeezing her arm painfully.

The leader jerked his head at the attaché case clutched in her free hand. 'Take that,' he ordered, and it was snatched from her. She began to feel sick with apprehension.

'Where do you intend taking us, *citoyens*? Can you tell us that?'

'To the police station, where else?' The guard jerked his head at the others. 'Let us be gone, with no more time-wasting.'

'But our baggage?' cried Eugénie.

'We will have it brought to us, and searched.'

'I will see to it,' cried the landlord, desperate to please.

As Eugénie was marched past Hortense, she turned and stared at the young woman who had once been her governess and closest confidante. Into her gaze she summoned all her contempt and fury. Before the guard could silence her, she hissed, 'Is loyalty to the

Republic now more important than loyalty to another human being?'

In the parlour doorway Hortense stared back at her. Her expressionless face seemed carved from wood.

TWENTY-SEVEN

It was midnight, and the barred window of the dank, cramped cell in the police station held a patch of sky that was inky black, apart from a single star that kept appearing from the clouds in a blaze of light only to disappear seconds later. Eugénie kept her eyes on the star's progress whenever she was asked yet another question.

'*Who are you?*'

'*Your destination?*'

'*The purpose of your journey?*'

The questions went on and on. In the adjoining cell, Julien would be being questioned too. She answered in a flat tone now, all hope of charming this guard gone. He was coarse and ill-educated, but he was dogged and brutal. She could see it in his face. She had a horrible

318

feeling that he knew she was a hated aristocrat and that he would trap her in the end. She could only eke out the hours until they took her back to Paris, to a token trial and death beneath the guillotine.

She was seated on a hard stool, and was stiff and cold, but at least her hands were free. *I shall use my nails if he touches me*, she thought. *I shall go for his eyes*.

He was looming over her as he asked the questions now, whereas at the start he had been sitting on a chair and a small table had separated them. Her attaché case was on it, its lid forced back.

'It is all in my papers, *citoyen*,' she answered wearily at last. 'You only have to look there for the answers, and we shall both be spared this tedium.'

She jumped as he punched a fist into the attaché case and the papers shot to the dirty stone floor.

'I have been through these papers. They tell me nothing.' He brought his face close to hers so that she could see the forest of black bristles jutting through the flesh of his chin. His breath stank of rotting teeth. 'They are forgeries!'

'I would like to know, *citoyen* –' she said with dignity, trying not to flinch from his sweating, frustrated presence so close to her, for it was the first time she had been alone with a man, and one so unpredictably violent '– I would like to know how it was that you felt you had the evidence to arrest Monsieur Coveney and me.'

'You had been reported. We knew you were coming.'

At one of the tiny isolated stops they had passed, Hortense must have sent word on ahead to Bernais, the first town with a proper functioning police force. *This is what the Revolution has done to people*, she thought. *They are willing to betray those whom they once professed to love. It has swept away their humanity.* She did not feel anger or hurt; she felt numb, and so tired.

At last her interrogator rose to his feet and summoned the guard outside the door. 'Bring the other prisoner to me.'

Julien was pushed, stumbling, into the cell, his hands bound in front of him.

Eugénie was shocked. He looked haggard, and was bruised and bleeding about the face.

'At first light tomorrow, you will both be taken back to Paris for trial,' said the guard shortly.

'This is an outrage . . .' Julien began, and was silenced by a blow to the head. He fell into a corner, where he sat slumped against the mildewed wall. He raised bloodshot eyes to Eugénie's horrified gaze and shook his head slightly.

They were not left alone, even then. Another guard came in, armed with a pistol, which he laid close to hand on the table, its muzzle pointing towards them.

They heard the sound of the bolt sliding into place on the other side of the door as Eugénie's interrogator left.

The new guard made himself comfortable on the vacant chair, stretching out his legs and yawning. He was younger than the first, with long lank hair beneath his hat and an evil grin. He took off his hat, gave the greasy cockade that stuck out from it a smacking kiss and laid it on the table beside the gun.

'I sleep light, so don't move a muscle, either of you – understand?'

An hour went by, perhaps. The candle on the table burnt lower. The guard's head fell forward as his eyes closed. On the floor Julien shifted his position slightly and they opened to slits at once.

Eugénie prayed the guard would fall asleep and give them some respite from being watched. She saw his eyes close again, and after a few minutes, when it seemed he was breathing deeply, she moved on her chair. There were pins and needles in her feet and she wanted to walk about. Immediately the guard's eyes opened and he winked at her, shifting the pistol slightly closer to his hand. He began humming the 'Marseillaise' under his breath, his eyes on her, taunting her.

'Do you know it, little aristo? Can you sing? Or will you save that for when you meet Madame la Guillotine?'

He winked at her and, wetting a finger, drew it across his throat.

From where he was on the floor Julien had to force himself to keep quiet. He trembled with fury and cold. But it was not worth antagonizing the guard.

He could see the gun from where he was, dangerously close to the man's hand and no doubt loaded. It was old-fashioned but it would do its job efficiently. Besides, there was the other guard in the outer room to confront, even if by a miracle he managed to overcome this one. His head hurt abominably and his wrists were already raw and bleeding from his tight bonds. He knew it was impossible to break free.

The silence was so deep that he could hear his blood pumping. He thought Eugénie might be drowsing at last, for her head was bowed. The guard most certainly was not.

Then they all jumped. There were voices in the outer room, breaking the silence. The guard who had questioned Eugénie – and a woman, surely? After a moment the conversation stopped, and their guard rose to his feet yawning, as the bolt was drawn back on the door.

'Come to check up on you, he has,' he said. 'Don't trust me, eh?'

Julien recognized the beautiful young woman from the chaise. She was alone.

His heart sank further. Had she found further evidence against them? She did not meet his eyes, or even glance at Eugénie, who was now sitting bolt upright, her head averted.

The woman spoke quickly to the guard. 'I am a government agent,' she said in a low, even tone. 'This is my identification.' She drew a piece of paper from her bodice, showed it to the guard, who nodded and stiffened perceptibly.

'I have been notified to tell you that there has been a mistake. These two prisoners are not impostors. Their papers are in order. They are whom they profess to be. They must be freed forthwith.'

The guard began to protest. She held up a hand.

'I understand that you and your colleagues have only been doing what you consider to be your duty. You will not be judged for this error in Paris. I will make sure that you are all here cleared of any misconduct.'

The guard looked bewildered and angry. 'But the woman what informed – the man too – they was in the same *diligence* as these two, stayed at the same inn. They'd had their suspicions from the start. They were—'

'Mistaken.'

'But the girl . . .' He pointed at Eugénie. 'Her

baggage is suspect. Our chief did the search, he found nothing but stuffed sacks with a bit of stuff wrapped round. Deliberately made to look like bolts of material, they was.'

'These are hard times, *citoyen*,' said the young woman calmly. 'There would be customs duty to pay on a full bolt. Whether she was going to cheat her English customers I do not know, but that is another crime altogether and she would not be committing it in France.'

'*Citoyenne*, with all due respect, I know aristocrats when I sees 'em,' said the guard doggedly. 'I know Englishmen, too. I've had plenty of both through in my time. Can recognize 'em, sense 'em, smell 'em. It is you and not the informers what's mistaken. These two are running, and their names ain't their own. I'd bet my good boots on it.'

Twenty-Eight

The guard came round the edge of the table. 'Let me call my partner in.'

'No need, *citoyen*. I have already spoken to him about the mistake. He is happy to let the prisoners go.'

There was a pause.

Julien saw Eugénie move her head and look round at the young woman. He felt amazement, confusion and the beginnings of relief. But the guard looked stubborn and unconvinced.

The woman seemed to acquiesce. She nodded, smiled. 'I understand and respect your reluctance, *citoyen*. We must always be vigilant for traitors to the Republic. Let me see their papers before we go any further and make double sure.'

'I have the girl's here.'

The guard turned and reached for the attaché case.

There was the glint of a blade in the lamplight, a sudden swift upward thrust and the guard fell heavily forward over the table. His eyes were open in astonishment, but did not blink. Blood began to trickle from his mouth.

'Come,' said Hortense. 'We've little time.'

She moved swiftly across to Julien and cut his bonds. He flexed his hands, looking dazed. He felt his head gingerly and staggered to his feet.

Eugénie rose unsteadily. The dead man was so close, the face with its gaping mouth, the blood congealing. The eyes, already glazed, looked straight at her.

'You are not going to faint,' said Hortense briskly. 'There is not time.'

'Of course not,' Eugénie retorted weakly, gathering the frail remnants of her pride. 'De Boncoeurs never faint.' She took a deep breath. 'But I thought . . .'

'You thought I had informed on you,' said Hortense, picking up the pistol from the table and tucking it beneath her cloak.

Eugénie nodded silently. She knelt with difficulty to gather the papers scattered on the floor: after hours of sitting on a hard chair her limbs were cramped and stiff with cold.

'Leave them,' ordered Hortense. 'I have new passports for you both.' For a moment she glared at Eugénie. 'However did you think you would escape the authorities with such a ridiculous alibi? I have risked everything to come after you.'

'We have done well so far,' said Eugénie proudly. 'If it had not been for that horrible woman at the inn . . .' She stared at Hortense. 'But why have you done this? If you truly are what you say, a government agent, why do this?'

'Lord knows,' said Hortense grimly. She shook her head. 'Now come, follow me. I have made arrangements.'

'It is good of you, *citoyenne*,' said Julien awkwardly, rubbing the circulation back into his hands. 'I beg you not to take offence, but how do we know we can trust you if you are a government spy? You may be taking us into even graver danger.'

'She's risking her life for us, can't you see?' cried Eugénie.

'But who is she?'

'She was my governess.'

'In a different world,' said Hortense.

She pushed them through the door, Julien walking painfully, a hand to his head. Eugénie's own legs still felt weak. Gasping, she almost fell over the prone body of the other guard. He was lying face down in a pool of blood. She looked away as Hortense ripped off his sash and gave it to Julien.

She was thankful she could not see his eyes.

An oil lamp still burned on the desk, and Hortense took it up. In the corner their baggage had been thoroughly investigated. The material covering the 'bolts' had been ripped apart, exposing the sacks of straw, which in turn had been cut open and strewn all over the filthy floor. The pretence seemed now pitifully inadequate.

Eugénie saw her precious *toilette* box on the desk, its delicate flowered lid forced back, the bottles unstoppered. Their possessions had been flung to all corners of the room; her thick shawl lay in the dust and dirt.

'Take it,' Hortense insisted. 'It will be cold outside.' She looked Julien over. 'At least the English know how to dress for bad weather. Your tailor has done you well. Here . . .' She grasped a heavy sword, a guard's sabre, lying on the chair, and passed it in its scabbard to Julien; he buckled it on beneath his greatcoat and the guard's sash.

They emerged into darkness and damp. It was about three o'clock in the raw January morning and, though not raining, the sky was overcast, apart from the steadfast star that Eugénie had seen, drifting behind cloud and then reappearing. She shivered and enveloped herself in the shawl, tying it at the front. She was horribly aware that they were putting all their trust in Hortense, who had killed two men without a qualm; and now they had not the slightest notion where she would take them.

The cottages round the police station were in darkness. A crude farmer's cart had brought them there, Eugénie pushed up roughly against one splintered side, her hands bound, while Julien lay half-stunned on the floor planks, their baggage jolting between them.

She had been too apprehensive to take in their surroundings. Now she followed Hortense over what seemed little more than a muddy track across flat fields. In the light of the lantern, Hortense's wavering figure waded through mist that was waist-deep. In the distance the black shapes of animals moved against the lighter sky.

She trudged on blindly, not daring to question Hortense, hitching her skirts up further, although the hems were already wet and sticking to her legs. She was uncertain how Julien with his battered head was faring. She was conscious of him moving silently in the darkness beside her, once offering his hand when she was stuck in a rut. She grasped it dumbly; it was as cold as her own.

When their eyes became used to the darkness, Hortense extinguished the lamp. They struggled on; Eugénie's boots had now collected so much mud she could scarcely lift her feet. She was trembling with weariness and delayed shock; in the darkness tears ran down her face and she did not bother to brush them away.

A dwelling reared up before them, heavy thatch almost covering closed shutters in the crumbling walls. Somewhere within a dog barked and was silenced by a curse. Beyond the farmhouse lay a scatter of barns and outhouses. They stood in a cobbled yard; there was a strong smell of dung.

'Wait here,' whispered Hortense. Her figure disappeared into the darkness. They heard the dog bark again as a door opened and closed. A light gleamed briefly between the slats in the downstairs shutters, and there was the mutter of voices.

After a few minutes Hortense came out to them, the oil lamp now lit again; she was carrying a wicker basket in her other hand. 'This way,' she murmured, holding the lamp high so they could pick their way through the effluence that covered the cobbles.

She led them round to the other side of the building,

past closed stable doors, to a flight of wooden steps that led up to a low door in the windowless wall.

They climbed up after her. She opened the door, and they found themselves inside a loft below the roof, rafters above them beneath the thatch, and under their feet broken boards and the sound of horses, aware of strangers and restless. It was warm and humid from the animals, with a pungent smell of rotting grass and fresh droppings.

Something scurried away into a corner as they entered. Eugénie stopped herself from clutching Julien; she looked around, wide-eyed.

'Listen carefully,' said Hortense urgently. 'I must leave you before my absence is discovered at the inn.' She set the lantern down on the floorboards and the basket next to it. 'There is food in the basket. Bread, cheese and wine. It must last you all day while you remain in hiding here.'

'What of the farmer?' said Julien.

'He knows I am a government agent. I have bribed him well and he wishes to keep on the right side of the Republic.' She spoke quickly. 'These country people go in mortal fear of us. There has been much slaughter of rebels in the provinces. He will leave you alone. When darkness falls again, I shall come to you and we shall ride by the old farm ways to an inn outside Montreuil, where I have hired a private chaise to take us to Calais. It is best you travel with me. No one asks questions of government agents and their companions.'

She brought out papers from somewhere in her skirts. 'Here are new identities for you both.'

Julien looked briefly at the papers in the light of the oil lamp. 'But these belonged to that couple in the *diligence* – the ones who . . .'

Hortense nodded. 'The informers, yes. Do not ask how I have their papers. It is best not to know.'

Their eyes met. 'I understand,' he said.

She turned to go.

'Wait. Tell us something first – it was no coincidence that you shared our chaise today, was it?'

She looked back at him steadily, hesitating.

'Hortense?' said Eugénie fearfully. 'Does someone in the government know of Julien's activities? Were you sent after us?'

Hortense nodded. In the lamplight Eugénie saw how hard her face had become in the years since she had first known her: her eyes like stones, her lips compressed. The Revolution had taken its toll of her. A man would think Hortense beautiful, but he would not look to her for flirtation and romance now. Something within her had shrivelled and died.

'Your name is known to my master, who works

332

directly for Robespierre,' said Hortense to Julien. 'It is known that you were a ringleader behind the attempted rescue of the King. I was sent to kill you.'

'But you have ended up saving us, Hortense,' said Eugénie softly. She put out her hand to her, but it was ignored.

'Who is your master?' said Julien.

'Do you not know? He is the man known as Le Fantôme. He is based in Paris, but has agents working for him all over France.'

'Le Fantôme? I saw you with him once,' whispered Eugénie. 'How did you become involved with such a man?'

Hortense turned to her. 'You poor child, did you not know that you are betrothed to him when you turn sixteen? My mission was to kill Julien and return you to him. The marriage contract was signed by your guardian some years ago.'

'That cannot be true!' said Eugénie in bewilderment. 'I can't believe it, I will not! Armand would not let me marry such a man!'

'It is the truth,' said Hortense. 'Your brother knew of it at the time.'

Eugénie whirled on Julien. 'Do you know anything of this?'

'Armand spoke to me of it,' he said haltingly. 'At the

time it was arranged, he felt it would be a good marriage and see you well settled financially.' He paused. 'He has, of course, changed his mind. It is why he hid you away, why he wanted you to leave France.'

Eugénie sank down on the dusty floor and put a hand to her head. 'I can't believe it of Armand! That hideous old man!'

'Do not blame Armand,' said Julien gently. 'It was not he who signed the contract. He was only a boy then, and knew nothing of Le Fantôme. Nor, I am certain, did your guardian, save for the fact that he was wealthy.'

Eugénie shook her head. 'But all this time Armand has kept it from me! Who besides you knows of this?'

'No one else, to my knowledge.'

'But you, Julien! Couldn't you have warned me? You were Armand's confidant.'

'It was not my place,' he said stiffly. 'All I could do was plan your escape as best I could.'

'And look where it has got us,' said Eugénie bitterly. 'We have aroused suspicion the whole way!'

'That is not my fault,' snapped Julien. 'It was you who insisted on taking those particular identities and our ridiculous disguises.'

She glared at him. 'If Armand had been with me – if you had not taken his place . . .'

'You may not be able to forgive me for that, but

it is outrageous to make me a scapegoat for all that's happened!'

Footsteps crossed the boards and there was a chill breath of night air. Hortense had gone.

'Perhaps she will not come back to us,' said Eugénie. 'Perhaps she will be arrested on her return to the inn.' Her voice trembled.

In the stalls beneath them, the horses shifted, their hooves knocking against the brick floor.

Julien sat down and unsheathed the sabre. The naked blade gleamed dully in the light. He laid it across his knees and watched the door. He would keep awake all night, he thought. It would not be long before the bodies of their informers were discovered. 'Hush,' he said. 'You should try to sleep.'

'I do not believe I can. I see –' her voice wavered '– those murdered guards in my mind's eye. Were they bad men, or only doing what they thought was their duty as Republicans?'

Julien shook his head. 'A little of both. Times like these create bullies. Tyrants, too.'

He had carefully sat a little way from her for propriety's sake, though he found to his surprise that he wanted to put his arm around her. She looked so young and vulnerable, with matted hair and red-rimmed eyes, crouched against the wall.

'But what shall we do if Hortense does not . . .' she began again, then stopped suspiciously and put her hands to her face. 'Why do you stare at me so? I am sure I must look a positive fright.'

He could not help smiling; her vanity was suddenly touching to him. 'You do not – not at all,' he assured her, 'but if we were to go to a party at Victoire's now, I dare say we both would be refused entrance!' He hesitated. 'That time I took you away – have you forgiven me for that?'

'It seems so long ago I declare I have forgot all about it,' said Eugénie, though she had not.

She thought of Guy, of her feelings for him, which seemed now to belong to another person. Yet if he were here with her instead of Julien, how quickly her heart would remember! And Guy would see immediately how much more mature she was than that evening at Victoire's, when he had kissed her.

But then, perhaps he would not want to kiss her again, with straw in her hair and a great dirty face.

'Do you think there will ever be salons and balls again?' she asked wistfully. 'The Revolution has changed everything, hasn't it? All we know is lost.'

'At the beginning I thought we were forging a new era of civilization,' said Julien quietly. 'And the constitution was to give it us. Freedom, brotherhood and equal rights for all men, rich or poor. Both Armand and I wanted it, our friends likewise – all the best and most virtuous of men. The old regime was corrupt and had to go. We thought it could be accomplished without bloodshed. But then we lost our way to the extremists. And now we have become victims of our own revolution. We were fools. And the biggest fool of all was the King.'

'How can you say that? I thought you a royalist. You tried to save the King!'

'I do not know what I am any more,' he said wearily, running a hand through his black hair so that it was more tousled than ever. 'I did not want him to die, nor did he deserve to for all his faults. But many would say he brought his fate on himself, through listening to unwise counsel and his own bad governance. And now who knows what will happen?'

'You mean – you do not think his death will be an end to it?'

Julien shook his head. 'The Queen and the Dauphin, though they're prisoners, are still alive and a threat to the Republic. The Dauphin could be put on the throne if we lose the war with Europe and are invaded. And war with England is inevitable, now that Louis has been executed.'

'I pray that Armand does not take it into his head to rescue the Queen,' said Eugénie. 'He has admired her ever since he was small. I don't trust him without you.'

Julien gave an ironic smile. 'Though it was I who dreamt up the plan to rescue the King.' He did not mention that he suspected Armand already had ambitions of his own regarding the Queen. That confounded note: *save us*. He thought of Armand, hiding alone in Paris, unable to rescue anyone now.

'Poor Armand,' said Eugénie. 'If only he can remain safe until he is able to join me . . .'

Julien kept his doubts to himself. He could not foresee a time now when it would be possible for a nobleman to travel safely through the countryside, especially one wanted by the National Guard.

'What will happen in Paris, do you think?' Eugénie murmured, settling herself uncomfortably against the wall. She could scarcely keep her eyes open, but was determined to stay awake to watch for rats.

Julien shook his head. 'I don't know, but with food scarcer and more expensive, the people will take to the streets again. The government will have to find a way to control them, otherwise the mob will rule.' He sighed. 'The Revolution may be over, but something far more terrible may take its place.'

There was silence. He thought she was asleep, but

suddenly her eyes snapped open. 'You will not – take advantage of me, will you, if I sleep?'

The impudence of it! Did she not trust him after everything?

'Do not flatter yourself, mademoiselle!'

'I thought not,' she said meekly.

She was asleep now, or at least her eyes had been closed for some time. She had slipped sideways. He laid the sword down and stood up, taking off his coat and folding it. Then he slid it gently beneath her head. She did not stir. He found himself transfixed for a moment, staring down at her face. How extraordinarily pretty she was, even with patches of dry mud on her cheeks.

Daylight was already filtering in through the gaps in the outer walls and the farm animals were waking. Noises he had not heard since he was a boy on his father's estate in Gascony came to him, and he felt a pang for all that he had lost.

He sat up, unblinking and grim-faced, his hand gripping the sabre's hilt, waiting, and remembering, as the hours went by.

Twenty-Nine

When darkness fell again, Hortense came to them with horses from the post inn. She paid off the ostler who had brought them for a hefty bribe, and climbed the outside stairs to the loft. On the threshold she smiled tightly to see the two of them fast asleep, but separated by a proper distance.

Julien jerked awake as she entered, half lifting the sword. Eugénie blinked at the lamplight and brushed straw from her skirts.

'It is time to go,' Hortense said, without greeting.

They stumbled out after her and saw the dark shapes of horses tethered at the bottom of the stairs. They were muscular, placid creatures, used to pulling carriages and treading through mire and ruts. Two had side-saddles strapped incongruously to their broad backs. 'Take the smaller mount,' Hortense said to Eugénie.

Eugénie never forgot that night ride: the press of darkness around them, for Hortense had had to extinguish her oil lamp, the chink of bridles and bits that they could not silence, the strange yet familiar rolling motion of the horse beneath her, the creak of her saddle, the agonizingly slow walk through countryside that she could scarcely see below a cloudy sky; and all the time the fear that they would be stopped.

'You ride well,' said Julien in some surprise to her, as she rode along a narrow track in front of him.

She thought she detected admiration in his voice and smiled in the darkness. 'My groom taught me at Chauvais. He was an excellent rider himself.'

It was still damp and misty, but windless and not cold; the weather had improved. In single file they picked their way endlessly along muddy tracks until eventually they came to an area of worked turbaries, where peat had been dug from the ground. They could see the ramparts of the town of Montreuil rising against the night sky.

'I know of a little church near here where we can shelter for the remainder of the night,' said Hortense. 'We'll go to the inn at daybreak.'

But the church was securely locked, and a notice on

the stout wooden door, roughly scrawled, read, 'No Jews and émigrés.'

'Things have changed since I was here last,' said Hortense grimly.

She found a barn in a field beneath the town. They dismounted and tethered the horses inside, where they would not be seen. Hortense went in first, holding the lighted oil lamp before her. Its glow fell on winter straw, stacked up in the corners, which would serve well as bedding.

Eugénie looked up and stopped, appalled. She opened her mouth to scream but no sound came out. All she could do was point with a shaking hand and gasp.

There were men hanging on the walls.

Hortense held her lamp higher and saw the skinned carcasses of two dozen sheep, fastened on the wall in readiness for market next day. She and Julien burst into laughter.

Eugénie could not join in. She sank down in the straw, horrors in her head.

They made good progress in the chaise they hired at Montreuil, passing the checkpoint at Samer without a problem once Hortense had shown her papers. They travelled through woods, past abandoned châteaux, and came at last to a meandering river with the ramparts of Boulogne rising above it.

It was already growing dark but, as the chaise began to climb, the air that blew through the cracks into its interior carried a cold, unfamiliar and invigorating scent.

Looking out, Eugénie saw a flat strand of firm yellow sand and, rolling over its edge, grey water frilled with white, as delicate and intricate as the most superior Flanders lace. The last time she had seen the sea she had been four years old, on her way to be shown off in England by her proud *maman*, her darling mother who was to die only a year later.

Hortense looked at them both. 'Shall we rest here tonight, or continue? It might be wise to travel on through the night if we can.'

Julien raised his black brows at Eugénie. 'Are you fatigued?'

'Not in the least,' she lied brightly, determined not to show weakness in front of him. 'Let us go on to Calais.'

They reached Calais at about five in the morning, when it was still dark. A deep ditch ran round in front of the walls and the gates were shut, as with all fortified towns at night. The chaise clattered up to the drawbridge and the coachman reined in the horses. Eugénie had been dozing inside the chaise and woke with a start.

'Will they let us through?' she said, peering out. There was no one to be seen. Then their postilion driver let out a great shout and a figure appeared on the parapet wall.

Hortense climbed out. 'Stay here,' she said. 'Keep your faces hidden.'

They heard the centinel shout down, 'What have you within? No rioters, no disturbers of the peace here!'

A conversation followed that they could not hear, though they strained their ears. Then Hortense climbed back inside, bringing a draught of cold sea air into the fug of the chaise.

'They are always surprised that a woman should be a government agent!' she said, smiling wryly. 'He has gone to the commandant to fetch the keys. For all that Calais has cut itself off from the Revolution, if you are an agent and have your bribes ready, it opens all doors. I said that I and my two colleagues had urgent business in the town.' Her smile faded.

'You cannot afford to linger here. We shall leave the chaise at the coaching inn, then I shall set about securing your passages to England while you both have a few hours' rest.'

In the bleak dawn light, Eugénie found Calais, with its narrow cobbled streets – no more than eight of them, she discovered – small and dirty-looking, for all its spacious market places and fine fortifications. Her heart sank as they left the chaise at what looked to be a prosperous and decent coaching inn, and followed Hortense on foot through the town, passing inns each more disreputable and sordid than the last. There was no wind, and the heavy clouds seemed to touch the tops of the houses. A sea mist filled the streets, dampening their cheeks.

A peeling placard on a wall suddenly caught her eye and a surge of delight filled her. She grasped Julien's arm.

'Fabrice is somewhere here! See what it says? He is to fly his balloon across the Channel, from Calais to Dover!'

She looked around wildly, in the ridiculous hope that she might see him coming through the waking town in the costume Belle had made for him.

Julien shook his head. 'Look at the date, Eugénie. The flight, if it succeeded, took place a year ago.'

She looked closer. Julien was right. She gulped in disappointment and turned away. 'Why didn't he tell Belle what he was doing?' she whispered.

'I doubt he can write,' Julien said gently.

At last Hortense stopped beneath an inn sign. 'The

innkeeper is discreet here and won't ask questions.'

Above them was a tall, leaning house in a long, cavernous alley that led away from the quay. At the end of the alleyway, they caught a glimpse of the harbour, masts rising through the mist.

Inside, the inn was modestly furnished, but clean; it seemed almost empty. The innkeeper, a small, eager man, with a spotless apron, recognized Hortense and with delight showed his three guests to rooms on the first floor. If he noticed the bruising on Julien's face, he said nothing. A *fille* came at once to light the fires, and they gathered in Eugénie's chamber, rubbing their cold hands gratefully before the flames.

'Won't you rest a while yourself, mademoiselle?' said Julien to Hortense. She had shadows beneath her eyes, he noticed, and must be at least as tired as they were; but she shook her smooth dark head. After breakfast, which she ate silently and hastily, she went to her own room to fetch her cloak.

Eugénie knocked timidly on the door and she opened it, frowning impatiently.

'Hortense?' Eugénie whispered, for Julien had been given the maid's bedchamber next door. 'May I speak to you?'

Hortense waved her brusquely inside. 'What is it?'

'Why not come with us to England and leave this life you lead?'

Hortense narrowed her eyes. 'Because I work for the wrong side, you mean? Because I am not a royalist aristocrat like you?'

Eugénie shook her head. 'There is no wrong side, Hortense – I have learnt that.'

Hortense stared at her in contempt. 'You are a fool if you think such a thing! But then you never were interested in politics.'

'All I wish is that Armand and I should live at Chauvais,' said Eugénie humbly. She tried to read some softening in Hortense's expression, but there was none.

'We were happy once, when I was a little girl,' she said in a low voice. 'You were my governess and I loved you and I believe you cared for me. Is that why you are helping me now?'

Hortense looked away. 'I cannot bear to see you the wife of a man like Le Fantôme! There is no other reason.'

'Not even – loyalty?'

Hortense gave a bitter laugh. 'Loyalty? To a family of aristocrats who dismissed me, both in Paris and in England, for my views? I had no other position to go to in England, and no money.'

'I am sorry,' said Eugénie, shocked. 'I didn't know

347

what had happened. I never heard from you.'

'Your guardian forbade me to write to you. He told the convent to destroy my letters. He made sure I was out of France by arranging for me to work for your uncle, Monsieur Coveney, in Deal, where he thought I could do no harm.' Her voice went on, furious but quiet. 'I learnt English, I learnt to despise the English respect for royalty, but to admire their constitution and parliament. When I was dismissed there, too, for filling my charge's head with revolutionary ideas, I returned to Paris.'

'And now you will be in danger for helping us!'

'If discovered, yes.' Some of the anger left her face as she looked at Eugénie. 'But I am careful, very careful. Now go and rest.'

Eugénie hovered in the doorway, troubled. She knew what the answer would be, but still some remnant of her old feeling for her governess made her ask wistfully, 'Shall we be able to meet again one day, do you think?'

Hortense's lip curled. 'A republican agent and an aristocrat? I do not think so!'

The innkeeper came out of the kitchens as Hortense came down the stairs. 'There is a message for you, *citoyenne*, brought in last night. Let me fetch it.'

He saw that the young woman, who had stayed at his

348

inn several times before, did not look surprised. She had her cloak hood pulled up around her face as if she were about to go out, but she waited while he bustled away and came back with a plain white envelope. It was sealed, but there was no name or address written upon it.

He watched her, for he was curious about this mysterious, independent young woman with the beautiful but stern face who always stayed alone and, though unmarried, always had the money to pay her bills; but she did not break the seal to read the note inside. She tucked the envelope away after a brief glance and said only, '*Merci, citoyen.*'

He caught sight of the bundle of assignats in her pocket as she put the envelope away. 'If there is anything you or your companions desire, mademoiselle . . .' he said quickly. 'I had made arrangements to be out this afternoon – we have no others guests staying, you understand – but if there is anything at all, ring for the *fille.*'

She bowed her head gravely in acknowledgement, before disappearing out into the mist.

No fisherman among her contacts was taking his boat out in the next few days, nor could be bribed to sail over to any of the Cinque Ports on the English coast. They sat morosely in the drinking houses along the quay, waiting for the weather to lift.

It was risky for her to enter such places, for a respectable woman alone stood out and was cause for comment, but she kept herself discreet, well covered by her cloak and hood.

They all told her the same, and in no uncertain terms: that war with England was imminent and they were waiting to hear the news before venturing out in the mist into a Channel filled – all the twenty-one-mile width of it – with English gunboats, waiting like ghosts to fire on them as they sailed blindly, slap-bang, into their gunwales. And if they avoided that, what would wait for them when they reached port on the enemy's coastline?

England was an old foe: Calais's past, with its years of English occupation, still haunted the town even now, and they were taking no chances, especially in this weather.

At one of the drinking houses Hortense was overheard. A man, sitting alone with a mug of small beer and a plate of pickled herring, listened as she asked around for passages for her two friends. He looked at the tall, striking young woman with decided interest. As she left, he rose lightly to his feet, unremarked in the hubbub about him, and slipped out after her.

THIRTY

Dessin's was famous for the best food in Calais and had once been a popular venue with travellers on the Grand Tour. At midday it was still crowded and noisy, though the days when the sooty beams rang with the sound of young English voices calling for wine were over.

The man who had followed Hortense saw her enter the inn, and followed her. He was not altogether surprised to see her go up to a young man, who bowed and kissed her hand, though she quickly pulled it away. They sat down together at a table to one side of the fire.

Hortense's pursuer sat down himself at a nearby table, ordered wine and waited.

'Why did you want me to meet you, Le Scalpel?' said

Hortense, waiting to speak until a jug of wine and two glasses had been put down on the tablecloth. 'It is dangerous. We should not be seen together, especially here, in Calais.'

She looked around, but there was no one she recognized, nor anyone who looked conceivably like an English spy. The man at the nearest table, brawny and weather-beaten, was wearing sea boots: another fisherman making the most of a day's holiday. In any case, in this racket it was impossible to hear what anyone at a neighbouring table was saying, which was why it was such an excellent meeting place for agents.

She did not wish to sit close to Le Scalpel, for he still had the power to disturb her senses, but she was forced to do so in order to talk quietly. He had placed an arm about her shoulders as if they were lovers still, and was whispering into her ear, stirring her hair with his warm breath.

A tremor ran through her and she tried to ignore it.

'Fortune has not been on our side, Hortense. Our two quarries were sighted and arrested, but they escaped. You know of this, I am sure.'

What did he mean? For a moment she froze, feeling his arm heavy on her shoulders, but then she spoke calmly. 'I had heard through our contacts. Has nothing been seen of them since?'

He shook his head. 'They have left a trail of dead. Two guards and the brother and sister who informed on them. De Fortin appears as adept with the dagger as any agent.'

He pulled away a little and examined her face, her eyes, lingering on her lips. His eyes, always sharp, missed nothing. 'You look fatigued,' he murmured. 'Has this mission been so frustrating? I had thought you'd have better fortune than I in pursuing them.'

'Why so?'

'You know Eugénie de Boncoeur so well she would trust you. It would be easy for you to trap her, I would have thought.' He watched her carefully, but she kept her face immobile.

'If I had found her, yes,' she said.

'Where are you staying?'

'One of the inns on our list,' she said vaguely. Not long ago he would have come to her as night fell. It still gave her pain to think of it.

His eyes flickered. Did he remember too?

'When did you arrive?'

'Early this morning,' she said.

'So you have not yet met up with Le Fantôme.'

Her heart lurched. 'Is he come to Calais?'

'Indeed he is, hotfoot after his bride and the royalist traitor. I fear he is most displeased with us both for failing him.' He gave a rueful grin that reminded her of how much she had once loved him, and drank deep of his wine. 'Still, all is not lost. We have only to sit and wait, and our quarries will come to us.'

'What do you mean, Le Scalpel?'

'We know that they intend to sail from Calais.' She struggled to hide her shock and look merely surprised. He nodded. 'I have just warned the guards to double-check the papers of all those travelling in and out of the town. If they are here already, the mist will keep them from sailing.'

'But what makes you think they will come to Calais? There are other ports.'

He smiled again, showing his excellent white teeth. 'Ah, you did not know that we have arrested de Boncoeur. He has – talked.'

Hortense forced herself to keep her voice calm. 'What has he said?'

'Little that we did not know – or suspect – already.' He ticked them off on his fingers. 'That he and de Fortin were two of the ringleaders in the plot to rescue the King. That de Fortin took his place on the escape from Paris. That de Fortin and the sister intend to sail from Calais to Deal on the English coast.'

He bent his head closer to hers again. 'And most damning of all, the burnt remains of a map were found in the fireplace of the tailor's house used by de Boncoeur. The map showed the Temple, with inside knowledge of the interior and the rooms where the Queen and Dauphin are being kept prisoner. It seems that de Boncoeur was about to plan yet another rescue!'

Hortense stared at him dumbly. He gulped down more wine and set down his glass. 'De Boncoeur is now in prison in La Force awaiting transferral to La Conciergerie, after which he will be tried. With the evidence we have, he will most certainly go under the guillotine.'

However was she going to break this to Eugénie? But no, she could not do it. If she did, Eugénie would never leave France.

Le Scalpel's tone altered and became slow, seductive. His eyes looked deep into hers, searching. 'You are not drinking. You are pale, my love, distrait. A little wine will do you good, bring blood to those beautiful lips. Why, your glass is still full.'

She gazed back at him, caught helpless in the intensity of his gaze. Her mind stopped functioning. He traced a finger over her mouth, then pressed the thick glass painfully hard where his finger had been, bruising her lips and forcing them to part.

She choked as wine gushed into her mouth. Red drops spattered over the white tablecloth.

* * *

Eugénie was too tired to sleep. She had had the *fille* bring her some lunch in her chamber, and now she lay back on her bed fully dressed, her thoughts, as always, turning to Armand.

She wondered how soon a letter from him would arrive at their uncle's house in Deal – whether it would mention anything about the marriage contract with Le Fantôme. It was hard not to feel betrayed, though there was nothing Armand could have done to prevent it. He had kept it from her all this time! Yet what would she have done had she known? She could have done nothing.

She tried to comfort herself. Once she was out of the country there was no danger that she would ever be Le Fantôme's wife. When she returned to France eventually, it would be with Armand, and with his lawyer's training she was certain he would think of some way of annulling the contract.

She did not think about meeting her uncle and cousin Henrietta, and of her new life in Deal; she did not dare to do so yet. Once she had stepped on to the boat and they were sailing, then would be the time. But this felt like wasted time: she and Julien resting here, instead of escaping.

How oppressively quiet this inn was, save for the

distant screams of the seagulls and the footsteps of the *fille* on the back stairs beyond Julien's room. Why was Hortense taking so long? It seemed an age since she had left, and what with the mist outside it was almost dark in her chamber already, though scarce two o'clock. They might have to spend the night in this silent little inn after all.

Eugénie sat up restlessly. She would slip downstairs to the entrance and see if Hortense was coming back along the alleyway.

Hortense came out of Dessin's alone, and was aware, though she did not turn her head, that someone had followed her out: someone who was not Le Scalpel. A flicker at the corner of her vision; the tread of boots over the cobbles not far behind her. Her scalp prickled; at once all her senses were alert.

She pulled her hood further up around her face, and decided to take a longer, more indirect, route back to the inn.

As soon as Eugénie stepped out of the inn she saw to her dismay that the mist had thickened. Now through the opening at the end of the alley she could no longer see the masts of the ships lying out in the harbour. A grey wall had descended, merging with the sky and narrowing the harbour to the empty fishing boats moored against the quay, lying almost motionless on the still, dark water. The air was heavy with unshed moisture. She could feel it against her face; her cheeks were wet already. She pulled her shawl up hastily to protect her hair.

Not more than twenty steps took her to the end of the alley, but now it had begun to drizzle in earnest. She stepped into the doorway of a shuttered warehouse on the corner and looked along the empty quay. There was no sign of Hortense; she had better return to the inn.

She was held, however, by the rectangle of sea before her and her dim memories of her first voyage. The ocean had no white lace in it today, and its uniform mass seemed to bulge slightly, like a jelly before it sets. But who would wish to eat a jelly of so disagreeable a colour? She fancied she felt a little sick merely looking at it.

Someone was walking along the deserted cobbles in the distance, someone carrying one of the new-fangled umbrellas. It was a man, a gentleman, or possibly a wealthy merchant, for she could see that beneath the wet black silk of the umbrella his breeches were of the finest cut and his boots gleaming with polish. She pressed back nervously against the door, for she should not be out alone, unattended, in a strange town.

But then the man must have lifted the umbrella a little. Although he was some way away still, she saw his face. Relief and joy flooded her. What good fortune had brought *Guy* here? All would now be well. She could tell him everything, for he would know what to do. Once more he would rescue her, and then . . .

But as she was about to move out of her shelter, about to run up to him, crying out his name in delight, to her enormous frustration another man came along from the opposite direction, holding a hand out to Guy in silent greeting. She would have to wait.

He was older, this man; she could tell by the way he moved. His black redingote shone with damp. Beneath the cocked hat his hair was powdered in the old style, and his face had an unhealthy pallor.

She recognized him immediately. It was Le Fantôme.

THIRTY-ONE

Julien was at the unshuttered window, staring out at the darkening afternoon. The maid had not yet been in to remove the remains of his luncheon, or to bring fresh logs for the fire, and he thought it must be her at last when he heard a knock on his chamber door. Then he heard Eugénie gasp out his name.

She burst in without waiting for his '*entrez*'. But they had long since stopped observing the social formalities between them.

'Where have you been?' he said, seeing that her shawl was over her head and the curls around her face were wet with rain. He was exasperated at her foolhardiness.

He bent to light the candle on his bedside table, but she stopped him.

'No, leave it! It is safer in the dark.'

Now even in the poor light he could see she looked distraught, her face white, her eyes huge and fearful. 'What is it?' he said in alarm.

'Le Fantôme!' she gabbled breathlessly. 'He is here, in Calais! I saw him on the quay! Oh, what shall I do?'

'Did he see you?'

She shook her head. 'No, I took great care that he should not.' She cast off her shawl and sat down on the bed. He saw that her hands were trembling. 'I cannot marry him, Julien. I cannot!' She looked up at him imploringly with her big blue eyes and his heart melted.

'You are not going to marry him,' he said firmly.

'But what am I going to do?'

'You are going to stay here with me until Hortense returns and tells us her news. Le Fantôme has no idea that you are here. You are quite safe.'

She nodded, seemingly comforted, but then hesitated. 'Guy is here too.'

'Guy?' said Julien, frowning.

'He spoke with Le Fantôme. I did not know they knew each other – but everyone knows that odious man, of course. I was about to ask Guy to help us . . .'

'Then thank God you did not!' exclaimed Julien. 'The fewer people involved in our escape, the better chance we have.'

'I do not know why you dislike him so! I know he would have helped us if he could.' After a pause, she admitted reluctantly, 'But I daresay he might have mentioned me by chance to Le Fantôme, so perhaps it was just as well.'

'Exactly. Now let us both calm down. We do not want the entire inn to know of our predicament.'

Eugénie opened her mouth, then shut it obediently. Julien sat down on the rickety three-legged stool, for there was no proper chair in the maid's room. He could see that Eugénie's hands had stopped shaking, but they looked so tiny and cold, he longed to sit beside her and cover them with his own. The fire had burnt down and the room was chill.

For a moment they sat in silence in the shadows, Eugénie thinking regretfully of Guy, whom she would leave without ever bidding *au revoir*, Julien wondering with growing anxiety what had happened to Hortense.

Then they both turned to each other in relief. There was a light footfall in the passage outside, the scrape of the latch lifting against the wood of Hortense's door and the sound of it closing. Hortense was back, perhaps taking off her cloak. In a minute she would come to them.

But instead they heard heavier footsteps walk swiftly over the creaking floorboards and past the door to

Julien's chamber. Someone had come up the back stairs. The latch on Hortense's door lifted again and they heard voices.

Eugénie's mouth opened. 'There is a man with her!' she gasped.

For a moment she felt shocked at her old governess's impropriety, though she knew that Hortense had long dismissed the conventions of female behaviour.

Who could he be? She looked at Julien, her eyes wide with questions. Julien put a finger to his lips, frowning.

The murmur of voices continued. Hortense seemed to protest. Then suddenly they heard her cry out a frightened 'No!' and there was an abrupt silence.

Julien rose quietly to his feet and gestured that Eugénie should move behind him. He drew the sabre from its scabbard.

They waited. Julien felt as if his every sense was alert. His heart began to beat faster. He faced the door.

They heard another door open, then close after a pause. That was Eugénie's chamber. Julien glanced back at her and she was staring at him, her eyes wide with surprise and growing fear. The footsteps came back towards Julien's door, quieter this time, evidently taking care to avoid the creaks.

Then it was flung open and a dark figure stood

framed on the threshold, armed with a drawn sword.

'Who are you to enter in such a way?' Julien gasped out.

But he scarcely had time to utter the words before the man had taken a couple of paces within the chamber, slid his right foot forward and lunged at him deliberately.

He means to murder me! Julien thought incredulously, as he parried the blow with a violent clash of steel that echoed in the small room, bringing his sword across the other man's blade and pushing it away from him.

His opponent disengaged swiftly and lunged for him again.

Julien parried and disengaged, unbalanced by the guard's heavy sabre, which was intended for cutting, slicing movements. His assailant had a dress sword, a much lighter rapier. He danced around Julien, manoeuvring him where he wanted with its darting, flickering point. Julien was unable to get into his own rhythm of fencing; all he could do was to parry the blows, to keep the rapier's naked point away from his flesh.

He had no idea where Eugénie was; he could hear her give little cries from behind him somewhere. It gave him strength and courage to fight on. Whatever happened, he must protect her.

His assailant lunged *en carte*; Julien disengaged clumsily.

The rapier was moving too fast to follow. *Always watch your opponent's eyes, not his blade.*

In the half-darkness he could see the man's eyes fixed on his, glittering above a black scarf that covered the lower part of his face. Soon Julien knew he would be defeated, would feel the sharpness of the rapier's point piercing the bones of his chest, cutting into the softness of his heart.

I cannot die! What will happen to Eugénie?

Desperately he struggled to keep the rapier away from his exposed front. He parried each thrust, but he could not attempt a riposte and he needed to attack to win. This man was too fast, too fit, too nimble and experienced, whereas he was out of practice and sluggish after a week of travel and lack of sleep. This was not like the old days of fencing with Armand, when their practice foils were tipped.

Besides, this man was not fencing for sport: he was a deadly and skilled assailant out, it seemed, to murder him.

The walls rang to the clash of blades as they engaged yet again. Both of them were breathing fast now, the man's pale breeches scissoring beneath his dark coat as he moved, the soles of his boots striking the floorboards in a sharp staccato. The black silk around his face billowed in and out as he panted. He was trying to force Julien to thrash wildly in defence and lose control.

Julien could feel sweat breaking out on his forehead; his legs felt weak. His opponent's blade flickered across into an undefended opening before he could parry it, and he felt a sudden stinging pain in his sword arm. He let out a cry and staggered back, struggling to keep hold of the sabre though his arm felt on fire. He could feel a warm stickiness inside his shirtsleeve. If he lost much blood it would make his defence weaker still.

His opponent disengaged and came at him again, his eyes alight above the black scarf. He knew he was winning; he was enjoying himself. He was pushing Julien further and further across the room. Soon his back would be against the wall.

Another lunge. Julien parried feebly. He could step back no further. He knew he was defeated.

His assailant laughed in triumph, the black silk blowing out. His eyes gleamed, cat's eyes in the half-darkness. He drew back a little to choose where to place his final, fatal thrust.

Eugénie screamed, and with both hands brought the seat of the maid's three-legged stool crashing down on his head.

* * *

'Have I killed him?' she whispered, her hand to her mouth. She shook from head to foot.

The man lay unmoving, face down on the floor, surrounded by broken pieces of stool. His rapier had slithered across the boards and jammed itself, still juddering, into the corner of the skirting.

For a moment Julien could not answer her. He licked his dry lips and thought he might vomit. His arm burned and throbbed painfully and there was blood on his shirt. With difficulty he sheathed his sword.

Then the sickness faded and his heart calmed a little. He was not dead after all: Eugénie had saved his life. And for the second time, he realized.

'I do not think so,' he said, and managed to kneel down and look at the back of the man's head. No wound in the thick hair was visible in the gathering dark, but there was no wetness when, with distaste, he ran his hand over the man's head; the thin black ribbon that tied his hair back was scarcely disturbed.

'I believe you have knocked him clean out,' he said with admiration.

'Is it a National Guard come after us?' said Eugénie fearfully, kneeling beside him.

Julien felt for a sash beneath the black coat but there was none, though his quick search discovered a dagger tucked into a sheath on the man's belt.

'I have no notion who he is.'

'Hortense!' whispered Eugénie. 'What are we thinking of? We must go to her!'

She rose to her feet at once and rushed to the door. 'Wait!' said Julien urgently. He wanted to see his assailant's face, but he knew he could not let Eugénie go alone to Hortense's room.

There was not time to light a candle. With difficulty he turned the man's head sideways so that he could see his profile. His eyes were shut, but he was breathing. The scarf had loosened, exposing the lower part of his face, the finely moulded lips, the clean jaw.

Julien knew that without a doubt he was looking at Guy Deschamps.

In shock he looked up to tell Eugénie, but she had already gone.

He could not kill him. Murder in cold blood was abhorrent to him, the murder of a defenceless, unconscious man even more so. It was his immediate reaction, and he had no time to give it thought, or to dwell on Guy's treachery. He got to his feet, picked up Guy's rapier in place of his own with his good arm and sheathed it. As a precaution, he took the key from the door and locked it on the other side. Then he went after Eugénie.

* * *

The candles had been lit in Hortense's room, perhaps
by her on her return from the quayside.

But now she was lying on her side, her cloak spread
out behind her like a bird's wing. Beneath her left breast
there was a rip in the material of her bodice, which had
already turned from white to red. More blood had
pooled darkly on the floorboards beside her. Her dead
eyes were open and full of hurt.

Eugénie knelt down without knowing she was doing
it, and horror prevented her from weeping.

THIRTY-TWO

Julien came in, grimacing with pain, his arm close to his chest. His dark gaze took in Hortense's body and Eugénie crouched beside her.

Eugénie looked up at him, her face haunted. 'She was murdered because she helped us!'

'We cannot know that,' said Julien, 'but it means we are in grave danger.' He bent to help her to her feet with his good arm, but she thrust him away angrily. Tears began to run down her face.

'We must make haste to leave this place,' he said urgently. 'Someone knows we are here.' He could not bear to tell her of Guy's betrayal yet. 'It might even be Le Fantôme.'

She started up in alarm at that, and wiped her tears away with her sleeve.

He bit his lip at the throbbing in his arm, wondering how long he would be able to walk without losing too much blood. She stared at him, as if suddenly she saw him properly for the first time since the fight.

'Julien, you are wounded!'

'It's trifling – a scratch, that's all.'

'Come, sit on the bed and let me look at it.'

It seemed to help her grief and shock to take charge. Besides, it was sheer delight to have her fuss over him although he was in such pain. She swiftly took clean linen from beside the jug and bowl on the little table, and used one towel to staunch the blood, the other she tore into strips. After a while her hands stopped trembling.

'I did not know you knew how to tie a tourniquet.'

'My groom taught me – in case either of us should ever have an accident while out riding, be bitten by an adder or some such thing. There! The wound is clean and should heal well in a while. Let me make a sling for you. Take off your shirt. I will avert my eyes.'

She did so, while Julien sheepishly obeyed, but then he felt her little fingers folding and knotting the material against his flesh; she struggled not to meet his gaze and he did the same.

He found he felt a little better for her ministrations.

'Now,' she said, trying to be brisk, 'you are all set up. Your greatcoat will hide the sling.'

It had taken too long; he wondered how soon the innkeeper would be back and the bodies discovered, one of them so very dead. They had both tried to avoid looking at Hortense, so he was astonished when Eugénie went over to the body and turning her head away so that she should not see Hortense's face, unfastened the cloak and gathered it up. Next, she was rummaging in the pocket attached to a belt around the waistband of Hortense's skirt and had pulled out her papers and bundles of assignats.

Eugénie caught his gaze. She looked shamefaced but defiant.

'A government agent accompanied by a member of the National Guard will have much more chance of leaving Calais than a couple of suspects!'

Julien was impressed. For a girl who looked so delicate and, indeed, conveyed such delicacy of feeling, at times she could display great presence of mind.

'But we cannot steal her money.'

Eugénie's eyes flashed. 'It is not hers, but the revolutionary government's, which has paid someone to kill you! Anyway,' she said quietly, 'she has no need of money now.'

That was true enough. 'But if we leave Calais, where shall we go?' His mind felt woolly: he could not think.

'To Crozier Saint-Clement, where else? It is the

closest port and where we were to sail from when you first planned our journey, wasn't it?'

'On foot?' he said doubtfully.

'We'll take nothing with us, no baggage. It is only a few miles' walk – if you are able to manage it.'

He nodded; he would not admit to her that there was nothing he felt less like doing.

'We can follow the line of the shore,' she said. 'Do you still have the map?'

In affirmation he tapped his boot, where he had tucked it away, and tried to pull himself together. She was right, of course: if they followed the coastline to the east, they should come to the tiny fishing village after a few miles. He had suggested it to Armand originally because it was so small and isolated. He had felt certain they could pick a boat up there and bribe its skipper to take them across. Now, with a war with England looming, he wasn't so sure.

Eugénie was already fastening Hortense's pocket belt around her own waist and stuffing the papers and money back inside. 'Fetch what you need, Julien, then we must leave!'

Left alone with the body, she hesitated. Then she knelt down and gingerly closed the dead eyes. She pulled the counterpane from the bed and covered Hortense with it. 'Forgive me for taking your identity,' she whispered; but she knew that Hortense would have approved.

Julien returned after a few moments. 'He's still motionless – breathing though,' he added grimly, as he put the key on the table.

Perhaps it would have been better if she had killed the unknown assailant with the stool, Eugénie thought as she helped Julien on with his greatcoat. How long would they have before the dreadful pursuit started again?

They took one of the lighted candles and went down the back staircase, passing the shadowy kitchen on their way out, where the *fille* was asleep by the stove. Eugénie caught sight of the bottle she had been drinking from, tiptoed across and grabbed it. It was brandy, exactly what a patient required, she thought. She forced it on Julien, who took several gulps and seemed to look better for it.

Eugénie tucked it away into Hortense's pocket for future use, and they left a handful of assignats in the doorway as payment for the rooms and the brandy, though whether the money would ever reach the innkeeper was doubtful.

There was an unlit lantern by the back door. She lit the oily wick with their candle and picked it up. Then she pulled Hortense's hood up around her face and turned back to Julien. His eyes glittered black in his white face, but his jaw was set and he nodded at her to open the outside door.

They stepped out together into the dark.

The man who had followed Hortense from Dessin's, and who had been loitering for some time at the head of the alley, saw two figures emerge from the house. The woman, well wrapped in her cloak, the hood over her head, was now with a young man, who carried himself awkwardly. The shape of a sword was visible in the darkness, sticking out from beneath his coat.

The man fingered his pistols thoughtfully and crept after them. They appeared to be heading for the gate on the east side of the port, moving swiftly under the hanging lanterns. He hung back when they reached the town wall and customs house, but without baggage they were waved through to the guards' room, to present their papers to those manning the gate.

There seemed to be no difficulty within – not that he would have expected any; they emerged shortly afterwards and the gate was raised for them.

Their pursuer gave them what he reckoned to be a ten-minute start, for he thought he knew the particular route they would take and, since he knew it of old, needed no giveaway light himself to find it; then he went into the guards' room. He was a familiar face, and they did not demur about giving him the identities of all those who had passed through that early evening.

His suspicions were confirmed. After the customary joshing with the guards and a patriotic exchange of '*Vive la République!*' he went through the gate himself, with a lantern that he had borrowed from them but which he did not bother to light.

The pair he was following had taken the path along the coast towards Dunkirk, and avoided the road. That was interesting. He could see the glow of their lantern bobbing among the sand dunes, appearing and disappearing, blurred but magnified by the mist drifting in from the sea.

He turned the collar of his coat up and pulled down the salt-encrusted brim of his battered round hat. He was not certain where they were heading, but it wouldn't be long before he found out.

It was bitter chill, not weather for a woman, and the going was heavy in this damp sand, especially with so little light to guide them. He wondered how soon it would be before she gave up. She'd lay herself down to rest in the sand, and, once he had shot her companion, he would put his pistol to her little white throat.

THIRTY-THREE

It was concern for Julien that made Eugénie stop at last.

In the still, heavy night, she could hear him grunting with pain behind her every time they sank deep into a damp sandhill and had to struggle out. Her boots had become weighted with the sand that had trickled its way in, making her legs ache abominably, and the bottom of her skirt was damp and gritty. She was relying more on her own night vision than the lantern, which gave only a frail gleam and was fast burning down.

She was not certain whether they were following a proper path or not, or simply a line in the wind-bent grasses that fringed the endless dunes. It was exceedingly cold, a deadening cold that had come with the invading mist. They could scarcely hear the roll of the sea, not far from where they toiled, only their own panting breath. To make things worse, the air could no longer hold so much moisture and it had begun to drizzle in earnest; she could feel wetness against her face, getting inside the hood of the cloak. It would not be long before the wick in the lantern went out.

'I believe that is a byre,' she said, pointing to a dark shape on their right. 'We could remain there till daylight.' For good measure, to make it seem her own desire: 'I am much fatigued.' She added, through chattering teeth, 'And frozen also.'

Both the last were true. In fact, a rest would be a most welcome alternative to this endless battle with soft, sticky ground and creeping cold. She had felt jubilant when they passed the guards so easily, but now that feeling had evaporated and she hated the eerie silence, the feeling of being absolutely alone under a vast, dark sky, not a star to be seen. And when they reached Crozier Saint-Clement, who would take them in at this time of night? There might be no inn in a tiny fishing village.

She was alarmed when Julien did not answer, but gave a muffled groan.

She took out the bottle of brandy. 'Drink some,' she ordered.

She gulped some herself – too much – and choked as

an astonishing fire went down her throat and burned its way to her stomach. She had never drunk brandy before: it was, she thought – as the fire died down to leave a pleasing warmth – remarkably restorative.

She took Julien's good arm. The sand gave way to rough grass, overgrown and boggy. They came to a fence, and in the tiny, diminishing gleam of the lantern they found a stile a little way along, which they negotiated somehow.

'Much good am I to you!' Julien was sufficiently recovered to mutter. 'A swordsman without a sword arm!'

'Hush, we're nearly there.' She found herself whispering. There were no cows, no sheep either, no movement or sound in the utter silence. Even the ceaseless turning over of the sea on the shore was lost now. The dark horizon was flat and empty, save for a few twisted trees rising through skirts of mist.

The building they had seen was not a byre after all. As they struggled across wet grass they could not make it out. Then they recognized the shape of the windows and saw it was a little church, built of stone. It was a ruin, long abandoned in the bleak landscape, its windows dark gaping holes in the moss-covered walls. There was no cross on its crumbling steeple and half the roof had fallen in.

Eugénie looked at it in dismay. 'Is our poor

benighted country so godless now that we allow our churches to fall down?'

For a moment she hesitated on the threshold, full of dark superstitions. But they must spend the night somewhere. Out of long habit, she crossed herself as she entered through the gap where the door had once been. She held the lantern up as Julien followed her. Shadows leapt at them. For a moment she wondered if the Devil entered such places after God had left, and looked about fearfully. But the Devil was in men's hearts and they were alone.

It was men, though, who had so wickedly ransacked the interior, stolen the cross and altar cloths, leaving nothing but broken stones on the floor, where mud and water oozed between the cracks. Wind-blown sand lay in drifts up the walls. Where the altar had once been there was a pile of rotting hay where a farmer had been using the church for storage; it was the only place where there was still a roof overhead. It was chill and dank, but at least it was out of the rain.

Eugénie helped Julien over to the pile of hay, and spread his coat for him and, looking half dead, he lay down and closed his eyes for an instant.

A hand grabbed her throat from behind.

Startled, she screamed and let the lantern fall, and it went out with a hiss on the slimy ground. The sudden darkness was almost blinding. Something small and hard was pressed into her back.

'Don't move, *citoyenne*. Pistols go off easy in the dark.'

Eugénie recognized the local dialect, but in her shock she was scarcely able to muster any coherent thought.

The object was removed from her back. 'Stay where you are.'

A tinderbox sparked, and light glowed from a lantern on the ground. Eugénie took a step forward to go to Julien, but she was seized and this time she felt something sharp against her throat. 'I've a knife, lady,' the horrible voice whispered behind her. 'Knife, pistols – I got them all. And you, young man, you don't move either.'

Julien had crouched forward, cradling his wounded arm. 'Don't hurt her!' he said fiercely.

'Your identity, *citoyenne*.' The hand against her throat moved down to grip her shoulder; she rubbed her throat and wondered if he had drawn blood. She found she could speak, though she was trembling violently.

'I work for the republican government!' She tried to control her voice. 'You will be in serious trouble for assaulting us like this.'

'Your papers, *s'il vous plaît!*'

'Our papers are in order. We had them checked and passed at Calais. What right have you to demand them?'

'Is there some query?' demanded Julien. 'Were you sent after us?'

'Enough. The papers!'

Eugénie pulled Hortense's papers from the pocket at her waist. She could see Julien fumbling for his with his good hand.

'He's hurt,' she said tremulously. 'Can't you see? Give him time.'

'He'll have all the time he wants when he's dead,' the voice growled.

She was released and the papers seized from her hand. But the pistol was still pointing at them both, wavering between them, and there was an expanse of glistening ground before she could reach Julien.

The dark figure bent over the lantern to examine her papers, but when she moved slightly the pistol came up in warning. She stood there, trapped and trembling, trying to see in the lantern light the face of the man who was threatening them.

It was indeed fiercesome: swarthy, bristles on the coarse cheeks, the devil incarnate. A member of the National Guard sent after them. He must have been at the guardhouse: she had not seen all their faces. She and

Julien had passed through so easily, but afterwards the guards must have become suspicious. Perhaps Hortense's body had been discovered. And what about Julien's assailant?

Her heart sank. All was lost.

The man hawked and spat disgustingly on the ground. 'These are stolen papers. You are not Hortense Thierry, government agent. She is tall and dark. I have watched her for some time. She works in Calais and Boulogne. Today she wanted passages for two colleagues. Tell me,' he came close to Eugénie and stared into her face, 'why do you go to England? To spy?'

Eugénie shook her head violently. She felt outraged, and in her outrage she blurted out the truth before she could stop herself. 'Why should I spy on my own country?'

The man went very still, like a beast about to pounce on its prey – all but his eyes, which flickered to Julien and back to her.

'Hush, Eugénie,' said Julien warningly.

'He knows we are not whom we profess to be, Julien. There is no point in remaining silent. Besides,' she stared straight back at the man's weathered face so close to her own that she could see the glint of gold in a front tooth and smell the drink and garlic on his breath, 'you are English too, if I am not mistaken!'

He pursed his lips warily at that, but he was taken aback, she could see. In answer he grabbed her again and breathed more garlic into her right ear. 'What makes you think so?'

She turned her face away and answered haughtily in English. 'Your dialect is good, but not quite accurate. I have a musical ear. I know it. And I am half English myself, so I recognize a countryman. Now kindly unhand me, sir.'

'Wait a minute, girl,' he said suspiciously, in English. 'Your English don't sound right to me.'

Eugénie drew herself up. 'And neither does your French to me. I admit I may have lost the nuances and refinements of the accent, but that is scarce surprising. I have lived my life in France and am only now seeking refuge with my English relatives.'

'Who the hell are you then?'

Eugénie drew herself up. 'I am Eugénie de Boncoeur of Chauvais.'

'A damned Froggy after all!'

'Half of me, yes,' she said with dignity, 'but my late mother was English.'

He looked suspicious still. 'And is he English too?' he said, pointing at Julien, who was struggling to his feet.

Julien caught the gist of it. 'Certainly not!' he said

in French.

'Sit down!' snarled the man. 'Didn't say you could get up, did I?'

'But who are you?' said Eugénie, as Julien subsided angrily. 'I have told you my true name. You must do the same. It is only fair.'

'No must about it, girl.'

The man went and sat down on the hay not far from Julien, who crouched back and glared at him, fingering his sword with his good hand. The man pulled a lump of tobacco from a pouch and sat chewing it reflectively while he squinted at Eugénie. The pistols were beside him, within all too easy reach.

'Tell me your story first,' he said at length, 'then I'll decide. I want to know what you have to do with Hortense Thierry.'

'How do I know we can trust you?' said Julien at once, in French.

In answer the man suddenly pulled aside his coat and grimy shirt to reveal a tanned muscular chest and a tattoo over the heart. He spread the square hairy fingers of his right hand over it.

'I swear on my dead mother's grave. If you convince me, then I'll give you my name. Otherwise –' his hand went down to stroke the pistols '– if I don't believe you, then I've got my lovelies handy, haven't I?'

'Hortense risked everything for me, you understand, and was murdered for it,' Eugénie finished.

She had become so caught up in the telling of her story that she relived the moment of finding Hortense's body, and had to blink away a tear. She scrutinized the man's countenance as far as she could in the dim light to see if he believed her. He had settled himself down comfortably in the damp hay, as if he was there for the rest of the night, but the pistols still glinted black and sinister at his side.

'Is that all?' he growled.

'All?' said Eugénie indignantly. 'It has been quite enough for both of us. We shall be thankful to reach the peace of Deal.'

'If we ever do,' muttered Julien.

'Deal peaceful?' scoffed the man. 'A hotbed of smugglers and what you might call lowlife, more like.' He appeared to detect no irony in what he said. 'Half the Navy's sheltering there too, while they prepare for war with France. I should know. It's where I'm from.'

'You recognized Hortense from Deal?' said Eugénie.

The man spat again. 'Nah, I'd heard of a French governess in the doctor's house, but I wasn't in this business then.'

'What business is that?' said Julien sharply, sitting forward.

He eyed them craftily, but seemed to relent. 'Same business as Citoyenne Thierry, but working for the other side. Mr Pitt, he's the Prime Minister no less, he said that since I knew the coast and the lingo, he could make good use of me and I'd escape the hangman's noose. 'Course he didn't tell me face to face. He sent an official from London, stood out a mile, he did, but he came looking for me. I'd been watching him a time already. Nearly killed him in my hut, I did, until he gave me Mr Pitt's proposal. Good money in it, better than smuggling – not that I've entirely given that up either, between you and me.'

'So –' said Eugénie, her eyes wide '– you're a . . .'

'Government agent, employed by Mr Pitt, paid by Mr Pitt, investigating the goings-on in France for Mr Pitt.' He got up nimbly and bowed. 'Jem Cuttle, at your service.' Then he reverted back to his old ferocious manner. 'But if you ever lets on – I'll cut your throats so deep the blood won't run. I'm good at it.'

'I'm certain you are, Mr Cuttle,' said Eugénie hastily. 'But we are most discreet, are we not, Julien?'

'Got rid of one or two Froggy spies that way, what had the audacity to think they could come over to England,' Jem Cuttle said reflectively. 'Gave 'em a nasty surprise.' He stopped and fixed her with a beady eye. 'So how was you thinking you'd reach Deal then?'

'We hoped to take a passage from Calais to one of the Cinque Ports on the south coast, and thence by coach,' said Eugénie. 'Now we are trying to find a place called Crozier Saint-Clement, where we believe we may be able to find a boat to take us across.'

'Crozier Saint-Clement? You must have muddled it with Crozier Saint-Christophe. This is the church of Saint Clement in Crozier. You're standing in it, girl, or what remains of it! You'll have to walk to Dunkirk to find a boat.'

Eugénie put her hand to her mouth. 'We can't do that! You can see the state of my friend. But what has happened to Crozier Saint-Clement? It's marked on our map.'

'Map must be out of date then. No new maps drawn since the Revolution.'

She turned to Julien in despair, but he had been frustrated by the quick exchange of English and shook his head, frowning. She explained, hating to see the hope go out of his eyes.

'Can you tell us what happened here, monsieur?' he said quietly. '*En français, s'il vous plaît.*'

'Bad harvests. Starvation. High taxes. Tenants gave up. Them aristocratic landlords, they didn't care. And the church, well, it's given in to salt. Nothing corrupts stone like salt.'

Eugénie sank down on the hay beside Julien, and Jem Cuttle didn't stop her. She put her head in her hands. 'I do not know what we are to do.'

Julien put out his good hand and touched her arm. 'We shall think of something.'

Not long ago he would have said 'I'. That at least was an improvement, she thought dully.

Jem Cuttle squatted on the soles of his feet, the whites beneath his pupils rolling up beneath his heavy brows as he watched them, and his hand going out to fondle his nearest pistol. There was a long silence.

'Mr Cuttle,' Eugénie began tentatively. 'Do you have a boat?'

His face was blank.

'We can pay you well,' Julien put in.

A gleam came into his deepset eyes. 'Ah, now you're talking. It happens I do have a boat not far away. We'd have to wait for a wind.'

'We can wait,' said Julien, his face lighting through the pain.

'For money, you said? Mr Pitt would not want me away from my work overlong.'

'Yes, indeed,' said Julien. He let Jem Cuttle glimpse the bundle of assignats he still had in his pocket.

Eugénie wondered if that were unwise, but she was beyond caring.

'Oh, please, Mr Cuttle! I don't know what we'll do otherwise!' She clasped her hands together, and turned her eyes on him imploringly. That always seemed to work, and did so now. Jem Cuttle looked at her and the hard bones of his face seemed to soften slightly.

'If there's money in it, I'll do it. I know the Goodwin Sands and they're treacherous for those what don't.' He eyed Julien's pocket. 'Payment before the trip, or I'm not taking you across.'

Julien sighed and pulled out a wad of money. He counted it before he gave it to Jem Cuttle. 'Half now, half when we're in the boat,' he said firmly.

Jem grunted, but pocketed the money. 'First light, we'll be off.'

'But Monsieur de Fortin is too weak to walk much further, Mr Cuttle,' protested Eugénie.

He nodded his greasy locks with a grim smile. 'T'ain't far. The boat's moored at Crozier Saint-Christophe. He'll do it unless he wants to be left behind in France.' His eyes flickered disconcertingly between them in the light. 'Got to keep you both together, haven't I? I've given you my name. He –' he jerked a thumb at Julien '– might see fit to give me away if he's discovered here before I get back. So now you're both my hostages in case they try to arrest me before we get to Deal!'

THIRTY-FOUR

They waited for morning, speaking in low voices. After tucking his pistols back into his belt, Jem Cuttle had rolled on his side and was snoring loudly. He had told them in no uncertain terms that if they tried anything he would wake immediately, and their chance of reaching England would be lost for ever.

Eugénie had an opportunity to empty her boots at last; she turned away modestly so that Julien should not see her ankles.

She wondered if he had a fever. His face was shining with sweat, and occasionally he caught his breath with pain, though there was no blood leaking through on to his coat. She offered more brandy, but he shook his head.

'I need to keep a clear head, Eugénie. I worry that he

might hurt you when I am not fit to defend you. A man like that with a young innocent girl, and such a scoundrel as he . . .' He clenched his teeth.

'There may be good in him, we do not know yet.'

A deafening snore sounded forth, magnified in the little church.

'I doubt it.'

'He could have shot us both and pocketed all the money, but he did not. He is all we have. We have no alternative but to trust him.' She went on, partly to reassure herself, 'And it was not he who murdered Hortense, though he must have had the opportunity to do so.' Her eyes widened. 'It may be that he is able to guess at the identity of her murderer, the man who assailed you, if we ask him.'

'There is no need. I know who the murderer is,' Julien said sombrely.

She frowned. 'Why, how . . .?'

'Eugénie, I am so sorry. I can keep it from you no longer. It was Guy Deschamps who murdered her and who tried to murder me.'

She looked at him incredulously, wondering again about the fever. His eyes did seem uncommonly bright. 'Whatever do you mean? Guy?'

'It was Guy who fought me, whom you knocked out.'

She stared at him for a moment as if he had escaped

from a lunatic asylum, then she shook her head. 'I do not believe you.'

She was as blindly trusting as her brother. 'It was a shock when I saw his face. But it was Guy Deschamps, no other.'

'Guy is our friend,' she said gently. 'You were mistaken. You had just been wounded and were confused.'

She leant over and put her hand to his forehead, noting with dismay as she did so how grubby her fingers were, the broken nails grimed with grit and sand. Julien shut his eyes briefly as her fingers touched his face. He was hot, certainly, but then her fingers were so cold.

'Do not believe me if you do not wish to do so,' he whispered. 'What does it matter when we are leaving France? We shall not see him again.'

'Do not say that,' Eugénie said. 'I intend to return with Armand as soon as the Revolution is over, and then I will renew my acquaintance with Guy, I am sure of it.'

Julien's eyes opened for a moment. There was pain in them indeed. Then they closed. 'Let us try to sleep.'

'In this filth?' She shuddered. But he did not answer.

'Oh, God, send us a wind tomorrow,' she prayed. 'Without it, I do not know what we shall do.' A prayer in a church, even a ruined one, surely had a better chance of reaching Him? 'And forgive me for being so lax in my devotions of late,' she added hastily.

An hour or so later when she woke, she found to her embarrassment that somehow in her sleep she had curled herself against Julien and was warm in the hay, despite the cold grey light that was outlining the ruined stones. It was Mr Cuttle who was awake and on guard, sitting in the entrance, his pistol cocked at the misty dawn.

Julien seemed worse in the morning, his face drawn. He staggered to his feet silently when Jem Cuttle growled, 'We should be off.'

Eugénie's stomach rumbled and she was exceedingly thirsty. She hoped fervently that there would be some cottager on the way willing to sell a loaf of bread and a bucket of well water.

'I taste a little wind coming,' said Jem Cuttle, lifting his face to the empty windows.

He set the pace, pushing them before him, a pistol pointing at their backs, as they tramped over the dunes, leaving the desolate little church and the remains of the few farm dwellings behind them in the mist. At each step Eugénie wondered if the pistol might explode of its own accord, jolted by the uneven movement. The sky was lightening all the while and beneath it the sea moved slowly in little glassy waves; the air was cold and clammy.

Jem Cuttle looked at the whiteness of the far horizon and shook his head. 'Fog banks,' he said. 'Let's hope the breeze comes soon and blows 'em away.'

Soon Eugénie's boots were filling with sand once more. Her eyelids felt gritty after so little sleep and she wondered if sand clogged her hair and scalp.

After about three-quarters of an hour they came to an indent in the coastline. Crozier Saint-Christophe was a huddle of mean fishermen's cottages and a little church around a tiny harbour, with a wooden jetty rising over the mud; but the coast road to Dunkirk ran behind the village, and Eugénie saw immediately that on the road stood an inn, modest but well-kept, with a stableyard.

Julien was failing: his footsteps faltered and he breathed in hard gasps. When she looked at him she saw his eyes were half closed.

'My companion needs a rest before we sail,' she said desperately to Jem Cuttle. 'I must change his bandages. Can we not seek shelter at that inn a while?'

Jem Cuttle pursed his lips as he glanced at the fishing smacks moored beyond the jetty. 'Best to catch the end of the tide. We don't want to find ourselves in slack water.'

'We needn't be long,' pleaded Eugénie. 'We should have some sustenance before we sail, Mr Cuttle – something to eat and drink.'

He nodded reluctantly. 'I grant you, it'll be good to warm ourselves before a fire and they won't ask questions there. Used me too often in the past.'

All the same, the innkeeper seemed curiously agitated when he saw them, though who might not be, thought Eugénie uncomfortably: the three of them looking so dishevelled and disreputable, wisps of hay clinging to their grubby clothes, their boots caked in sand, and one of them with filthy, bloodstained bandages. No doubt she and Julien smelt as strong as Jem Cuttle after the previous night.

But fortunately on an early January morning the inn had little custom, and they were hurried into the empty coffee room, where a fire had been lit.

Jem Cuttle stretched out immediately in one of the comfortable chairs, legs thrust forward in the most shamefully abandoned way, pistols on the table in front of him pointed unerringly at his two hostages. His gaze did not leave them for a moment, even as he lit an evil-smelling pipe.

Shortly afterwards the wife appeared with clean dressings for Julien, averting her eyes from the new arrivals as she put the tin basin on the table. She gulped as she saw the pistols, and ran away at once despite Cuttle's greeting. Then the innkeeper returned with refreshments on a tray: coffee and rolls, and watered wine.

'I cannot serve you here again,' he said in a low voice to Cuttle, his shocked gaze not on the pistols, but on the bloody cloths Eugénie was unwrapping from Julien's arm. 'It is too dangerous. We can have no business together now.'

'I understand, friend,' said Cuttle. 'Times have changed, eh?'

The innkeeper bowed his head apologetically and hastened out.

After Eugénie had retied his sling, Julien lay back in the chair, his eyes closed, his face ashen. He did not look as if he would ever move again. Jem Cuttle took out his pipe and whistled through his teeth as he saw the long cut, still seeping blood.

'Someone tried to skewer you, sure enough, lad! You need a stitch or two. There's sail twine and a needle on the boat should do it.'

Julien shook his head weakly. 'Thank you, Cuttle, I'll do well enough till England.'

Eugénie poured a glass of the watered wine. 'You must drink it, Julien,' she whispered. 'Don't die, I beg you – for my sake!'

A smile curved his lips and he opened his eyes. 'I have no intention of doing so!' he murmured, and took several gulps of the wine before closing his eyes again.

Jem Cuttle turned to Eugénie, heavy brows drawn together. 'Is he in trouble?' he said in a low voice. 'Is that why he flees?'

'He is not fleeing,' said Eugénie indignantly. 'He is no coward, but if he remains in France he will die under the guillotine for what he has done.'

'Ah.' Cuttle narrowed his eyes and puffed reflectively. 'There is a description out for someone very like your companion. I know these things sooner than most, being in the business, so to speak. If he is who I think he is, then Mr Pitt will be interested in talking to him.'

'Then you had better deliver us safe to England,' said Eugénie tartly.

Two hours later there were three new horses tethered in the stableyard. They had been ridden hard; their flanks were mottled with sweat despite the weather.

In the front parlour the innkeeper faced the gentleman from Calais, and the two National Guards with him. 'I did indeed have two strangers here earlier,' he said carefully in answer to their question. 'They wanted breakfast.'

'If you gave them breakfast, you must have had a chance to observe them. What did they look like?'

The innkeeper licked his lips nervously. 'The girl – very fair and young. The young man – dark. He had been injured, but both were in some – disarray.'

'Which room did they occupy?'

'I put them in the coffee room, *citoyen*.'

'Show me.'

It was the gentleman who had been questioning him, while the two guards eyed him in surly fashion, shifting their muskets; and it was the gentleman who now entered the little room and paused. His nostrils quivered fastidiously. 'Tobacco. A pipe, recently smoked. Someone was with them. You have not told me everything.'

The innkeeper began to stutter. 'There was another man, yes, monsieur. They left together.'

The gentleman stepped closer. 'Did you see in what direction?' he rapped out. His skin was dry, and mottled with the heat of his ride, his breath sweet with peppermint, as if he had taken some quantity of it earlier that morning. 'Tell me, or I shall have you arrested forthwith!'

'Towards the harbour – it was above an hour ago,' stammered the innkeeper.

The gentleman looked at the guards. 'We must alert

customs,' he said grimly. 'We'll give chase. They'll not get away.'

THIRTY-FIVE

The smack, the *Charlotte*, stank of fish. Wet nets filled the cockpit, and Eugénie stumbled over coiled ropes in her long skirts as the boat's hull moved alarmingly beneath her boots.

Jem Cuttle had brought her out in the rowing boat as hostage, leaving Julien on the quay. Now he motioned her to sit down, waving a pistol at her. She wasn't certain where would be out of his way, so she sat on the damp plank to one side of the helm, clutching the bulwark behind her in case the boat lurched unexpectedly. She looked anxiously back at the end of the jetty, where Julien stood waiting, a lone figure blurred by drizzle. Between them was a wide expanse of cold grey water.

Her heart was beating hard. She did not like being

alone with Jem Cuttle; he was a little too wayward with his pistols.

He stowed the nets away in the stern locker. 'No time to leave her shipshape before,' he muttered. 'Urgent work on shore.' And he winked at her wickedly.

To her relief, after that he ignored her, as he busied himself with the sail bag. There was only a single sail, which he hoisted after he had brought the boat head to wind and cast off the anchor. Then he pulled in the sheet, turning the boat expertly back to the jetty and towing the rowing boat behind.

As Jem Cuttle brought the *Charlotte* up alongside, Julien clambered in, hampered by his sword and bad arm. Though he protested, Cuttle pushed him none too gently across to an open hatch in the deckhouse, pressing the pistol into his back. 'You're best out of the way in the cabin,' he said curtly in French. 'Can't have a wounded man falling about on deck. And I'll take that sword off you while I'm about it.' He glanced at Eugénie as he slid the rapier into the starboard locker. 'You'd be better off down there too, girl.'

Eugénie had already put her head down the hatch out of curiosity when they first boarded the boat, and knew the stench of old fish down there would make her sick. She shook her head decidedly. 'Perhaps I can help you if I stay above, Mr Cuttle.'

He grunted, sticking the pistols into his belt. 'You ever sailed before? Thought not. Well, you can keep your eyes peeled for other boats.'

'What sort of boats?'

'Any sort is bad.'

From below Julien looked up suspiciously, unable to understand what was being said. She tried to smile back at him as Cuttle cast off once more, pushed the smack away from the jetty and the sail filled.

At least the motion of the boat was not as bad as she feared, though it was achingly cold on deck. She struggled to keep her hood up round her face in the damp air and watched the little harbour recede into a patch of mist. There was grey water all around them, the crests of the waves breaking now; no land in sight, and all their hopes rested with a ruffian.

'How are we doing, Cuttle?' Julien called, sticking his head through the hatch.

Jem Cuttle squinted up the sail. 'Beam reach, lad – force three, I reckon, only making about five knots and not enough wind to rid us of this mist yet. Still, if we can steal away in it, so much the better.' He checked the brass compass, and nodded. 'If I keep to this course and the wind don't drop altogether, we'll make Deal in about four and a half hours.'

After an hour, Eugénie was so cold she was forced to

go below. She climbed into the dark, cramped cabin, hampered by her skirts, and saw that Julien was asleep, stretched out on his back on the single bunk, his wounded arm cradled against his body.

It seemed an agreeable opportunity to study his face awhile: not handsome, exactly, she granted, but in sleep he lost that arrogant, supercilious expression and looked as soft and young as a boy. The bruises on his face were fading. Beneath the arched brows, how dark the curve of his eyelashes seemed against his cheeks – and surprisingly long for a man. How straight his nose was, how firm his chin! The sooty hair, though thick, was very fine, like threads of black silk.

But if she were to touch it, he would wake.

Out of the little window she tried to see if she could glimpse the English coast, but the visibility was too poor. She wrapped herself in a greasy blanket she found in the forepeak and was just becoming warm, when abruptly above her head she heard Jem Cuttle utter a swear word she had never heard before. She had no notion of its meaning, but it did not bode well.

She stuck her head out of the hatch apprehensively. 'What is the matter, Mr Cuttle?'

'Customs boat after us – two-masted clipper. She'll overhaul us in no time with that sail area.'

'What shall we do?'

'We can't bluff it out. They know me of old. Given 'em the dodge many times in the past. Let's hope we can do it now. The mist will help. I'm going to harden up. Stay below.'

He pushed the tiller away from him, hauled in the sheet and the boat heeled sharply. He was changing course, pointing closer to the wind, hoping to sail into a patch of mist perhaps, Eugénie thought, as she clung to the cabin ladder. After all they had been through, to be stopped by customs men searching for smugglers!

On this tack, the movement of the boat was more violent. Julien rolled on the sloping bank, groaned and opened his eyes.

'Oh, Julien, we are being pursued!' Already they could see the clipper had changed course and was riding full-sail out of the mist, small but swift, still a distance away but bearing straight down on them.

Julien struggled off the bunk and went to the hatch. 'Give me a pistol, Cuttle! We've got to get out of this.'

Jem Cuttle shook his head. 'I'm not wasting a gun on a left-handed man!'

Eugénie gulped and pushed past him determinedly. 'I can handle a gun, Mr Cuttle,' she called up a trembling voice. 'I used to shoot rabbits at Chauvais. My eye is good – so said my groom.'

Julien looked at her in horror. 'You can't go on deck, Eugénie!'

'Send the girl up and be done fussing!' Jem Cuttle bawled down.

'Then for God's sake, take care,' said Julien. 'Keep your head down!'

As Eugénie climbed up, Cuttle gave a final satisfied turn to the barrels of both pistols with the wrench. 'Primed and loaded!' He glanced at her anxious face. 'Best to keep your shot for when they're close, girl.'

He seemed to have confidence in her, and that stopped her hand from shaking as she took the long screw-barrelled pistol from him gingerly. It was heavy, but the butt was surprisingly comfortable in her palm.

She pulled back the cocking-piece, holding the barrel away from them both as she looked back at the clipper. Jem Cuttle had wound the sheet round the winch to sail one-handed more easily while he gripped his pistol in his free hand.

Spray flew over the bulwark and into Eugénie's eyes and she blinked it away. She feared it would be impossible to keep her aim steady, even though the sea was slight; and she had only a single bullet before she would have to reload.

One chance.

The customs clipper was on their port bow, closing

the gap between them. It was so close they could see the dark figures of the men on board. 'Wait until I say before you shoot,' said Jem Cuttle.

Eugénie nodded speechlessly.

A voice came over the water, carrying easily in the light wind. 'Proceed no further, in the name of the Republic! Heave to so we can board you!'

Jem ignored it. A sudden shot exploded in the water just aft of their stern.

'Trying to frighten us,' he said through clenched teeth.

Eugénie was staring across at the men standing behind the clipper's black bulwark. 'Le Fantôme!' she breathed.

He was not wearing his hat, and his face was clearly visible above the dark redingote as he gazed across the water at the smack.

Was it he who had sent the clipper after them? But how could he know she would be on board?

Another shot, by the bows this time, sending a plume of seawater up and over them.

'Right!' said Jem Cuttle. He levelled the long barrel of his pistol, aimed, squeezed the trigger and fired. There was a flash that almost blinded Eugénie, and then the loud, flat report, terrifyingly close in the confines of the *Charlotte*'s cockpit. On the clipper one of the crew crumpled and in slow motion toppled over the side and into the water.

'Got 'im,' said Jem with satisfaction, his thick fingers working swiftly with powder and bullets to reload, while he held the freed sheet between his teeth and wedged the tiller between his knees. In a trice the reloading was done, the barrel screwed back.

The shouted command came again. 'Obey, or we'll fire!'

'We cannot hope to outsail them, Cuttle!' Julien shouted from the hatch, as a bullet from the clipper ripped the wood on the boathouse. 'Stop sailing, man, or we'll all die!'

But Jem Cuttle was a man possessed, relishing the fight, his eyes gleaming with excitement and desperation. He fired again, rocking the *Charlotte* with the pistol's discharge, and another man fell on the clipper. 'Nothing better than my lovelies for long range!' he muttered to himself. 'We'll not give up easy, will we?'

Le Fantôme had stretched out an arm and was pointing at them. He must have given the order to shoot.

Eugénie's heart was beating so hard it made her hand shake. She levelled the barrel of her pistol and squinted along it, aiming it at Le Fantôme's tall dark figure in the stern, standing motionless and sinister while others moved about him. He should not be so very hard to hit. Her finger was on the trigger. She only had to squeeze it. *Could she – would she . . .?*

A bullet split the air above their heads and tore through the sail, leaving a neat, singed hole. They both ducked automatically but Jem was frowning, almost as if he were disappointed.

'They could kill us easy now if they wanted, but they're shooting wide. What's their game?'

Eugénie crouched low in the cockpit.

'It's me, Mr Cuttle. They want to take me alive!'

Then the clipper was past them, sailing a course across their bows, cutting them off. Jem Cuttle swore as he brought the tiller across to avoid collision and they both ducked as the boom swung over.

Julien's white face was at the hatch. Jem flung back the locker and brought out the rapier. He sent it skidding across the boards. 'Fight for your life, lad, left-handed or not, soon as they board us!'

The clipper came round on to their course, taking their wind so that the *Charlotte* lost all headway. The smack rocked helplessly against the side of the clipper as Jem Cuttle let go of the helm, grabbed the other pistol from Eugénie and leapt on top of the deckhouse.

His eyes were wild as he brandished a pistol in each

hand. 'If they board us, I'll shoot!'

'Your papers, *s'il vous plaît*!' came a shout from the clipper. Faces stared down at them, the hard, ruthless faces of men who scoured the sea each day, hunting illicit traders of tea, brandy and silk between France and England; they would not show mercy to counter-revolutionaries who threatened the Republic.

Eugénie pulled her hood around her face to hide it. 'We have nothing to declare!' she called up. 'We are good French citizens. Why do you pursue us?'

'We know who you are. Your captain is a wanted man, and we have reason to believe you have another on board, Julien de Fortin. Is your name Eugénie de Boncoeur? Answer, or it will be the worse for you!'

'Enough.' It was the quelling voice of Le Fantôme. His figure loomed over the last speaker. 'Let me see her.'

For a moment they stared at each other, the girl and the pale assassin. Even from that distance Eugénie felt the triumph in his gaze as he ran his eyes over her, his lip curling a little with distaste at the state she was in, her hair windswept and falling about her dirty face, the cloak filthy and draggled with seawater.

Then he flung out his gloved hand beneath the black sleeve of his redingote and pointed, as if he were fixing a butterfly with a pin. 'It is the girl. Board the vessel, arrest the men but bring *la petite* Boncoeur to me!'

THIRTY-SIX

The customs men prepared to leap on the deck of the fishing smack. Jem Cuttle danced a lunatic's dance on the roof of the deckhouse, shouting an encouragement to certain death at them that was littered with obscenities.

Then, on the misty horizon, a ship, vast and magnificent, hove into view on the horizon.

It was a British frigate, three-masted, with a Union Jack flying on each mast: a forest of white sails and branched rigging above an immense hull that cut through the water, sending a bow wave ahead of it that made both the smack and the clipper rock violently. On its decks were the sinister lines of gunports.

Commotion broke out on the clipper. Boarding the *Charlotte* was abandoned in the terror of seeing a

British gunship at close quarters. The captain shouted orders, sails billowed, sheets were tightened, and suddenly it was sailing away from them with all the speed it could make, trying desperately to avoid the frigate by taking a different course. Le Fantôme's furious pale face gazed back over the stern, but he fast became a blur.

It was the last Eugénie would see of him for a while.

The little fishing smack was alone on the water, drifting towards a towering black hull.

'What should we do, Mr Cuttle?' Eugénie cried. 'We'll be mown down! Can't we sail a different course?'

'Too late, girl. Let's hope they see us.'

Eugénie began to wave her arms wildly. 'They won't fire at us, will they?'

Julien emerged from the hatch and looked aghast at the size of the frigate. 'We're not officially at war yet,' he said doubtfully.

Jem Cuttle leapt down from the boathouse roof. He rummaged in one of the cockpit lockers and brought out a Union Jack ensign. 'I'll run this up on the mast.' He winked at Eugénie. 'Got one of each in here, French and British. Best to be prepared.'

'We should shout!' said Julien. 'Shout as loud as we can, in English.'

'We *are* English,' said Eugénie. 'We don't want them to think we're French!'

'I doubt they'd understand the words anyway,' muttered Julien.

They began to to yell across the water.

On board something was happening. Tiny black figures ran about on the decks. There was the sound of creaking as the rigging slackened, and the great sails began to billow as the bow came round into the wind. As gracefully as it had sailed, the frigate stopped, moving gently with the rhythm of the sea. A long rowing boat was lowered over the side.

'They are coming over to us,' said Eugénie half fearfully. 'I suppose they intend to inspect our papers.'

'Let's hope not,' said Julien ironically. 'An agent of the French government and a National Guard?'

Jem Cuttle looked over at the frigate in admiration. 'Don't she make you feel proud to be British? What a beauty.'

'The French have a one-hundred-and-twenty-gun ship, also very beautiful, and with superior sailing qualities,' Julien pointed out stiffly.

Already the rowing boat, which was the entire length of the *Charlotte*, was nudging up alongside. Sailors in the blue coats of the British naval uniform, armed with muskets, leapt on board.

After that things happened bewilderingly fast. The three of them were guided politely but firmly down into the rowing boat. When Jem protested at leaving his smack, his hands were swiftly brought behind his back, he was disarmed and forced at gunpoint into the boat.

'Apologies, sir, but the Captain wants you particularly,' said the young midshipman.

Grunting and swearing, Jem subsided sullenly in the stern and gazed at his beloved boat, floating rudderless and abandoned on the sea.

This was not the reception Eugénie had been expecting. She should be welcomed as a fellow countryman! She had spoken in English and given her name, but had received blank looks. The closer the frigate became, the more ominous it looked, with its great black side like a prison wall above her.

And, *mon dieu!* there was a flimsy rope ladder dangling down the side that she would now have to climb! How would she preserve her modesty, let alone not fall off?

Julien leant towards her as she stared up. 'If you fall, I'll catch you. Look upwards as you climb, not down. Do not fear, I shall be behind you.'

'I am not in the least fearful,' she lied, through clenched teeth. Was he such an expert climber of rope ladders? 'When I was a little girl, my groom knotted a rope and taught me to climb it. There are chalk quarries around Chauvais and it's easy to fall down them.' She turned on him. 'Besides, how will you catch me with one arm?'

'It is a very strong arm,' said Julien.

She had been concerned about her skirts lifting in the breeze as she climbed, but she soon realized other things were much more important: placing her boot on exactly the right part of the rung below to keep her balance, the gleaming water waiting far below her if she fell, the painful grazing of her knuckles on the wood of the hull every time she took hold of the rung above.

She had left her cloak in the boat, for it seemed too cumbersome for such a climb, but the breeze caught her off guard with its chill, buffeting her skin and hair and making her eyes water so that she could scarcely see where to grip.

The climb seemed endless, but it was Julien about whom she worried, for she could hear him groaning behind her as he struggled up slowly and painfully, clinging like a spider to its web with his one good hand, and relying on his legs to push him up. When he eventually collapsed on deck, he was half fainting.

'Get this man down below,' said a voice. 'He requires the ship's doctor.'

A strong hand helped Eugénie to her feet with the

utmost courtesy, and she found herself standing on scrubbed boards, looking into the steady eyes of the officer of the watch, a telescope still under his arm. He bowed his head. 'Mademoiselle, I apologize for the inconvenience you have just suffered.'

Eugénie was panting with the effort of the climb. She struggled to regain her dignity. After a moment she gulped in English, 'Sir, I am very much obliged to you for rescuing us from our predicament.'

He said gravely, 'The Captain wishes to question you. One of the men will escort you to the quarterdeck.'

That sounded ominous. She looked around for Jem Cuttle and saw that he was fighting the grip of two sailors, who were trying to tie him to the rail with a length of rope.

'Oh, sir, is it necessary to treat him in such a way?' she said in alarm to the officer of the watch. 'He is my friend, and English, you know.'

'We know who he is. I recognized the name of his boat from our list. But he is threatening to jump overboard and swim back to her. Perhaps you can dissuade him.'

She rushed over. 'Jem, Mr Cuttle! Please desist. We have just been rescued by these kind sailors, have we not?'

Jem Cuttle glared up at her with a fiercesome,

desperate eye. 'I'm not losing my *Charlotte*, girl. Look at her, bobbing about out there on her own! She'll be lost to wind and tide if I leave her. And where am I – *what* am I – without my boat? Can't do my job for Mr Pitt, can I?'

A man in the uniform of a captain was descending the steps from the upper deck. Around him sailors straightened and saluted as he made his way over to Eugénie and Jem.

'Jem Cuttle,' he said solemnly. 'If you try to regain your boat, I shall give the order to open fire. Both you and your boat will be lost in a single puff of smoke. You will be lost anyway, man, if you return to her. The French gunboats are massing. You're safest with us.'

Cuttle eyed him darkly. 'Mr Pitt will have to stand me another boat, Captain Harkness.'

'Oh, I think the Prime Minister will do that. You are one of our most valued runners on the Channel.'

Cuttle looked slightly mollified. He nodded at the sailors who had tied him. 'Get these bonds off me, lads. I'll not move.'

Captain Harkness turned to Eugénie and bowed. He raised a bushy eyebrow beneath his cocked hat. 'Are you another émigré, mademoiselle?' he said in impeccable French. She thought she caught a hint of weariness in his tone. '*Votre nom, s'il vous plaît?*'

'No, indeed I am not,' she said, with spirit, in English. 'My name is Eugénie de Boncoeur. I am half English on my mother's side, and I have an invitation to stay with my uncle, Thomas Coveney of Deal.'

The Captain's gaze warmed; a smile lit his heavy features. 'Thomas Coveney of Deal, eh? He is a surgeon at the naval hospital. He did a splendid job on my nephew, a midshipman who fell off the rigging and broke his collarbone, silly boy. And Deal is where we're bound now, back to rest at anchor in the "Downs" for victualling before action with –' he cleared his throat as he looked at her '– the French.'

When he had first arrived in Calais, Le Scalpel had taken the precaution of bribing the captain of a sloop to take him across the Channel as soon as the weather was sufficiently improved. If you worked for someone as powerful as Le Fantôme, you could always get what you wanted.

The Captain had already had dealings with both government agents in the past, and they had paid most excellent well for his services. He needed the money: he had a family to feed, and this was his last chance of earning so much before war was declared and put a stop to all Channel crossings.

Two hours earlier than the smack, the sloop had

ridden the tide out of Calais, and now Le Scalpel, a bandage around his head that only seemed to complement the handsome face beneath, was watching the misty coastline of England draw closer. He had been there several times before; his English was fluent and, with its faint accent, irresistible to women.

'I want you to get over there as soon as you can,' Le Fantôme had said, before he had left Calais himself. 'There is a chance I may not catch them. If they get away, we know where to find them.'

His eyes had narrowed to slits as he looked at Le Scalpel. 'I want the girl back alive, you understand? But kill Julien de Fortin.'

That would be pleasure indeed.

But then Le Scalpel's smile faded, as he fingered his bandaged head and thought of Eugénie de Boncoeur. He still had a headache, and had spent upmost of an hour the previous evening shouting for the *fille* to unlock the door. For a moment his face hardened into vicious lines, so that those who knew him as the charming Guy Deschamps would not have recognized him.

He would punish La Boncoeur in due course, but first he would dally with the little minx a while longer. Then, when he had finally finished with her, he would deliver her to his master.

* * *

Eugénie had been below for some time in the tiny cabin they had assigned her. She had not been able to change her clothes, but had washed her face and had been brought a comb and metal looking glass by an embarrassed little midshipman. It seemed luxury after the privations of the last few days.

In place of Hortense's cloak she had been lent a uniform coat that she fancied brought out the blue of her eyes. She found herself a little bored already, and thought she might sally forth on deck before accepting the Captain's invitation to luncheon.

The mist had descended again, in a fine wispy curtain that hid the horizon and any land there. She had hoped to glimpse the white cliffs of Dover and was disappointed. A sudden dread assailed her as she stood alone at the rail, for the horizon seemed to be darkening in an ever more forbidding way even as she gazed. What did it hold for her, this alien country of England? And if she felt she did not wholly belong in England, what must Julien be feeling?

There was a step behind her and she turned to see him, his fresh sling startlingly white. He was smiling his crooked smile, his dark eyes holding hers.

'Julien!' she said half shyly, for he had seemed to step out of her thoughts and was there before her as if she had wished for him.

He bowed low. 'Mademoiselle,' he said, his eyes taking in the coat, clean face and freshly dressed hair. 'I feel I should address you formally once more, for you do look so very elegant!'

'And as for you, monsieur, I do believe you look much recovered,' she stammered, with great and unexpected relief. 'English doctors are excellent, are they not?'

'The one below was disappointed that I presented with a mere sword cut. He stitched it up most efficiently and my arm will soon be good as new.'

He stood beside her at the rail, but did not look at the hidden horizon; he looked at her. Eugénie found she felt oddly nervous; she was conscious of his left arm very close to hers. She began to talk in a bright, brittle way.

'It will be strange indeed to meet my uncle and cousin again after so long! Why, my cousin and I are of an age. And you, Julien – I am sure they will extend their hospitality to you, you need not concern yourself about it . . .'

Her voice trailed away as she suddenly wondered if Julien might not wish to leave Deal immediately, and travel on to London to stir up support for the Queen and Dauphin – or perhaps meet with Monsieur Pitt. The thought made her feel startlingly bereft.

'But perhaps it is not your intention to remain in Deal?' she faltered.

'Oh, it is, Eugénie,' he assured her solemnly. 'My intention is to remain at your side wherever you are.' He paused. 'That is, of course, if you want me there.'

'I do, Julien, I do!' she cried in a rush, and blushed at her forwardness. She tried to explain it away. 'For it is so very much better when one can face whatever the future may bring with – another person.'

A smile lifted the corners of Julien's mouth, so that she wondered how she had ever thought him morose. 'Especially when that particular person is close to one's heart, do you not agree?' he asked.

Eugénie nodded; she could not speak.

Julien looked away for a moment, towards the dark line of approaching land, his face serious. 'Something must survive this terrible time, Eugénie, something positive and good, even if there is yet more bloodshed to come.' He gave a little shudder, as if premonition had brushed him like an icicle.

But then he turned back to her, and gently prised her hand from the rail. Looking deep into her eyes he kissed her fingertips slowly, one by one.

'There's a little time left before we reach Deal. Time enough to tell me about your childhood and that so-efficient groom of yours.' Before she could demur he had leant towards her, still imprisoning her hand, and said softly in her ear, 'For I do confess, I find myself mightily jealous of him!'

The plot to rescue the King

There really was a plot to rescue Louis XVI from the guillotine at the last desperate moment, and the Baron de Batz - shady financial speculator, elusive adventurer – was involved, bribed by the Baron de Breteuil, an ex-minister of the King's. But on the bitter January morning of the King's execution, none of de Batz's supposed contacts turned up as planned, to rush the King's carriage and sweep him away. Perhaps it was because the Commune, alert for any last-ditch rescue, had become aware of the plot – who knows?

Some books about the French Revolution

I tried where I could to read contemporary accounts of the Revolution, pre-Terror. A fuller book list and details of the historical figures mentioned in the story are given on my website, www.patriciaelliott.co.uk.

The French Revolution (a collection of eye-witness reports) by Georges Pernoud and Sabine Flaissier, Secker and Warburg, 1960

Memoirs of Madame de la Tour du Pin, Harvill Press, 1969

Daily Life in the French Revolution by Jean Robiquet, Weidenfeld and Nicolson, 1964

Travels in France During the Years 1787, 1788 and 1789 by Arthur Young, Cambridge University Press, 1950

Patricia Elliott

An extract from the second book in the Pimpernelles *series:*
The Traitor's Smile

Eugénie took the letter over to the little dressing-table, where the light of the candles was reflected in the looking-glass. As she did so, she caught sight of herself: the half-smile hovering on her lips, her eyes shining with anticipation. *It is a billet-doux, I am sure of it!* she thought. *A love letter – from Guy!* For a moment her despair at Armand's imprisonment and the constant ache in her heart over Julien's coldness lessened a little.

The letter had her name upon it in unfamiliar handwriting; the pressure on the nib had pierced the paper. Eugénie hesitated a moment, staring at the seal. The letter was not from Guy at all. The crest imprinted in the wax was disturbingly familiar. She had known it all her life: the stag's head surrounded by a wreath of ivy. It was the proud, ancient crest of her ancestors, the de Boncoeurs of Chauvais. Though her name was not written in Armand's hand, he must have sealed the letter himself with his signet before it left his prison cell.

Her heart thumped with hope. She would hear news of him at last! She broke the seal with shaking fingers, then tried to hold the letter steady under the candlelight and take in what it said.

And that was how Hetta found her, minutes later. Hetta had come in dressed in her nightgown to bid Eugénie a chilly goodnight for the sake of politeness between cousins, but saw her sitting motionless at her dressing-table. She approached, and Eugénie looked up. In the glass her eyes were desperate.

'Hetta, what must I do?' She put her hands to her face. 'However can I agree to this?'